THE PECULIAR
MISSING MONDRIAN

K.J. HERITAGE

The Peculiar Case of the Missing Mondrian

Published 2022 by *Sygasm Publishing*

Cover design: *K.J.Heritage*

This is a human book. Artificial Intelligence (AI) was not used in any way in the writing or plotting of this novel, nor in its cover design, or in any other aspect of its production. Machines are far too busy trying to take over the world.

Sygasm Publishing
http://sygasm.com

ISBN-978-1-7391068-0-5

Not so serendipitous happenchances...

CONTENTS

NINE MONTHS AGO

WHITEWASH

"THIS IS IT!" Dan Kowalski said, repositioning his easel and canvas, whilst performing a little dance, adding "C'mon!" and an awkward fist pump for good measure. Dan was doing this for a particular reason. And that reason was *Art*. You see, Dan Kowalski was a committed landscape painter, and more importantly, a life-long lover of colour, of every single part of the spectrum. From amaranth (reddish pink) and celadon (a beautiful pale green) to gamboge (orange with a smidgen of blue) and phlox (a stunning violet void of any green).

"I live for colours and would die for them," he often told anybody who would listen, although they mostly wished they hadn't, especially when Dan then went on to list those colours and their many variations in alphabetical order.

The scene before Dan was awash with colour. His eyes drank in the majestic vista like a thirsty student on a Freshers' Week pub-crawl. The varied greens of meadows and hedgerows, the swathes of yellow rapeseed and purple lavender in bloom, stretched away from him to a horizon dominated by small, wooded hills. All set against a fantastic bright, bluer-than-blue sky. Cumulus nimbus clouds, white and nimbussy, drifted fluffily over the English countryside, catching the first crimson rays of sunrise. And stabbing over this wonderful scene? A chiaroscuro of stark shadows and shafts of intense, angled sunlight. Dan was proud of that word. *Chiaroscuro.* He would drop it into conversations with impressionable young ladies and smile inside as their eyes widened.

Regardless of Dan's proclivities regarding some of the more gullible members of the opposite sex, this scene was indeed a landscape painter's dream. It even had the imperfection of a busy highway curving through it like a twisted scar—ugly, glaring road signs, stained concrete, and a tacky twenty-four-hour garage. Cars and trucks, the sound of their engines a noisome drone, raced past upon the grey of tarmac, intent on their early morning commute to wherever on earth they thought they needed to be. Dan smiled. He needed to be right here. It was a scene he'd searched for all his life. He stood back, took a long pull on his electric cigarette, stroked at his voluminous hipster beard—one Rasputin would be envious of—and adjusted his topknot. "Take your dreams seriously, yeah? And success will come your way," he whispered, blowing out his favourite go-to phrase in a plume of electric go-to smoke that dispersed on the gentle early morning breeze, adding, "You've got this, Dan! It's in the bag!"

Dan possessed what was known as an *optimistic soul,* although his friends had another take on things. "Dan was deluded," they would say behind his back, "a dreamer who just didn't possess the tools for success. Not even a metaphorical screwdriver." Of course, they never told him this. Not directly. Instead, they would say things like, "It's great how you keep pushing yourself, despite all the setbacks," and, "I really love your stuff, I just can't understand why it doesn't sell," and, "No, I don't have room for one of your daubs on my living room wall…"

His friends knew exactly why Dan's art didn't sell. His paintings were spattered with the most awful garish colours.

Rainbow splats that looked like a toddler had chewed a box of crayons and copiously vomited over his canvases.

Of course, none of this put Dan off. If anything, he viewed his lack of success as a sure sign that artistic triumph was soon to be his. He'd studied enough art history to realise that every famous artist that had ever lived had started off as a failure... mostly. Which meant he was doing exactly the right thing, and therefore, nothing so far had dented his confidence. And yet, faced with this picture-perfect scene, with its picture-perfect light, and its picture-perfect imperfection, his hand wavered over the canvas. It was something that had never happened to him before. Dan felt... *uncertain.* A singular and unfamiliar sensation. What was it that Sylvia Plath had said? he thought to himself. *The worst enemy to creativity is self-doubt.* It was a great saying. One of the best. And yet his hand still hesitated. What if this scene, this light, and these colours were too much for him? What if he should fail? He pondered this new and quite terrifying concept for a moment before shaking his head emphatically, like a precocious child being force fed broccoli. "No Dan. Don't believe the haters! You can do this!" he bellowed as much to himself as to the painting gods, before boldly choosing the brightest red he could find and splashing it onto the canvas. Meanwhile, the painting gods looked at each other and grimaced.

Dan worked feverishly, his brush adding greens, blues, and brightly obscene purples and yellows. Shapes emerged and disappeared as if by magic, his hand darting up and down, and left and right, dabbing at his canvas like a one-handed man fighting for his life with a blunt knife. Finally, he dropped his brush and stood back to proudly assess his work.

It was a masterpiece of dripping, congealing, competing colours. "I can't wait to show this to all those doubters," he said to himself, happily wiping paint from his beard. And yet... the painting was very similar to all the others that he'd produced. Others that he'd not sold. But he was sure this was the breakthrough. It had to be! He'd used nearly every colour in his extensive palette. That must mean something…

Dan had left art school bright-eyed and clean-shaven five years ago, keen to start his life as a painter, but hadn't quite found his artistic mojo. He'd searched everywhere for it. Even under his bed and down the back of the sofa, but the thing refused to make an appearance. Of course, his classmates found their mojos early on, showing them off willy-nilly to anyone and everyone like it wasn't anything remotely special. Indeed, many of them had gone on to great success while he'd been waiting, his only solace those impressionable young ladies who sadly didn't stay impressionable for very long. Especially after they found out he was flipping burgers for some horrible food chain as a means to get by. Nevertheless, Dan had been confident that his moment would come, his breakthrough. But those five years had been hard on him, especially when he was forced to watch his classmates make careers while he stood comparatively still. He'd stopped communicating with them a long time ago, thinking that the zeitgeist he was so desperately waiting for could only ever be compromised by his association with them. And besides, he needed freedom from all the distraction of their ongoing success. Or so he told himself. He was doing it the proper way, by struggling, by not selling even a single painting, by being actively despised by art dealers and other artists, and by flipping greasy burgers…

Dan nervously reassessed the canvas. The colours were bold, sure they were, but many of them had run together to make a muddy brown. And, if he was brutally honest, it bore little or no resemblance to the fantastic scene in front of him, literally or figuratively. The uncomfortable feeling of self-doubt descended upon Dan for a second time accompanied by a profound feeling of revelation. It was like a veil had been lifted from his eyes and he was seeing his work properly for the very first time. And Dan didn't like what he saw. "This is rubbish, isn't it? All my work is utter, utter—"

The loud roar of a heavy engine, the screech of brakes and an almighty crash. A massive silver tanker left the road at speed, traveling too fast to make the corner, and smashed through the roadside hedge, rolling towards him. Dan could do nothing but watch, dumbfounded. The cab bit into the thick earth, flipping the truck onto its back, halting its forward motion, and spraying a wall of dirt upwards. Seconds later, with various cracks and pops, the tanker split open, geysering thick white foam in a series of frothing albino oil-strikes, bathing everything in the immediate vicinity in blinding, beautiful white, a white that grew like an alive thing. And with it came a familiar smell. A smell that Dan hadn't smelled in a long, long time.

Shaving foam.

A creak of metal and a teenager crawled out of the smashed cab, took one look at the carnage and at Dan, and ran away.

"What the—" Dan said, staring at the scene before him, suddenly aware of more movement. A previously unseen figure stood up amongst what was now a sea of white. A man in his thirties, dressed all in black, seemingly untouched by the foam explosion. The guy took in the scene without much interest, shrugged, and ambled away.

It is said that the dividing line between idiocy and genius is a fine one, and unbeknown to Dan, he was not only going to step across that line but take one giant leap over it. His trained eye focused in on this new person, drawn to the black figure highlighted by the almost total absence of colour. And within seconds he was working on the same garish canvas, painting over it in glorious strokes of white.

SKANKY MIKE

NINE MONTHS AFTER Dan's moment of *Gillette, the best a man can get* inspiration, Skanky Mike shambled into the small, unlit London alleyway that had been his home for the last twenty-six years. An icy chill followed him, cutting through his dirt-encrusted, second-hand rags like they weren't there. Icy chills in London had come into their own in recent years and had somewhat got above themselves. These days, icy chills roved in gangs who would chase you home and mug you on your doorstep.

It was 3am or thereabouts, not that Skanky Mike owned a watch or cared about time. He didn't care about very much these days. He was fifty-seven years old, tired, and felt the freezing cold deep in his bones. He thankfully reached his little makeshift shack and crawled inside, knocking over a quarter bottle of whisky with a note pinned to it.

> *It's gonna be a cold one tonight so I got you this to keep you warm.*

Skanky Mike barely took in the words, opening the bottle without a second thought and put it to his mouth, guzzling the free booze like a man dying of thirst, the whisky dripping into his unkempt, manky beard. After teasing out the last drop, he threw the bottle aside, burping loudly.

Who is Skanky Mike? Let's just say he's one of the many unfortunate individuals left to fend for themselves on the increasingly cruel streets of London. Mike had been living here since the 80s with less and less support.

Over these long years, Skanky Mike's home in the alleyway behind an old unused gallery had grown from temporary cardboard and plastic sheeting to a small hut-like crawl hole with a corrugated roof and sturdy, wooden posts. He even had a newish mattress and two sleeping bags, as well as a small table and a place where he kept an old plate and some rusting cutlery. It wasn't much, but it was home. Indeed, compared to most of the homeless people forced to survive on the cold streets in recent times, he lived in a comparative palace.

He'd stayed there relatively undisturbed for decades... until a few months ago that is, when the abandoned gallery had been taken over by some young rich types whose attempts to get rid of him had so far failed.

Skanky Mike is a fixed part of the local community, and no one can force him to move...

...was how the young journalist had written about him in the local newspaper. Skanky Mike had told her to *get lost* when she'd first come to interview him. Until she promised to get him a burger and to pay him twenty quid that is. After that, he was putty in her hands. Rather smelly, sweary putty, but malleable all the same. She'd gotten her story and, as a result, the local community had banded together to keep Skanky Mike where he was. These *upstart gallery owners* couldn't remove him. He was a *local character* and *part of the rich community fabric of the area*.

The fact that most of the story was made up and that Skanky Mike wasn't quite the lovable character he was portrayed as—Skanky Mike was in fact a miserable, cantankerous loner—meant nothing to him. He got to stay where he was, and that's all that mattered. For a few weeks, well-meaning visitors would drop off food and bags of clothes for him, until they realised what a disagreeable character he really was and went back to their uptight, guilty middle-class lives.

Skanky Mike wasn't his real name of course. It had been given to him by his first and only love, Pauline. A young, skinny, and petite but no less dangerous Glaswegian punk who he took under his wing in the mid-90s. Pauline had been, as far as he could guess, abused by her stepfather, and forced out of her family home when she tried to tell her mother. There was more to it than that, but she never said what that was. And he never pushed her. *Skanky Mike* was her pet name for him. He never knew why she called him that, but keeping the name kept her alive in his mind. She'd been a great gal, until…

He didn't know who gave her a beating or why, only that she'd come to him bruised and swollen with a badly cut lip. Her injuries didn't appear to be that bad, the little of them he was allowed to see. Even so, Mikey had wanted to take her to the hospital to be checked over, but Pauline wouldn't let him.

"A dinnae wantae gang hospital," she'd told him most emphatically in her thick, Glaswegian tones. "A'm afrad they'll pat me awa', Mikey. A've hud worse, haven't ah?"

One thing was for sure, they needed a place to hole up while she recovered. That's when Mikey decided to move into this alleyway with its large rubbish and weed-filled courtyard beyond. It sat at the end of an East End backstreet near Spitalfields Market that almost no one knew existed. He'd walked past the road before, hundreds of times, and never noticed it. At the end of this road was the small alleyway that was to become his home for over a quarter of a century, half-blocked with bins and more rubbish. He'd discovered the place a few weeks earlier when on one of his *scavenging hunts* as he used to call them. He'd found open doors leading into a maze-like gallery building filled with boxes and crates and had snuck inside for a looksee. And may have picked up one or two things before sneaking back out again. The next time he visited, the doors were closed, and the building deserted. All the better. Skanky Mike saw the potential of the alleyway straightaway, planning for him and Pauline to live there, once she recovered that is.

But she never did.

The day after the beating, she'd mostly slept, making him promise to go and get antibiotics and painkillers. As they were homeless, neither of them could get a bank account and so the pittance they were paid by the government was given out to them in cash on a daily basis. Normally, they'd go to the dole office together, but with Pauline unable to walk, he'd queued up to get both their money. There was a disturbance, and the police were called. By the time he got paid, he needed a drink. Really needed a drink.

His plan was to buy a couple of ciders, drinking one himself and taking the other back to Pauline—after popping to the local surgery that supported those on the street to pick up the medical supplies. But he never got there. He drank both bottles and went back for more, spending both his and Pauline's money on a ten-hour bender. By the time he returned to the alleyway, he was steaming drunk, belligerent, and angry at Pauline for making him feel guilty about spending her money.

"Where hae ye bin? Ah wis wrong afore, Mikey. Go get th' man. Tak' me tae hospital. A'm hurting bad," she'd said, grabbing him with sharp, urgent hands, her black and blue face twisted in pain. But Skanky Mike did nothing. "Mikey!" she screamed, "A'm dying 'ere! Mikey!"

"You're never happy!" he drawled at her from a drunken haze, pushing her away. "I've had enough!"

She screamed in pain, clutching at her side. "Mikey! I need

help! Mikey!"

"Leave me alone!" Mikey had shouted, putting his hands over his ears, lying down, and passing out. At various times during the night, he was awoken by Pauline's desperate screams, but he was too far gone to notice or care.

The next day, Pauline was screaming no more. Dead and unmoving. It was his fault. If he'd gotten the antibiotics like she'd wanted instead of drinking all that cider, maybe she'd still be alive. He'd dragged her away and dumped her where she'd be found as just another dead homeless girl.

Skanky Mike had never forgiven himself. Living in the alleyway was his punishment—to remind him of what he'd done to his best friend. He'd been here ever since.

He pulled out a half-eaten kebab from his coat pocket, pushed his long greasy hair behind his ears, and took a bite, chewing mechanically, its contents spilling onto the floor. A rat poked its head out of the outer gallery wall that his little shack backed onto. "You made it, huh?" he said to the rodent, offering a piece of pitta bread that it snatched off him before disappearing.

Mikey had seen the exterminator van earlier in the day. It was parked right outside his little hideaway. He hated pest exterminators for deeply personal reasons that only the reporter from the local paper knew about.

"The gallery is riddled with vermin," he was told by Bill, the pest control guy, although Mikey received the distinct impression that the man was talking about him and his little shack.

Feeling a little woozy, Mikey lay back on his mattress, his head buzzing, his hands clammy, and his jaw tense. A few months ago, there was no room for a van to park here or any other vehicle. The new gallery owners had cleared away all the rubbish he'd collected over the years, as well as the weeds and overgrown vegetation, dumping it all into a large skip. The clearance was undertaken to uncover the gallery's back doors.

A way to move art and paintings in and out of the downstairs gallery space. The upshot was that, apart from his little shelter, the place was nothing like how it had been. And now the cold wind whistled where before it only rustled. Tonight, the blasts of air sounded strangely distant.

Mikey!

He sat up shaking his head, the shack spinning and twisting around him, the wooziness replaced with a feeling like he was falling.

Mikey boy!

"Pauline," he whispered, his own voice sounding weird and phased. "Wha'…?" he gasped. "Wha' tha he—"

His voice was cut off by a dreadful screeching, a twisted, painful shriek, the sound stabbing into him with a force that knocked him backwards. He crawled outside his makeshift den into the cold night, but he no longer felt the chill. He was hot and sweaty. The sky glowed with an overpoweringly bright amber from street-lighting that smothered everything in dripping marmalade. He stood up onto trembling legs, reaching out his hand to touch the sticky liquid, his arm extending so weirdly that he snatched it back in fear.

"Wa's happening to me?" he whispered, his words echoing and taking actual form in front of him, before turning to ash and blowing away.

The screeching repeated, its sound sharp, vivid, and unearthly, blasting down the alleyway and straight into him. Mikey knew what the sound was, it had haunted his dreams for over twenty-five years—Pauline screaming for him to help her!

A hand on his shoulder and a voice whispering into his ear. *Mikey?*

Skanky Mike twisted around to come face-to-face with Pauline, her skin swollen, bruised and black. Her finger stabbing at him in accusation! "It was yay who did this ta me, Mikey! Yay did this!"

Skanky Mike turned and ran, screaming dementedly into the night.

THE BANGING AT THE DOOR

TWO DAYS AFTER Skanky Mike ran away from his alleyway home never to return, Jim Riven was awoken by a loud banging on his front door, and the rude shouting of his name.

He rolled over to his bedside table and glared at the glowing blurs of his ancient digital clock. The bright green numbers told him what he already knew. It was not anywhere near noon. Not even close to it. It wasn't even bloody 10am! Riven was just contemplating the horrific truth of this when… more banging and some wholly impressive shrieking.

Riven knew what he must do. He lay back down and closed his eyes. Whatever was going on outside his front door in the real world could stay there thank you very much. This was his special time for lazy sleeps, for snoozing the morning away, and for nothing much else. Getting up and facing the day was one of his least favourite things to do. The world, with all its demands, needs and necessities, was a place he preferred to enter on his own terms. No. He preferred to stay within the confines of his soft, white, gently yielding oblong. Add a pillow, a warm, tea-stained duvet, and an offed-phone, and he was as happy as any number of people who are confident to call themselves *Larry* on an almost permanent basis.

More bangs. The shrieking now reminiscent of some kind of drunken Tolkienesque Nazgul get-together.

What on earth was going on out there?

Riven gave it no concern. It would soon stop, and he could slip back into his preferred, lazy, and restorative sleep. He was about to stick his head under his duvet when the reprehensible happened. The one thing that was strictly forbidden. The singular action that all his friends, acquaintances, and everyone else in between had been warned against—a warning that involved many stern waggings of his finger, multiple threats, and more expletives than were strictly necessary. Whoever was outside his door had pressed the flat's buzzer and all hell and damnation was let loose!

Riven had lived in his North London flat, located a short walk from Camden Town tube station, for seven years, and in all that time he'd never been able to locate the circuit that disabled the buzzer welded to his front door. It was like his whole flat screeched and vibrated at him when it was pressed. A howling dirge backed by a shrieking chorus of demented and screaming lost souls. He'd purposely covered it up with tape and had added various warning messages over the years. Messages that became more gratuitously offensive and abusive as the time passed. Pressing the buzzer was beyond the pale! Whatever that actually meant. But it was beyond it, and by some considerable distance.

He flung off his duvet, flung himself down his hallway, flung open his flat door and flung the blurred person standing there one of his best frowns. Light stabbed into his eyes, blinding him. He was pretty sure that four-point-six billion years ago, the sun had been a neat idea—warming, kick-starting life and such and such—but this Saturday morning, hungover after a heavy Friday night chasing lagers and that girl with the spiky hair and the cheeky smile who'd totally refused to have anything to do with him, the sun was doing itself no favours whatsoever.

He squished up his eyes to no great effect and led with an "Ugh!" an "Arrghgt!" and a "Who on earth is this?" followed by some Olympic standard coughing. While he was trying to stop his lungs from bursting all over his doorstep, a cloyingly scented figure pushed past him.

"Get your act together, Riv," said a familiar female voice. "This is important."

An anxiety-infused name stabbed violently into his mind.

Landa!

And he'd let her in. To celebrate the acquisition of this knowledge, he indulged in some more coughing, combining it artistically with a series of nasty dry retches. It was a display worthy of a gold medal.

"I'll make tea," Landa said from somewhere inside his flat. "And put some clothes on, no one wants to look at that thing before 10am!"

LANDA

JIM RIVEN'S EARLY morning slumber was not always duvet-covered bliss. Sometimes he'd sit bolt-up in bed, sweaty and panicked, checking under the sheets for the presence of a certain ex-girlfriend, wondering what he'd do with himself if she ever turned up in his life again.

Landa's full name was Yolanda Osbourne, and she was loaded. Properly rich. Part of the Kensington Set. The daughter of Roy *Roo* Osbourne—a billionaire businessman, media tycoon and all-round git who owned Roo Corps, a rather nasty right-wing news and media organisation. He was one of those shadowy kingpins who whispered in the ears of politicians and used his newspapers and news channels to influence public opinion, openly boasting that he could make or break governments if he so wished. Which, it seemed he could. So yeah, Roo Osbourne was a top class S.O.B.

Riven had tried to talk to Landa about her father, about how he supported an elitist system of haves and have nots, but he just wasn't very good at all those annoying political conversations and usually ended up stumped and irritated, wishing he'd said this or that when he'd had the time to think it through properly. But despite his conversational feebleness,

Riven believed the little guy deserved more. The underdog. Those less well-off and those unable to look after themselves. Who doesn't think like that who's not decent? Live and let live and all that, was his favourite go to phrase. The fact that Landa was loaded and didn't really notice or understand society's unbalances, nor the role played in them by her father, had been a constant source of irritation to him.

Just the thought of Landa's name was enough to give Riven the Heebie-Jeebies. Luckily for him, she had announced one fantastic morning six months ago, that they were over, and that he'd just have to live with it, okay? Riven had certainly lived with it. And when she'd gone—collecting all her things and slamming his front door without even a polite goodbye—he was not ashamed to admit he'd punched the air and performed a set of complicated but euphoric little dances.

Riven liked having girlfriends, but they came with a whole host of horrible possibilities. They wanted to talk to him. To go to places with him. To get him off his sofa and to do all manner of things for them. Unfortunately for Jim Riven, Landa was all these girlfriends rolled into one. There was nothing wrong with Landa per se. She had all the required feminine bits and pieces in all the right feminine places. Some might say *very much in the right places* but her considerable physical charms were no match for her equally considerable lack of any emotional charm whatsoever. But on the rare occasions when Landa was not screaming, drinking, and snorting her way through life (usually when she was asleep), Riven had a soft spot for her. Troubled soul and all that. Like a sticky toffee that pulled at your fillings—after a while it became almost palatable, although you vowed to lay off the things in the future.

He closed his flat door, stumbled back to his bedroom, and hastily picked his way through the pile of clothes he liked to keep on his bedroom floor. Once suitably dressed—black trousers, black jacket and a black tee-shirt bearing the legend *Don't Mess With This Idiot*—he lurched with considerable trepidation into his kitchen, bemoaning the fact that Landa was back in his life again, something he'd been actively and successfully avoiding for the last six months.

How did he meet her? He shuddered at the memory.

He'd been forced out to a party of some sort about a year ago as a favour to his best friend, Dillon, who was attempting to woo a work colleague of his—the girl with the nice eyelashes and the look that was so very agreeable. The plan was to go to the party, get him bolstered with a few lagers and maybe some shots, and then for him to make his move. It was an awful plan. Not in the sense that it was doomed to fail—this was the same plan Dillon depressingly implemented every time he found himself under the charms of some wide-eyed bright young thing way out of his league—but in the sense that he always chickened out. Dillon would come up with some reason why now wasn't the right time to make his move, like he'd drunk too much, or he was wearing the wrong beige, corduroy trousers, or that the moment had inexplicably passed.

Riven would've taken him to the task on the matter if it wasn't for the simple reason that it's biologically impossible for some guys—guys like Dillon—to chat to girls they fancy. Riven, on the contrary, could certainly talk to the opposite sex, although, judging by their general reaction, it appeared to be something they wished he'd stop doing.

It was at this party that Riven met Landa. Or to put it another way, where Landa mugged him. It wasn't a conventional mugging. There was no knife, no sock full of pound coins, and certainly no knuckle-dustered fist to the face, but he'd been mugged all the same. No doubt about it. As already mentioned, Landa had the right feminine bits and pieces all present and correct—on this occasion, they were well-displayed to even the most casual observer. Riven had been altogether taken by her external attributes, thrust as they were into an impossibly small, red cocktail dress and never thought for one moment that this girl was going to come back to his flat with him and then force herself so completely into his life that he would seriously consider making a one-way move to a different continent. Sure, on the face of it, impressively proportioned girls throwing themselves at you at parties sounds just the thing guys and certain ladies would love.

On the face of it.

He'd been absentmindedly talking to Dillon about the things Dillon loved talking about, computer games, coding, 70s TV, spy movies and antique US guns—Dillon was a great guy, but his interests were somewhat niche—when Landa breezed over, fixing him with those sparkling green eyes of hers framed by a head of flowing, thick red hair, and grabbing his forearm. He often thought there was something very needy in the way some people needed to grab a hold. To say he was not touchy-feely was an understatement. He was neither to any great extent. Rather the opposite to be honest. The girl might be the hottest thing at this party, but that gave her no right to latch onto him like some dazzling, ginger limpet mine. He was about to tell her this when he spotted Dillon's face. Despite his friend's particularly voluminous beard, long shaggy hair, and thick-rimmed beer-bottle bottom glasses, he could see he was impressed. Very impressed. Dillon had that lazy grin plastered across his face. That same face he'd been using when talking about the girl from his work with the nice eyelashes and the look that was so very agreeable. And so Riven made the mistake of suffering Landa's attentions just for the sake of machismo.

Machismo is not a good look at any time, especially on Jim Riven and, unfortunately, things had progressed very quickly after that.

Usually, in the course of these things, waking up with an impressive specimen of naked womanhood draped over you, was a fine thing indeed. No matter that your neck was stiff, and you could no longer feel your arm, this was generally known among those less sexually successful guys—and those certain ladies again—as a 'result', leading to a cockiness of step and the recital of exaggerated sex-god-like details to envious friends. In this instance, as Riven lay there listening to Landa's snoring, he'd had an opposite take on the thing. He couldn't help but think he'd been sort of… used. It wasn't that he hadn't been pleasured in the required fashion, nor that Landa hadn't enjoyed her own intense moments of physical abandon—which she certainly had—but it was more of a feeling that, well, he could've been anybody. And there comes a time in your early thirties when that kind of thing just doesn't wash any more.

Nevertheless, Landa was not an unattractive lady, especially when she was as still and as quiet as she was then. But that was to change very quickly and rather radically.

Her phone, that she'd left switched on and that had been making gentle chirruping noises all night, started ringing and within seconds she was awake and rummaging through a red leather bag. One adept hand emerging with a lighter, cigarettes and the offending phone.

She answered the call with a pleased squawk—like the ululation of a parrot let out of its cage on a single-minded mission to terrorise the cat—and shoved the diamond-encrusted device into the crook of her neck, whilst pulling herself free of him and lighting a cigarette.

"Guess where I am?" she shrieked gleefully. "Yes! Some guy I picked up. Yeah. I'm at his place. Yeah. He's here now." She pushed the phone into Riven's face. "Say hi," she demanded.

"Um, hi," Riven replied, waving impotently at the surrounding cloud of cigarette smoke. There was a pause before a posh voice answered. *"Oh hi. You're with Landa, huh?"*

"Um, yeah."

"Right, okay, yeah."

Landa shrieked and put the phone back to her ear. "Yeah, yeah we did. Yeah. Lots of times. Every which way and then some. Hu-huh. Yeah, we did that as well. Ouch! Ye-ah."

There was a lot more yeahs and then some expletives before it became apparent that the person on the other end of the phone was not as pleased with recent events as was Landa. The sound of a man crying was not something Riven particularly enjoyed, not even second-hand, especially through a phone jammed to his ear, but Landa insisted he listen.

She finally offed the phone and lay back on her pillow, taking a long drag on her cigarette. "That will teach him!" she said gleefully, grabbing his favourite mug emblazoned with the phrase *I BLOODY LOVE TEA* from the bedside table and balancing it on the flat of her taut, muscled stomach to use as a makeshift ashtray.

Riven loved that mug. Using it as an ashtray was just heresy.

"So, what did he, um, do?" he asked, biting down his annoyance.

"Do!" she shrieked again, making dogs howl and bark in a half a mile radius. "I told him not to see that girl, but he wouldn't listen."

"He was having it away with someone else behind your back?"

"Oh no," she replied, taking such a large drag on her cigarette that it fizzled like a fuse in a stick of dynamite. "He wouldn't dare! But that girl at his work—I've seen the way he looks at her. Nasty, flirty, little cow. I told him point-blank, quit your job or I quit you."

"That's quite some ultimatum."

"If someone loves you, they do what you say," she blurted in an explosion of smoke. "It's as simple as that."

"I'm not sure it is," Riven replied. "I would go as far as to say that there's some debate allowed on such matters." Landa stared back at him with such an expression of confusion that he felt compelled to carry on. "I take it he didn't leave his job?"

Her entire face creased like a balled fist. "Said he couldn't. Said it wasn't possible. Said people were depending on him. You know the kind of guff guys come out with when there's a sniff of a lay? But I'd been very clear. He either left that hospital or I left him."

"Hospital? What does he do?"

"He's a surgeon or some whatnot. And you know nurses."

"…Right."

The conversation, such as it was, carried on like this for some time and, as the minutes ticked slowly by, Riven became less and less convinced that his recent life choice had been a positive one. He understood that there was such a thing as a *rebound leg-over*—not one of the most eloquent of terms, but it put across the meaning more than adequately—and he assumed that this was what had happened. Landa had used him to teach someone else a lesson, and the comprehensive list of sexual positions and practices she had engaged him in were in fact part of a particular plan of revenge that led to the possibility that, once Landa had finished her one-sided tirade about her boyfriend, men in general, and nasty nurse cows as she called them, she might get up, gather her scattered, red-themed ensemble, and disappear from his life forever.

Riven had never been so naïve.

It took six months of hard work to extricate himself from this girl. As to how he managed this impossibility? That's a story for another time. Suffice it to say, he'd now lived a blissful Landa-less six months and her sudden appearance at his front door had set alarm bells ringing and sirens blaring across the normally quiet and civilized world of Jim Riven's mind. Landa was back, she was in his kitchen, and she was banging and shrieking like a trapped cat being attacked by a vengeful parrot.

THE MISSING MONDRIAN

"**WE'RE NOT GETTING** back together, yeah?" Landa announced as he sipped at a mug of tea.

He'd been forced to make the tea himself after one of Landa's meltdowns—how she fed and watered herself was beyond him. Even trying to boil a kettle was a three-act drama. He said nothing. Keeping quiet or using one-word replies was the only way to deal with Landa. That and running away when her back was turned.

"So don't get your hopes up," she added. "I am in a serious relationship, yeah? With one of Daddy's friends. He's an architect. So I don't want you blabbing about me being here. Hush hush, okay?"

Jim Riven took in the news with a relieved sigh. Things were not as disastrous as he'd first imagined. But Landa was here and wanted something from him, that much was for sure. He decided, there and then, to do whatever he could to get her out of his life as quickly as possible. But it was still early and Jim Riven did not do mornings. He sat on the sofa wincing at the sunlight streaming into his living room. He kept a strict closed-curtain policy. Or he did until Landa arrived. The amount of light now entering his brain was reaching dangerous levels. He considered closing his eyes and hoping Landa would disappear. It was a silly idea, but mornings were a time when, more than any other, he was prone to half-awake idle fancy. Nevertheless, the idea took physical form and he wished her away.

"Open your eyes, I'm talking to you!"

He did as ordered, restraining himself from saluting. Landa had that kind of effect on a guy.

"I'm here about your skill. You know the one. For solving things."

"I am not a detective," he said, sounding more than a little defensive. "I've told you this time and time again."

Landa shook her head. The barest of shakes. But enough to inform him that his opinion on this matter was not relevant, important, or indeed needed at this time. Or any time in the future thank you very much. "Remember how you found Mum's Fabergé earring after we started going out?"

Riven did indeed remember. If anything, the whole episode had only cemented Landa's connection to him.

You see, Jim Riven had a certain talent—if you can call it that. A being-at-the-right-place-at-the-right-time sort of thing. Coincidence some might call it. Others living in a Jungian Universe would cite Synchronicity, whereas those with a more religious bent simply believed it was God winking at them. Whatever it was, Riven was a terminal sufferer. Things were just apt to happen around him, without any regard for what he thought about it.

Of course, everyone has experienced coincidences at some time in their lives. For normal people, these are wonderful little moments. Startling, confusing, and great fun to talk about in pubs on long Sunday pub afternoons when you've eaten and drunk too much and don't want to go home. Like when you're reading or writing something, and the exact same phrase is spoken on the TV or radio. Or when you're thinking of that idiot ex from years ago and then suddenly find a friend request from that same idiot ex in your social media feed. Or when you bump into Steve from IT on holiday in a bar in the back end of nowhere and he starts telling you about the new company laptop download and you want to kill him. You think to yourself, Wow! What an amazing coincidence! Before downing your overly generous Tequila Sunrise, making your excuses, and climbing out of the nearest window.

Except it wasn't amazing. Not for Jim Riven anyway. His life simply wasn't his own. That's why he preferred to stay in bed. It reduced the possibility of all that happenchance that dogged his existence. These coincidences certainly didn't happen all the time, instead they came in annoying waves, but they were regular and irritating enough to cause him a lot of problems. Like what happened with Landa's mother's missing Fabergé earring. The incident that had cemented Landa to him.

Landa smiled, her thick ruby lips parting to reveal a perfect set of expensive-looking teeth. "I need you Riven. I need your special talents. And you're not allowed to say no, okay? I don't care what time of the sodding morning it is for you. This is important."

Riven took another sip of tea and groaned inside.

"You are going over to Monty's Outtasight! gallery, okay?" Landa continued, seemingly able to speak at the same time as taking a drag on her cigarette and gulping a mouthful of tea. Monty was Landa's best friend and state-registered egomaniac.

"Monty's got a gallery? I thought he was something big in Bitcoin or whatever, or so he bragged to me."

"Yeah, about that. Ouch. Monty lost nearly everything. Some sort of investment thing gone wrong. Wiped him out."

"So why on earth did he open a gallery?"

"It came to him, when he was at the lowest of the low, a way for him to get back. He's always loved art. You've seen the way he dresses, he's like a piece of art himself. So of course I helped him with the financing and everything."

"Of course."

"He's my bestest, bestest friend, okay? He'd do the same for me if I was in a pinch."

"And what you want me to do involves Monty?"

"It was his opening night, last night. Everybody who is anybody was there. Celebs… just everybody. It went on until way past midnight. We had such a wonderful time. But… Oh Riv, when Monty arrived back at the gallery this morning, he discovered my Mondrian was missing."

"Your what?"

"My Mondrian."

"And what's a Mondrian when it's at home?"

"A painting by Piet Mondrian! You must've heard of him."

"Must I?"

"He's a very famous last century Dutch painter who only single-handedly kick-started the Modern Art movement." She thrust her bejeweled phone into his face.

Riven stared at an impressively sized painting made up of red, yellow, and white painted blocks within a trellis of thick black lines. Landa stood in front of the enormous daub, looking oddly colour coordinated. It was something he could've painted himself in a couple of hours. Then again, he never really understood modern art. Which didn't mean he poo-pooed it—certainly not—he just accepted that where some people engaged with moving, evocative shapes, colours, and sculptures, all he ever saw were squiggly lines and garish hues and bits of well-crafted stone and whatnot. It was an affliction more than anything else. No. Riven's area of expertise was more in the area of curry, of selecting the best individual Jalfrezis from the best local takeaways. And Shiraz. Lots of Shiraz. That… and the synchronicity thing that he didn't like to talk about.

"It's certainly… very blocky," he ventured. "Lots of squares and oblongs. Very nice. Was it expensive?"

Judging by the way Landa's eyes bulged in her rather beautiful face, he guessed the answer was veering towards 'don't be bloody stupid'. She snatched the phone away and threw it into her ornate handbag.

Riven invested in what he hoped came across as a sage nod. "How much are we talking?"

Landa sighed, the mask of her usually hard face suddenly dropping and Riven couldn't help but be impressed at her effortless beauty. Beauty now etched with fear.

"Millions and millions, Riv. What am I going to do?" Tears exploded from her eyes in a torrent, dripping down her high cheekbones to pool underneath her elegant chin. "The Mondrian belongs to Daddy and now it's missing. I should never have borrowed it."

"Art theft is a serious business," Riven said, watching the tears spill onto her expansive bosom, turning the red material of her dress crimson. "Why doesn't Monty get onto the police and the insurance companies? That's a job for them. Get the professionals in."

Landa shook her head vehemently, tears spraying everywhere. "I can't! It's all Daddy's fault!" she spat, her voice a gunshot ricocheting off the living room walls making Riven jump. "He knows I absolutely love Mondrian. He picked up the painting a few months ago. An absolute beaut'. I think he did it to spite me. I asked him if I could have it for my pad, it would look so cool in my entrance hall. You know the wall I mean?"

Riven had been to Landa's pad as she called it. A massive five-bedroom mansion in the heart of Kensington. The overriding theme was Landa's favourite colour red. It had been interior designed by one of those bouffanted and bearded fellows off the telly. As far as he could tell, he'd just sloshed different shades of red paint everywhere before presenting Landa with what he guessed was a bill of obscene proportions. From what he'd seen of the Mondrian, it would sit perfectly in her entrance hall, in the same way a clown would grace an abattoir.

"But Daddy wouldn't let me borrow it. Said I was too irresponsible. But he's been away for months—some Middle

East deal—and I sort of loaned it to myself," Landa continued, blowing her nose. "When Monty asked to display the painting at the opening night of his new gallery… I couldn't say no. And now it's gone missing! I told Monty straight. You can't go to the police! Daddy will find out and he's been threatening to stop my allowance for a long time now. This will give him the perfect opportunity."

"I see."

"You do? That's great, Riven, great. You'll help me then? Yeah?"

Riven let out a sigh, world-weary, with more than a hint of tired, fed up resignation. "Okay."

Landa squealed, throwing herself at him, her damp bosom pushing wetly into his neck. "There's a taxi outside waiting for you!" she wailed into his ear. "It'll take you right there." She pulled away, her emotion-twisted face suddenly all smiles, and again, Riven was hit by her stunning looks. "I know you can do it!"

"I can't promise anything, but sure, I'll go take a looksee. Just don't get your hopes up."

She squealed again. "Cool, I'll be waiting back at my pad."

"You're not coming with me?"

"I said a few things to Monty. You know the kind of things? Shouty, sweary things. I was angry at him for losing my multi-million-pound painting. He'll cool down, we both will, when you find the Mondrian for me." She grabbed the mug of tea out of his hands and replaced it with a showy business card for Monty's gallery, Outtasight! The name was pure 60s' slang and designed in a pure 60s' font, surrounding a large, yellow, winking smiley face.

"Off you go," Landa ordered, pulling him to his feet and pushing him forwards.

Riven lurched out of his flat into the bright morning of one of those spring months that couldn't quite decide if they want to be warm or not. Today it was going with the whole bright, sunny and shiny but freezing cold vibe. A taxi waited outside, one of the older ones, its diesel engine slowly chugging, clouds of exhaust rising majestically into the air and adding to the general misguided sense that global warming wasn't anything much to worry about.

Landa left the flat, loudly slamming the door behind her. "Remember how you found Mum's Fabergé earring after we started going out?" she said as if giving a pep-talk to a reluctant fighter. "It will be just like that."

Riven did indeed remember.

THE FABERGÉ EARRING

IT WAS A few weeks or so after they had started going out together. Landa had gone to some swanky do near where she lived in Kensington and had forgotten to pick him up on the way. She'd been forgetting about him for a week or two and had even left him to spend the night at a gas station one evening after she and her friends totally forget he was with them. Jim Riven only saw this as a positive sign. Perhaps soon, he had hoped, she would forget about him altogether, but regrettably, events were going to take an unfortunate, if not predictable turn.

With Landa away at her swanky Kensington do, he'd spent a good fifty-minutes pondering changing his name, his address, and finally his country by taking the next available flight to Lithuania or any other province he knew next to nothing about, but came to the conclusion that this was fraught with too many practical concerns and logistical problems. Instead, Riven decided to make his escape via a take-away curry and an expensive Shiraz. He was happily imbibing his favourite exotic spicy concoction when he bit into something very uncurrylike. It turned out to be a piece of costume jewellery.

Or so he'd thought at the time.

He washed it under the kitchen tap and left it on the draining board. And there was his mistake right there. But he'd learned he couldn't win against synchronicity. If he'd hidden the thing at the back of a drawer or thrown it away, Landa would've still somehow stumbled upon it.

Depressingly, this was just how things operated around him.

Landa arrived later that night, inebriated and in a bit of a state, which, for her, was nothing new. Drink? She was a booze and drug all-rounder. She'd lost one of her mother's earrings—the ones she'd been expressly forbidden to borrow. Rubies surrounded by a crown of diamonds. The spit of the stud he'd found in his Mushroom Jalfrezi. Landa spotted it almost immediately. After which, her shrieking hit new, previously undiscovered decibel levels.

Somewhere in her addled mind, she seemed to think he'd managed to find this important earring all on his own. And that he'd used some kind of detective ability, despite no logical evidence to the contrary. This wasn't the only incident that convinced her of his *talent*, but it was the one she remembered the most.

As to why or how an ear stud lost in Kensington ended up in a Camden curry house? That was beyond Riven. But he gave up trying to work this stuff out a long time ago. The whole thing was too perplexing and far too irksome. Suffice it to say, the incident with the earring had stuck with Landa. To be honest, that kind of thing would stick with anybody. It became lodged in her brain. And since that evening, whenever Landa found herself in trouble, she would pick up the phone and seek Riven out. It was also the reason, he guessed, why she stayed with him for so long, even when it became obvious that they were terminally unsuited. She had some notion that they were meant to be together, a notion that was difficult to shift. Landa had many, many notions. Without them, he guessed, she would just be a stunningly attractive rich girl who lacked any sort of purpose other than to cause trouble, mishap, and distress wherever she went. She wasn't bad per se—that sticky toffee again—but in the scheme of things, he really, desperately, hopelessly wished he'd never met her.

But he had.

He nodded his goodbye to Landa, who was already on her phone blathering to one of her mates, and slipped into the back of the taxi hoping for a little snooze.

BLOODY GRAPEFRUIT

ROO OSBOURNE CRUMPLED back into the plush chair of his private jet, sipped at his cup of morning coffee and grimaced.

"What on earth is this, Janey?" he shouted, his voice a mixture of thick Australian outback and the various and unsuccessful attempts of many fired dictation coaches.

Janey—real name *Jane*—a stunningly attractive air stewardess in her late twenties busying herself at her station, immediately stopped what she was doing and came over. A vision in the blacks, whites and golds that formed the uniform of all Roo Osbourne's private staff, golden hair pinned to her head with military precision, the clothes fitting perfectly around her invitingly curved figure. Her makeup and golden hair reflected the same perfection. Not a smudge. Not a hair out of place. A living doll, and Roo Osbourne was a collector.

She took the cup off him and sipped at it. "I'm so sorry, sir. It's the new girl." She flicked her long eyelashes in the direction of an equally stunning brunette who was responsible for the coffee. A modern reincarnation of the 50s' actress Rita Hayworth, with almost the same iconic smile and cleavage. "She was only doing as you ordered sir. You asked for decaffeinated coffee and she complied."

"But when I order decaffeinated coffee, that's not what I

want is it, Janey?"

"No, sir."

"I want the other decaffeinated coffee."

Jane knew exactly what Roo Osbourne meant. He was requesting the decaffeinated coffee with a massive kick of caffeine in it. A little ritual that she had purposely forgotten to tell the new girl about. This was a sweet gig, and she wasn't getting any younger. Unlike her competition. "I'm sorry sir. The fault lies with myself for not conveying your wishes as… exactly as I should've done. It can be easily rectified."

Roo shook his large ungainly head, his thick, wet lips wobbling. Janey was playing a dangerous game and they both knew it. "It's not good enough. You know what to do."

"Of course, sir," she said smiling inside, her gambit paying off. "She won't be flying with you again."

"She won't be flying at all. Fire her."

There was no one here apart from Janey to see how Roo Osbourne could treat beautiful women. No one to observe how they held no sway over him. But he didn't need women, not anymore. He'd proved who he was time and time again. He was a badass billionaire. A billionaire who could get anything and have anyone. A billionaire only a fool would even think about crossing. Money was one thing, but power was something else entirely. And Roo was one of the most powerful people he knew. A media baron who forged his empire in Australia and the UK and who moved it to the US and then the Middle East. He could have any woman he wanted. Or anyone for that matter. But the power buzz of treating people any which way he liked was just as strong. Men would kill for women like these, he thought to himself—as I would've done, back in the day—but now I can treat them as nothing but vassals. He had a soft spot for Janey though. He knew what she'd done, sabotaging the new, younger girl in an attempt to get her fired. He respected her for that, for removing the competition. But she'd have to go too. He'd let one of his minions take care of it after they landed. It would be unfortunate for her to ruin her perfect face with ugly tears. Yes, Roo Osbourne was a collector, but he'd been the kind of kid who loved to smash his toys.

Jane nodded at the instruction, taking care not to show the disgust she always felt in her boss's presence, and took away the offending drink, replacing it a few minutes later with a cup of freshly brewed caffeinated coffee.

Roo accepted the coffee in one of his peculiarly small hands and took a sip. "Perfection."

"As it should be, sir," Jane replied, smiling, the line of her red lipstick precisely outlining her curved lips.

"Tell chef I'm ready for breakfast." He tried not to sound too disheartened, but breakfast had become his least favourite meal of the day.

"I'll bring it over now, sir. We'll be landing in London within the next forty minutes."

Roo straightened the cuffs of his excellently tailored shirt, readjusted his grey jacket's top-pocket hankie, and ran a hand over his short, greying hair. Everything about him was trying its very best to be immaculate, which was unfortunate, as Roo Osbourne was a large, ungainly, uncomfortable looking marsupial of a man. His limbs sat awkwardly in their sockets, and despite years of deportment tuition—his various tutors had all invariably given up or were fired—and the very best tailoring, he still pretty much resembled twelve-stone of potatoes wrapped up in a rather expensive and unsuitable-looking sack. Most unfortunately of all, was Roo's lugubrious, toothy face that bore a striking resemblance to *Macropus Giganteus*—the Eastern Grey Kangaroo. And that was despite of some considerable and very expensive orthodontic work.

He leant backward to allow Janey to drape an elegant, ironed napkin across his lap, his eyes dropping down from within his loose-skinned face to view her perky breasts for the last time. He did this with no attempt to hide his gaze. She was his employee and if he wanted to stare at her rack, he would stare at her rack. While it was worth staring at, that is. It's what she was paid for. Paid very handsomely as it happened.

The food when it arrived, was colloquially described as an *Aussie breakfast*—two farm fresh eggs, smoky bacon, grilled tomato and mushrooms, sausages, hash browns, and beans, as well as two sides of fried bread dripping in oil.

He cut off the end of the sausage, stabbing it with an elegant silver fork, before adding mushrooms and bacon and dunking it all into the thick yolk of an egg and stuffing it into his over-large mouth. He chewed for long moments, savouring the glorious flavours before spitting it all out into a silver bowl dutifully held by Janey just for that purpose, her smile never wavering. Next, he attacked the hash browns and beans.

Roo's Diabetes Type 2 meant that ingesting his favourite breakfast was now a thing of the past. But that would not stop him chewing every morsel and spitting it out before moving on to his prescribed healthy breakfast. Health was one of those irritating things that he couldn't control. He'd fired doctor after doctor until he'd been forced to accept the diagnosis.

Janey took the now full silver bowl away and almost immediately, his actual breakfast arrived. Bloody blood grapefruit! As prescribed by his latest wonder dietitian. The thing may have been elegantly segmented by his personal chef, glittering with a thin coating of demerara sugar, but to Roo Osbourne, it was like gilding a turd. Grimacing, he removed a single red, fleshy segment and placed it on his tongue. To say the fruit wasn't to everyone's taste, was an understatement. But the same dietitian was sure his diabetes could be reversed with exercise and a strict diet. She based her reputation on it. And a helluva lot more, Roo mused, curling his lip, but this time, finally, he'd succumbed to her advice. He winced at the taste, the grapefruit's sourness barely hidden by the meagre dusting of sweet—something his first wife had alluded to the last time she'd met him, suggesting that his new breakfast very much suited his personality. He'd let her get away with it, of course.

She was the mother of his only child and as such was spared the full hostility of his bare-toothed, hyena-esque Harvard lawyers. He supposed that at one time he may have been in love with her, and maybe part of him still was. His wife and his Eton Mess of a daughter, Yolanda, were family, and they deserved special consideration. No one else ever received such privilege and no one else ever would.

Roo's phone trilled. A delicate, warm tone. High-pitched sounds and garish, tinny music were, to put it lightly, not to his taste. Indeed, all his execs, employees and anyone in his proximity were either told to use the same tone or be banned from using a phone at all. Many had been sacked for breaking this rule, but then again, he mused, he could fill a stadium with all the people he'd fired over the years. Stalin had nothing on Roo Osbourne, that was for sure.

The phone sat on a specially designed cradle attached to his seat. Modern smart phones were incredibly useful, but unfortunately too large for Roo Osbourne to handle in his ridiculously small hands. The call was from his investigation firm. The one he used to keep tabs on anybody or any organisation trying to pry into his private or business life. He tapped at the screen with a small index finger and answered, nodding at the report, before replying in threatening tones. "You know the drill. Keep ya eyes on her. If she looks like she's gonna to be a problem, neutralise that problem in the usual way, unless you think she may be of any use to me. Either way, she's made the biggest mistake of her life."

Janey twisted her head to look at him, a concerned expression on her beautiful face, an expression that was immediately replaced with a smile.

Roo smiled back. Yeah, it was definitely time for Janey to go. The shelf life of these girls was a short one at best, but he'd kept Janey on past her time due to a rare attack of sentimentality and she'd gotten cocky.

He offed the call and chose another blood-red segment of

grapefruit, chewed, and swallowed quickly, grimacing.

"We are beginning our approach, Mr Osbourne," the pilot said calmly over the intercom. *"Touching down in just under fifteen minutes."*

Roo Osbourne had led a charmed life, it was written, where Roo Osbourne was the charm. A rag to riches story. From an outback farmhand to a news media goliath. Of course, most of this was untrue. Made up and embellished by a comprehensive media team he'd employed for just that purpose three decades ago. But the story had stuck. The same nonsense was written pretty much verbatim in his Wikipedia profile. His clothes worn as a child were not rags, but neither were they tailored—although they might as well have been rags to Roo Osbourne. These days he only wore the very best designers—not that it made any difference to his unkempt appearance, but he did so anyway. He came from the dusty Australian outback, suffered a dusty Australian outback upbringing and an even more dusty Australian outback education. He did not shine academically or socially. If not for his shambling physicality, his odd looks, and his peculiarly small hands, he'd probably still be there, drinking tinnies and getting into fights in the local bar. But it was those looks that had led directly to where he was today. That young kid had had a lot to prove. And by God did he prove himself—and a helluva lot more…

"Your mum made out with one of those well-hung 'roos, ay?" was the common refrain at school. Indeed, that is where his nickname *Roo* came from. In those days, he despised it, but the same media team who had invented his past, had advised that he took control of his own image. "It's what everyone calls you behind your back anyway and I think you know that." The exec who had said those words in his presence was summarily fired and never worked in the marketing profession again, but the man had been right. It's what everyone called him, and besides, using it would be one in the eye for all those losers at school and everyone since then who had dared to speak that name against him. Now he wore Roo as a badge of pride. He even called himself that in his own thoughts, although in his mind, Roo was spelled *Rue* because many, many, many people had come to rue the day they crossed Roo Osbourne.

A NICE DAY FOR IT

"MORNIN'," SAID THE driver in the over-chummy way some taxi-drivers insisted on inflicting upon their passengers. "And what a beautiful mornin' it is."

Jim Riven's brain bristled inside his skull, his frontal cortex furrowing and twisting uncomfortably. "If you say so," he replied belligerently. Not only had he found himself suddenly at the beck and call of an insistent ex-girlfriend and been forced at tear-soaked bosom-point into solving a robbery, but he was also now expected to partake in small-talk before he'd properly woken up.

Even at his very, very best, say at a late-night party after imbibing one or six lagers, he might perhaps, maybe, possibly, be tempted into a light-hearted conversation with a stranger. Hopefully of the opposite sex. Indeed, he might actually think he was quite good at that sort of thing. Maybe rather spectacular at it. But here and now, in the back of a cold taxi, at a dreadfully early and inopportune time of the morning, small talk was the last thing he wanted to indulge in. No. If he wanted to listen to people talking about nothing in particular, he'd watch a daytime talk show while holding a large glass of something red and Shiraz-like after firmly wrapping his head inside a duvet.

"Sounds like you got out of the wrong side of the bed

today, if you don't mind me saying."

"The sides of my bed are not the issue here. No. The problem lies squarely with the getting out of it."

"Huh?"

"This wasn't my idea, okay?"

"What wasn't?"

"This," Riven replied with exasperation, emphasising the word in such a way as to hopefully encompass this pointless conversation, the taxi he was in, the utter earliness of outside, and the annoying task he had to perform.

"I see. Nice day for it, though."

"No, not really." Riven looked at the card Landa gave him. "We're going to Spitalfields in the East End."

"I know. Got the address off that friend of yours. Very swanky. The area, not your friend, although... are you her boyfriend?"

"No, no, no," Riven replied, adding an extra no to properly put across the message.

"It's like that, is it? An ex?"

"Very much so. And then some."

"Didn't end well?"

"It ended perfectly well as far as I was concerned. And not too soon." Riven eyed the taxi driver in the mirror. Fifty-something. Balding grey hair. Haggard. His eyes telling him Landa was well out of Riven's league and that he was some form of advanced idiot for letting her go.

"So what do you think about that ticket?" the driver asked.

"That... what now?" What was the man blithering on about?

"You must've heard about it? The winning rollover jackpot lottery ticket bought in London that no one has claimed yet? Me and the missus have been through all our coat pockets and drawers twice, just in case."

"Huh?"

"The Lotto. It was that double triple rollover from months

ago. Today is the six-month deadline to claim the prize."

"Oh. The lottery. Right. I never bother with it. The chances of winning are astronomically small. You'd need to play it once a week for something like five-thousand lifetimes to make sure of winning."

"That's why me and the wife always buy an extra ticket when it's a rollover."

"But the odds are fourteen million to one."

"You seem to know a lot about it."

"I did a study of it a while back. Thought I might, I dunno, have a bit of luck." The truth of the matter was that Riven had hoped that using his powers of serendipitous happenchance, he'd somehow win the lottery. Hundreds of pounds later and angry about the whole episode, he'd admitted defeat.

"I take it that it didn't work out for you?"

"You could say that."

"Ah, that's because you didn't have a system."

"Please don't tell me what—"

"You see, the trick is to choose numbers that mean something to you. Like a birthday or house number. Or a lucky number, but that's just the start of it..."

As far as Riven was concerned, he had already swapped far too many words with the taxi-driver than were absolutely necessary. "That's all very fascinating," he said, jumping into the taxi-driver's self-important monologue when the opportunity arose, "but I'm tired. Got home late and all that. You understand? So I'm going to take a nap. Wake me up when we get there, okay?" Riven lay down on the back seat, closed his eyes and drifted immediately to sleep.

Some indiscriminate time later, Riven was rudely awoken by the taxi driver. "We're here, mate."

"Huh?" Riven replied dreamily. Adding a disheartened "Oh!" as the morning's events replayed themselves across his mind. He checked his watch. Almost 11am. It was still a heinous time of the day, but the sleep in the back of the cab had cleared the fog out of his mind.

"That'll be eighty-five twenty. Call it a round eighty-five quid."

Riven rubbed at his eyes, the taxi-driver's words replaying inside his head until they made sense. "Eighty-five quid? Didn't Landa pay up front?"

"Your hot ex?"

A shake of his head.

Landa didn't maliciously expect him to pay for the taxi, but she was that type of rich person who assumes everyone has a few hundred quid on their person at any one time. To her, anything under two hundred pounds was small change. Luckily, Riven always kept his card in the back pocket of his jeans. He reluctantly pulled it free and showed it to the driver.

"Sorry mate, it's cash only. My card machine is down. I did explain that to your lady friend."

Riven was about to tell the taxi driver to take him to the nearest cash machine, when he spotted an odd-looking wallet poking out from under the seat on the cab-floor. He picked it up. It was made from alligator skin and fastened with a silver clasp, from which the gilt had been worn away by what appeared to be years of use. If he'd not been lying prone on the back seat, he would never have noticed it. He flicked it open to find four twenties and a fiver. Exactly eighty-five pounds in cash. The coincidence jarred him into stark wakefulness, and he sat bolt up. It was happening again. Bugger!

Riven made the easy decision. He took the eighty-five pounds from the wallet and paid the driver, vowing to get the money off Landa at the earliest opportunity and to return it and the wallet to its owner as soon as he could find out who they were. For now, he had more immediate concerns.

He stumbled out of the taxi onto a cold sidewalk and found himself standing outside a retro-looking building. Monty's Outtasight! gallery. It was hidden away on a small back road. Perhaps that's where the name came from? A large yellow winking smiley face dominated the façade, giving the place an eerie, cheesy look.

The taxi chugged away. He jammed Monty's gallery card into the alligator-skin wallet and stuffed it into his back pocket.

A sign on the gallery said *CLOSED*.

Riven pushed the door. Of course it was open. If a closed sign on an unlocked door was their level of security, he wondered how many other works of art had simply walked away.

Sighing, he stepped inside. "Hullo," he ventured, closing the door behind him. After the vivid and irritating brightness of the morning, the vivid and irritating brightness of the gallery interior was no comfort at all. Light dazzled from expensive looking fitments. There were wall lights, ceiling lights and floor lights. As well as various lamps and hanging bulbs dotted here and there, making sure that every corner was illuminated, whether it wanted to be or not.

A tall, pencil-thin girl in a pencil skirt and very nice knee-length boots emerged from the glare. "We're closed!" she said in a pencil-thin accent that seemed used to ordering minions around. "Can't you read?" She pushed back her long, pencil-thin hair and pursed her pencil-thin lips.

"Yes, I can read, actually," Riven answered, squinting against the lights. Despite the pencil thinness, the girl was lovely, especially her boots. He smiled his most winning smile. "I started reading at a very early age. So early that everyone really hoped I would become one of those annoying child geniuses. You know the ones I mean? Horrible little oiks. But I'm afraid the genius gene gave me a bit of a miss. Instead, I grew up to be just annoying, or so I'm told. Having said that, a lot of my exes have shed doubt on the fact that I grew up at all… if that helps?"

The girl looked him up and down and gave him a double take. "Oh no. Jim… Jim Riven?"

THE GIRL WITH THE NICE BOOTS

RIVEN GROANED INSIDE, the smile leaving his lips. "You know me?"

"You don't remember?"

In the absence of any suitable reply coming to his lips, Riven's throat made a peculiar squeaking sound.

"Why should I be surprised by that?" she continued. "You ruined my life and promptly forgot all about me. Typical."

Riven had no idea who she was or what he'd done to her, but there was no hiding the fact that it wasn't anything good. Riven's memory was not impaired. In truth, his little grey cells were of above average quality—it was just that he actively tried not to remember the bad stuff. And there was a helluva lot of bad stuff in Riven's life to forget about. Reams of it. Whole libraries. The girl knew his name though and had made sure to remember it. That, combined with the mean look in her lovely brown eyes, didn't bode particularly well for the next part of this conversation.

"I'm sorry," he said mechanically. "What's your name?"

She pointed a finger at her boots and glared at him.

He gave her fetching footwear another once-over but came up with nothing.

"How dare you forget me! How very dare you! I'm the girl

with the nice boots!"

Memories cascaded into Riven's brain in a mortifying flood of recollection. "Oh bugger!"

"So you've remembered?"

Riven nodded. He did indeed remember the girl with the nice boots. It must've been about ten years ago he surmised. He'd gotten a temp job at a local printshop. He was supposed to have worked there for six months but was sacked after just one day, which wasn't out of the ordinary. Jobs and Riven had never gotten on. He'd tried to make them work, but they had too many irreconcilable differences. Although his financial situation sometimes dictated otherwise.

It had been lunchtime and the girl with the nice boots, then a student at the local university—one of those arty ones with fashion design and art courses and other some such—had walked in with a flash drive containing her final year dissertation. A ten-thousand-word document she'd spent months writing. The deadline was in a few days, and she needed the thing printed out. Two copies on high quality A4. Riven had flirted with her, none-too unsuccessfully it turned out, nicknaming her after her very special and very sexy boots. High-heeled, leather and hand-painted in blocks of red, white, blue and yellow. She was free that evening it turned out and wanted to celebrate finishing her dissertation. She gave him her flash drive and her number and left.

So excited by the prospect of spending the evening in the company of the girl with the nice boots, the young Jim Riven somehow misplaced the flash drive. Quite simply, it disappeared. He searched everywhere for it. But it was like the thing had been swallowed by a wormhole. Still, it could only be a little fly in the ointment of their burgeoning romance, as of course, the girl with the nice boots would have a backup copy… of course she would.

When the girl with the nice boots returned, it turned out she wasn't as practically minded as he would've hoped. When asked about backup copies of her dissertation, she turned a very peculiar colour and began to emit loud squeaking sounds. Things moved on relatively quickly after that. There was a lot of screaming and shouting, multiple threats and expletives, and a whole host of sobbing and tears. Riven was immediately removed from the shop front and summarily fired. Later that evening, he'd texted her his apologies, asking to take her out to 'drown her sorrows' as he put it. Her reply was, shall we say, not a favourable one. Indeed, it contained a repeat of the expletives and threats from earlier, except they were now spelled in angry capitals with more than a few exclamation marks. And that was the last he'd heard from the girl with the nice boots until today.

"Did they ever find the flash drive?" he asked quietly.

"No. And with little time left, I had to rewrite my dissertation from scratch. You cost me a First, you know that, Jim Riven?"

"But if you'd made a backup, then—" The look on the girl with the nice boots' face told him that continuing this sentence would be a very bad idea. A very bad idea indeed.

Riven tried again. "I didn't mean to lose the thing. Of course I didn't."

"Luckily, I had other work to present but the dissertation was worth seventy-five percent. I scraped a pass with a Third-Class Honours degree."

"Honours? That's um… good… isn't it?"

"It's the lowest grade."

"Still a pass is a pass," he said brightly.

The girl with the nice boots said nothing, although her glare intensified.

"Monty is expecting me," Riven said, breaking the uncomfortable silence.

"That's Mr Fitzhugh to you," she replied, talking to him like he was a minion again. Her pencil-thin lips united to form a nasty sneer. "This way," she said curtly, stomping off.

Riven blew a sigh of relief and followed her, his eye

reluctantly drawn to her nice boots and her even nicer bottom. It was particularly inappropriate to ogle at her in this way, he thought to himself, especially given the recent revelation—ruining the poor girl's life and all that—but bottoms were bottoms and pretty much screamed for attention regardless of the situation. Why was that? he mused. Humans were complicated beasts, that much was for sure.

Despite the girl with the nice boots' rather fetching bottom, Riven had no particular type. He wasn't a boobs or leg man (or however that was now described in the days of political correctness). No, it was more how everything was put together that got him interested. Intelligence was also a major factor. And, unfortunately, looniness. No matter how sane the girls he fancied appeared on the surface, underneath there usually bubbled a host of eccentricities and a serious amount of general craziness. He should know better. But he didn't. It was human nature to repeat one's mistakes and it turned out Riven was exceptionally human in this one particular regard. With this in mind, he raised his eyes and thoughts away from the girl with the nice boots' bottom and instead studied the gallery.

The place was bright and cheery, lit by too many lights, and recently done up with what looked like expensive fittings and whatnot, but the building felt ancient, like it had been here for hundreds of years.

"When was this place built?" he asked.

"Victorian times. Lucky to survive the Blitz. It was converted into a gallery after the war. Was a popular hangout in the 60s."

"You seem to know a lot about it."

"I do my research. I pride myself on it," she said. "You think anything gets into this gallery without my scrutiny?"

"Um… no?" Riven ventured.

"Research is everything in a job like this. Everything."

"I'm sure it is."

"Monty, Mr Fitzhugh, had the building fixed up. The

under-gallery, where the problem lies, was only renovated this week, in time for last night's big show. But we still have a rodent problem, which, as you can imagine, is a no-no in a place housing such valuable art."

They passed big blue paintings with little white bits on them, sculptures that looked like they were made in a kindergarten papier-mâché class, and an amber-coloured glass statue of a half-woman, half-bird holding an enormous phallus. The sound of the Sex Pistols played from a small gallery room full of ancient-looking TVs broadcasting various looped videos of dogs humping each other. "This is modern art, is it?" he asked, a little bemused.

"It most certainly is. My specialty. That degree you ruined was in modern art of the twentieth century."

"Oh, so that's what your dissertation was about…"

"I may have only gotten a Third, but I know my stuff."

Riven looked around him and couldn't help but feel perplexed at what he was seeing. "But I just don't get it."

"Get what?" the girl with the nice boots said, turning to face him, the sneer reappearing on her pencil-thin lips.

"It's not that I don't want to understand modern art," Riven said, shrugging at what appeared to be a statue of the lower half of an over-sized baby, complete with a flannel nappy, disappearing into the floor. "But… well… it's all a bit confusing."

"Modern art is the response of artists and thinkers to the advances of the industrial and technological age," she began, like she was addressing a child. "Society began to change drastically at the beginnings of the last century, and because of this, artists began to represent society's experience of the newness of modern life in similarly innovative ways."

"And that's modern art, is it?"

"It's far more than just that. As a term it applies to a whole host of artistic genres spanning over a hundred years. It is characterised by the artist's intent to move away from creating exact or compelling representations of what they are seeing, like an accurate portrait or a landscape, but to instead look inside themselves, to use their own unique perspective to create their art. Imagine the shock of the first photograph? Overnight, a painter's skill was superseded by technology. It made artists focus more on their interpretation of what they were seeing and feeling. What these artworks are doing is rejecting the accepted or traditional styles and values of the past and creating something new and similarly innovative to the world that now surrounds us. Piet Mondrian, who was regarded as one of the greatest artists of the twentieth century, said *Art is higher than reality and has no direct relation to reality. To approach the spiritual in art, one will make as little use as possible of reality, because reality is opposed to the spiritual. We find ourselves in the presence of an abstract art. Art should be above reality, otherwise it would have no value for man.* And Piet Mondrian more than anyone in modern art history knew what he was talking about."

Riven nodded, still none the wiser but impressed that she could remember such a long quote with what looked like ease. And of course, she was referencing Mondrian. The guy who's painting had been stolen.

The girl with the nice boots turned and continued walking.

"You certainly know your stuff."

Her whole face beamed at him hatefully. "Of course I do. I'm also a buyer for the gallery as well as an accomplished restorer and modern art historian. Mr Fitzhugh employed me for that expertise."

"It sounds like you've done very well for yourself despite…"

"Despite you ruining my life and career?"

Riven said nothing, she was certainly piling on the guilt.

"Down there," she said, coming to stop next to a flight of steep steps. "This leads to the newly opened under-gallery. It's been closed off since the 60s. And during that time, the rats thrived down there."

Her tone seemed unnecessarily derisory but Riven didn't care. He was here for one reason and one reason only, to try and find or not find this Mondrian and afterwards to go back home to bed. This weird thing with the girl with the nice boots was perturbing though. Another coincidence. He didn't like where this was going. Not one bit.

"Okay," he replied, wondering why such a valuable Mondrian had been displayed in the basement, whilst simultaneously wishing he was somewhere else. But then he remembered Landa waiting for him. He was sure to disappoint her. A Fabergé earring was one thing, a six-foot Mondrian painting was entirely different. It certainly wouldn't fit in a Mushroom Jalfrezi take-out tray, that was for sure. They stepped down into the glare of the brightly lit stairwell and arrived at an impressive underground complex of small, but still brightly lit, whitewashed gallery rooms.

The girl with the nice boots took him into one of these and pointed to a series of what looked like small rat-holes where the walls met the floor. Around them was scattered bits of white plaster that had 'exploded' out. Stacked against one wall were three large blank canvases, next to which were scattered tubes of white acrylic paint. Riven was a little perplexed. "It's very interesting," he ventured. "An…" he dug around in his memory for the appropriate word, "…an installation of some sort I take it? A bit like that Banksy chap but understated. I like it," he added as an afterthought.

"Very droll," the girl with the nice boots replied. "I remember you as being quite funny, even if you did turn out to be somewhat of a giant prick who ruined my life."

Still confused, Riven half-smiled and half-frowned at the compliment/insult.

She nodded to the holes. "The plaster was a temporary fix for the gallery opening night, but as you can see, the little buggers are very persistent."

"Okay," Riven replied, becoming more confused by the

moment. "And the blank canvases and tubes of white paint?"

"That's for the exhibition next week. It's very exciting. Dan Kowalski will be here painting something brand new, inspired by the Outtasight! gallery. His use of white is just astounding."

"I'm sure it is," Riven replied.

"Right, I'll leave you to go get your equipment."

"Equipment?" Riven was taken aback. "I don't use any equipment. Whatever skills I may or may not possess do not require tools. Maybe a glass of Shiraz or a nice milky mug of tea perhaps. But anything else… no."

"You don't use traps or poison? What are you? Some kind of Pied Piper?"

"Pied Piper?" Somewhere in Riven's brain, the penny dropped, loudly clattering on the floor of his cerebral cortex and making a thorough racket. The girl with the nice boots hadn't brought him down here to see some incomprehensible and expensive art nouveau installation. No. Instead, she was showing him the evidence of a rather serious vermin infestation. He turned to face her with what he hoped was a suitably miffed expression. "I think you've made quite the mistake."

"You don't work for Bill, the rat guy?"

"No! I do not work for Bill the rat guy!" Riven spat back, feeling more than a little insulted.

"He told me he was bringing an assistant today, so I thought—"

"I'm here to see Monty, okay."

"You know him personally?"

"Unfortunately, yes."

"But you look like…"

"The local pest exterminator? You think a rodent control service guy would wear something as classy as this?" he asked, pointing to his *Don't Mess With This Idiot!* tee-shirt.

"I just assumed—"

"Well you assumed wrongly. Now please take me to see him."

They quickly passed a few more small side galleries and entered what Riven guessed was the main exhibition area proper—a long, thin, high-ceilinged room decked with artworks on either side, the walls exposed brick, painted white. A small, semi-circular platform sat at the far end under a blank wall—the focal point of the room. He guessed this is where the Mondrian would've been hung before it went missing.

The room's interior was filled by abandoned tables, littered with upturned and half-full champagne bottles, plates of half-eaten canapés and empty glasses. A small PA system sat at one end with a DJ mixing desk. The remains of last night's opening party.

Riven stared again at the blank wall. Landa's six-foot Mondrian would dominate this space, he surmised. In front of where the painting should have been, Riven clearly recognised Monty Fitzhugh. A thin, effete black man in sunglasses and what appeared to be an outfit made from garish carpet off-cuts topped by a Cossack hat that had very possibly been someone's welcome mat in a previous life. He sat agitatedly on a chair, while a younger man, a hunky white guy in classic blue jeans, white tee-shirt and a crisp and shiny black leather jacket, attended to him. Riven had only met Monty a few times and they'd not got on. The man had made a point of disliking everything about him from the start. And when Monty and Landa got together? All types of trouble would break loose. Riven couldn't help but wonder how he and Landa were allowed to be in the same room as one another without breaking some international accord. Monty did look genuinely upset though, that much was for sure. Then again, losing your fortune and a multi-million-pound painting belonging to a litigious-prone billionaire, must be a bit of a downer. Poor bugger.

"Oh, it's you." Monty said with a face like sour vinegar, his voice a posh-sounding whine containing peculiar-sounding, elongated vowels, and even more peculiar-sounding consonants—like an effeminate Chewbacca forced into a pair of very tight trousers. Monty's trousers were also very tight, Riven noticed with amusement.

"Landa's dreadful little oik has finally graced us with his presence, innit tho?"

MONTY, INNIT THO?

RIVEN HAD MET Monty early on in his relationship with Landa. It had been one of those supposedly regular kind of events—at a party, where Landa had presented her new beau to her friends. Except there was nothing regular about it. To call it a party makes the event sound like some relaxed do in a bar or around someone's house. What Landa had organised was as far away from an informal get-together as Mahatma Gandhi was from a KFC Boneless Bucket. Landa's party was a no-holds barred, three-day, sun-filled shindig aboard a billionaire's luxury yacht on the Côte d'Azur.

Landa flew Riven out there on her father's personal jet, which as far as Riven could tell, was solely inhabited by beautiful, and eager to please, living dolls.

Billionaire luxury yachts, the Côte d'Azur, and private jets stuffed full of stunning young women who laughed politely at his terrible jokes, would have sounded very appealing to Riven, if not for the fact that these things were accompanied by an over-excited and post-Fabergé-earring-obsessed Landa. Sure, he was flattered by the attention, but his life wasn't his own anymore. Instead, it now belonged entirely to his new and singular girlfriend. Being whisked off at the drop of a hat to a foreign country and to be force fed caviar and champagne—it seemed dreadfully clichéd, but that's what was on the menu—was not what Riven had been expecting after biting down on something unexpected in his curry the day before.

After arriving seasick and disorientated aboard the enormous yacht, Landa's friends had looked him up and down with bemused faces. Riven didn't mind that they obviously didn't rate him. He wasn't dressed in the latest—or any—designer wear, he wasn't remotely rich, and he didn't act like the world belonged to him. It gave him hope that one or all of them would have a word with Landa to explain how unsuitable he was. An intervention of sorts. However, this was early on in their relationship, and Riven hadn't quite grasped that no one would ever dare tell Landa she was wrong about anything. Especially as she was the leader of this rich-kid coterie. Although this wasn't strictly true. Her best friend, Monty, always said what was on his mind. Riven respected that, even if the man obviously didn't like him.

His first words to Riven were a withering, "Oh no!" before turning to Landa and saying, "I knew you were slumming it, Landa darling, but really? This dreadful little toe rag?"

"Now, now Monty," Landa replied. "Don't be like that. Riven saved my absolute life! I owe him everything. A sign we're meant to be together forever."

Riven became somewhat faint at this news and felt the need for a little lie down in their cabin—an obscenely vast suite of rooms. Billionaires absolutely loved yachts, doted on the things. The reason? They were such terrific tax write-offs, and heaven forbid that these selfish gits were ever forced to pay a penny in tax. Riven wondered if the twenty-four men and women who formed the crew, lorded it up when it was empty, having their own parties. He hoped so. They probably needed one after having to put up with Landa and her awful friends for a few days. He slipped into the circular double bed—fitting the sheets to this thing must be a nightmare—and closed his eyes, hoping to wake up back in the safety of his Camden flat to find out all this had been some horribly protracted nightmare. However, the door opened soon after, and his so-called quiet lie down was interrupted by a naked Landa crawling in bed with him, forcing him to perform all manner of horizontally themed gymnastics. Not that he put up much resistance. In the scheme of things, if Landa hadn't been the rather spoiled daughter of Roo Osbourne, perhaps she and him might've had a chance. But sadly, she was the rather spoiled daughter of Roo Osbourne, and that pretty much ruined any possibility of romance that may have been available to them.

That lost soul thing again.

Someone would save her soul one day, Riven was sure of it, but no matter how he looked at their relationship, that person wasn't going to be him. Nevertheless, he hoped that she would find that person soon. So far, her choices had been woefully inadequate, and Riven, regrettably, was forced to include himself in that list.

That evening, the party moved into full swing. There was a band, a lot more guests, and even more food. He'd asked one of the waiters if they could whip him up a Mushroom Jalfrezi, but his request was met with confused silence. Riven then managed to stay out of the way until that part of the evening where, apparently, everyone needed to strip naked and jump into the on-board pool whilst shrieking like hysterical hyenas.

Riven didn't swim, nor did he scream like a hysterical hyena—mostly—and no amount of pleading from Landa and her naked friends could encourage him to do either. They were about to drag him into the pool anyway when he was thankfully saved by Monty.

"Leave him be, innit!" he said much to Riven's relief, holding a glass of champagne and a smoking cigarette. Monty had pushed the boat out on tonight's get-up. His hair, previously in cornrows, was now teased out into full-afro-mode, giving the tiny man a good extra ten inches of height. He wore a pair of striped, rainbow-coloured, loose-fitting flares, an open-neck, purple shirt, 70s' sunglasses, and such a serious amount of gold strung around his neck that it was a marvel he could stand up at all. "Monty wants to talk to him, Mano to Mano, innit tho?" he continued, referring to himself in the third person, like an author forced to write their own bio. "You get me?"

And so they'd left them alone.

"I know who you are, Jim Riven, with your two-bit trainers, two-bit tee-shirt and two-bit looks, innit?" Monty said sitting down next to him and sucking at his cigarette.

"Okay," Riven replied, captivated by the array of glisteningly wet breasts, bottoms and male wobbly bits cavorting in the pool, and wondering why Monty was dissing his clothing choices. Riven was very happy in his black shorts, black plimsolls, and black tee-shirt. A classic beach come yacht combination in his opinion.

"Monty knows your game, innit?"

Riven pondered whether he should respond to Monty's overuse of the modern slang word, 'innit'. He was all in favour of English being a renowned bastard language, picking up words here, contracting words there, and making up entirely new words everywhere else it bloody well pleased, but there was something about 'innit' that quite got Riven's goat. It was a contraction of isn't it, or isn't he/she, or aren't they, isn't there and many other end-of-sentence questions that seemed to acquire its most annoying effect in places where it would make absolutely no grammatical sense whatsoever. It was the nonsensical nature of this particular addition to the English language that Riven had the most problems with. Nevertheless, he took a deep breath and bit his lip. Now didn't feel like the right time to discuss the ins and outs of grammar, pronunciation and dynamic languages. Monty had something he wanted to get off his chest.

"You don't think I know what's going on with you and Landa, tho?" Monty continued.

'Tho' was also an overused word of the English language

that Riven found difficult to get his head around. A contraction of the word, 'though', and also indiscriminately added to the end of sentences for no apparent reason other than to annoy people like Jim Riven, who were trying their very best to be supportive of the whole dynamic language thing but having difficulty with some of the actual bits of it.

"You mean that she's practically kidnapped me?" Riven replied, knowing full well this wasn't what Monty was getting at, but he was in a funny mood.

Monty sat back in his chair, perplexed. "You're suuuuuch a gold-digger!" he said. "That stunt you pulled with the Fabergé earring might've fooled Landa but it don't fool Monty, you get me?"

Riven sighed. "Indeed, I do. I get you very much so."

"You... do?"

"Sure I do. I get it. She attracts boyfriends who are most likely all money-grabbing spongers. And I'm sure the lot of them would be very impressed with all this...," he looked around him at the gleaming deck of the multi-multi-*multi*-million-dollar yacht, at the patient waiters and crew standing to attention, at the mountains of uneaten, extravagant food and bottles of the most expensive booze, and at the pool full of baying, drunken and naked twenty-somethings, "...all this... *this*. But I'd much prefer to be back in my Camden flat, thank you very much. It's brilliant that she has a friend like you to stand in her corner. I think that's very noble. I really do."

"Then you're saying you're not after her money, innit?"

"I'm only after a quiet life, and as much as there are parts of Landa that I have a soft spot for, I don't think a quiet life is on the cards, do you? I don't fit in here for a start. You're all rich kids. You've all been monied from birth. I've nothing against that or you, but it means we are from entirely different worlds."

"Well, I'm a self-made millionaire, innit?"

"You are?" Riven was genuinely impressed.

"I came from the streets. Made my money through hard

work and sound investments, innit?" Monty said sipping at one of his champagne flutes and taking another large drag on his cigarette.

Up to this point Riven had seen Monty as, well, a bit of an over-dressed idiot. "I didn't expect that," Riven said, meaning it.

"I'm a lot more successful than you'll ever be, innit? I'm a winner tho."

"Winning is a complicated concept that means a variety of different things to a variety of different people," Riven replied, deciding on a sage nod to accompany his unexpectedly profound words. He grabbed a champagne flute from a passing waiter and toasted the effete but deserving millionaire sitting next to him. "To a self-made man!"

Monty raised his own flute and drank, looking confused and a little annoyed. It was obvious that this conversation wasn't going how he'd expected.

"Now on to Landa," Riven said. "I think it's great how you watch out for her. She needs someone like you fighting her corner. You were right, earlier. What on earth is she doing with a toerag like me? I get it. I really do."

"You do?"

"She made a mistake, Monty. And you see it. So how are you going to help me make her realise that mistake?"

Monty gave him a sideways look. "Oh I see it now, innit? You're playing a very clever game. Well it won't wash, okay?"

"Look, I understand that you've probably dealt with a lot of gold-digging jackasses who've made a play for Landa and thumbs up to you." Riven held his thumbs up and straightaway wished he hadn't. "So, perhaps, if you could let her know that maybe she could do a lot better with someone else, I'd be in your debt."

"Don't play that angle with me, innit?"

"Perhaps some people don't have an angle. Have you ever considered that?"

"I don't care. I love Landa, more than any of you ever will," he blurted defensively. "And you're mistaken if you think I'm gonna be so easily fooled by your clever linguistics innit?"

"So we're not going to be friends?"

"Friends?" Monty scoffed. "Don't make me laugh."

"Fair enough. Still, many thanks for saving me from the pool—that would've been a fate worse than death. I'd better go and hide before they notice me again."

He stood up to sneak away, but Monty grasped his arm. "I will tell her to get rid of you. I will. I don't trust you or your effin' type."

Riven gave Monty what he hoped was an encouraging smile and headed off to the other end of the immense yacht hoping to find an empty lounge and an even emptier sofa. He hadn't taken the threat of being pulled into the pool lightly and he needed to be as far away from water as he could get on a yacht parked in the middle of one of the more popular recreational oceans.

And true to his word, Monty had spoken to Landa about him. But for the very first time, she'd put her foot down. Rebuking him in front of everyone else. Professing her undying love for one Jim Riven, who everyone, including Monty, had to pretend to get on with. And since then, Monty had of course hated him.

A HANKERING FOR SHAMAN

"YOU'RE FINALLY HERE, innit," Monty continued derisively. "Come to save the effin' day. Well whoopy effin' do"

"Apparently," Riven replied, looking down at him. He'd forgotten Monty was—how did they put it these days?—vertically challenged. A tiny man who always wore Cuban-heeled shoes and very tall hats. He liked the guy though. His heart was in the right place, but the rest of him, not so much.

Monty smirked. "All hail to our effin' saviour. Well I won't be clapping my hands tho, innit?"

"And it's nice to meet you again too," Riven said.

"Saviour?" The guy in the crisp leather jacket repeated in a thick, put-on sounding East End accent, a confused look on his face.

Now he was closer, Riven adjusted his description of the man. His jacket wasn't that crisp, he realised, and he was tattooed—blue, red, and green ink peeking above the white of his tee-shirt and crawling up the side of his neck. And unlike Monty, who radiated wealth, this guy didn't. His jeans lacked a certain cut and were slightly grubby. He was hunky though. Very much so. In that out there way that some people liked to dote on. With that whole stubble and jawline thing going on and the bluest of blue eyes framed by long lashes.

The girl with the nice boots pointed a pencil-like finger in Riven's direction. "I don't get it, why on earth is *he* here?"

"You know Riven, innit?" Monty replied with a furrow of his plucked eyebrows. "He's Landa's wonder detective, if she is to be believed tho."

The girl with the nice boots visibly baulked. "He's a what? A detective?"

"Detective is too strong a word for what I do," Riven said, feeling the need to speak up. "But people are somewhat put off by other terms like voodoo doctor, seer, or clairvoyant. None of which properly describe my talent, whatever that might be. I have a hankering for shaman, but then I'm sure people would expect me to chant something and wave around bits and pieces of whatnot while wearing a silly hat of some kind. So I suppose, in this instance, detective will just have to do. Even though I'm most certainly not a detective. And nor will I be doing any real detecting. Does that help?"

Monty, the guy in the not so crisp and black leather jacket, and the girl with the nice boots stared at Riven for a few moments. Their expressions were, to say the least, unsupportive.

Monty shook his head and removed his sunglasses to expose stressed looking brown eyes. "I'm so effed!" he ululated, the word reverberating off the gallery walls. "Properly effed effed!"

Monty wasn't the type to use bad language, Riven remembered, but then again, he surmised, this occasion did warrant the use of an expletive, even if Monty couldn't quite manage it.

"You mean… this is 'im?" the guy in the not so crisp and shiny leather jacket said disappointedly, playing at the perfect mess of his blonde hair. "This is the actual guy who's gonna get Landa off yer back?"

Monty replaced his sunglasses, his lips lifting in a garish smile, revealing a garish gold tooth studded with a garish diamond. "Harve-E, meet Jim Riven, innit?"

Harve-E grasped Riven's hand unnecessarily tightly, whilst

giving him an unnecessary wink. "Jus' call me Harve."

"And what do you do?" Riven asked.

"Not wot, but who?" Harve replied, beaming at Monty, his blue eyes shining with obvious affection.

"Huh?"

"I'm Monty's BF ain't I? Bin together for a few months. Best months of me life. True."

"I see," Riven replied. It was well-known that Monty occasionally liked what was known as 'a bit of rough'. Harve here—with his hunkiness and stubble, his tight tee-shirt and tattoos, and his not so crisp and shiny leather jacket and slightly grubby jeans—fitted that description perfectly. Having said that, the two of them made a handsome couple. Not that he'd tell Monty that.

Monty sighed, his Cossack hat slipping to perch at an odd angle on his small, rounded cannonball of a head. "Why Landa wouldn't let me go to the police I don't know!" he warbled in high-pitched tones. "She also wouldn't allow me to call the insurance people in. Let them sort out the thing, was what I told her, innit? Get the experts in on this. But Landa always gets her way."

"Going to the police was also my advice," Riven said. "But here we are."

"But what could the rozzers do any road?" Harve interjected.

Riven had always liked the term *rozzers*. It scored higher than the *filth,* and the *pigs*, and others, simply because it contained what he thought was a comedy element. The *pigs* might fit you up for a crime you didn't commit, and the *filth* might beat you to a pulp in the cells afterwards, but the *rozzers* would let you off with a caution before slipping on a comedy banana.

"There's no evidence of a break-in," Harve continued. "That'd flummox the rozzers no end. It's like some bloke teleported in 'ere, right, took the Mondrian an' teleported back out again."

"Really?" Riven said, finding himself annoyed with the way Harve said *tely-por-ud*—like an East End gangster in a cheap sci-fi movie. His accent was borderline ridiculous.

"The Mondrian was here last night when the place was locked up, innit?" Monty whined from inside his carpet-themed ensemble. "We have armoured doors and a top of the range alarm system." His voice became higher with every syllable. "But this morning, when we arrived, it was gone, innit?" The effort of speaking appeared to take it out of Monty who was forced to use Harve for support. It was quite the performance.

"Sounds like an inside job to me," Riven replied. He'd heard this phrase thousands of times on TV and was very pleased to be able to use it in real life. It gave him a professional air—like he knew what he was talking about, especially when Monty, Harve and the girl with the nice boots all looked at each other uncomfortably.

"Enough of this gabbing!" Monty said, breaking the moment and pushing Harve away. "I suppose you'll want to take a look around tho?"

"If you think that will help?" Riven replied.

"Don't you?"

Riven shrugged. "A tea wouldn't go amiss, and maybe a biscuit. Just to help me get started," he said hopefully.

Monty turned to the girl with the nice boots. "Yeah. Go do that for him, Jen-baby, okay?"

"And I want a proper tea," Riven continued, focusing his attention on the girl previously known as the girl with the nice boots, but now revealed as Jen-baby.

"I'm not sure making tea is in my job description," Jen replied.

"I want it properly brewed, milky with unsweetened soya milk and at least five sugars," Riven continued unabashed. "Not a paper cup of hot water and a teabag on the side. Brewed and in a mug if possible. With a nice digestive or ginger biscuit."

Jen said nothing for a few moments, although it was

obvious she was furious.

Monty rounded on her, his ridiculous high tones dropping to become suddenly threatening. “You think you’ve got problems? My bestest, bestest friend has had her badass billionaire father’s multi-million-pound Mondrian stolen, innit? If it’s not found, Roo Osbourne will take me to the effin’ cleaners. I’m gonna lose everything, or what’s left of it. And, honey, if he thinks you’re the slightest bit involved, he’s gonna ruin you as well. So if Jim Riven wants a mug of disgusting effin’ tea, I suggest you get him a mug of disgusting effin’ tea. Apparently, he’s the only effin’ hope we’ve got, innit?”

Jen gave Monty a thin-lipped smile of obedience, before pointing furious eyes in Riven’s direction and stomping off, her nice boots making clacking sounds in the large, underground gallery.

“I should sack her, innit?” Monty said when she was out of hearing.

“But she’s the only one who knows wot’s wot, ain’t she?” Harve replied. “Stuck up an’ all that, sure, but that’s wot you want for this sort of operation. Some snobby art genius wiv ‘er fingers up the backside of the industry.”

“I pay her too much tho innit? Costing me a fortune.”

“Landa told me about your money issues,” Riven said. “How are you coping?”

Monty pouted angrily in Riven’s direction. He’d touched a nerve, that much was for sure. “Oh, just eff off!”

“Wish I could, but you know Landa.”

Monty sagged and Harve rushed to his side again.

“It’s my own effin’ fault,” Monty said from inside the cradle of Harve’s overly muscled arms. “The Mondrian is worth effin’ millions. Millions! I pestered Landa to let me have it for my opening… it made such an impact, but it stressed me out having it here. I knew something like this would happen, innit? I just knew it.”

“You did?” Riven ventured.

"He was worried sick about it," Harve said. "That's why Jen an' me double-checked the place before we left. There's an access door ter an alleyway outside, but the gates were not only locked, they were also chained from the inside. They've not been unlocked since the Mondrian arrived on the day of the show. Monty installed an armoured roller shutter ter the front of the building. An' that was the only way in and out."

Monty pulled himself free from Harve and straightened his hat. "The windows were bricked up years ago, innit? Whoever took the Mondrian is some sort of effin' magician."

"Shame there's no CCTV," Harve added.

"It's being installed next week, tho. Too effin' late!"

Riven was surprised. "I know little next to nothing about security whatnot, but no CCTV seems like a dreadful oversight, doesn't it? Especially with such an expensive artwork under your roof."

"What're you inferrin'?" Monty said, taking the accusation personally.

Riven suddenly felt on firmer ground. Grammar was something he was somewhat of an expert on. "I'm not inferring anything. I am implying. An important difference."

"Well Monty ain't got nothin' to do with this, okay?" he said, the words spitting out of his mouth as little darts of anger. "Implyin' or otherwise. So you can strike me off your suspect list, innit?"

"Oh, I won't be making a suspect list."

"You won't?" Harve asked, confused.

"No, no, no. That's not how my thing works at all. Totally the opposite to be honest."

"Well I won't be accused like this, innit?" Monty whined. "I'm going to try and talk to Landa again. But she's been refusing my calls innit? This is so effin' effed up!" He took out a mobile phone and angrily tapped at the screen.

Riven stepped towards the blank far wall, his foot finding something on the floor. He stooped down and picked up a bright red Stanley Knife with the blade out. "Who does this belong to?"

Monty looked up from his phone and at the knife and shrugged.

"The rat guy, I fink," Harve said.

"Bill?"

Harve's eyes furrowed. "You know 'im?"

Riven turned the knife over in his hands. "Jen mentioned him to me."

"He left before the openin'," Harve continued. "Did some last-minute work, an' he's supposed ter be 'ere today, right? But so far he's a no show." He looked at the knife and frowned. "I'm sure that wasn't lyin' on the floor yesterday, someone would've seen it."

Riven slid the knife into his pocket.

"You wanna see the back doors?" Harve asked enthusiastically, adding, "that's not an invitation, haha!" Riven guessed he was trying his best to lighten the mood.

"If you think that will help?"

"They're still locked." He pulled out a keyring containing many keys. "This is the only set. I kept 'em wiv me at all times."

"And I can vouch for that," Monty said, lifting his head up from his phone and pouting. "I stopped at Harve's pad last night. Decided to slum it for an evening. He slept like a log. Harve was out like a light all night, innit. So don't start accusing him either."

Harve smiled lovingly at Monty, before his eyes returned to Riven. "We came in first thing this mornin'. Everyfink appeared normal. It were Jen who found the paintin' missing."

"She's a sneaky one if you ask me," Monty said, his hat slipping to an even crazier angle. "I wouldn't be surprised if she had something to do with it. She knows this gallery inside out, innit? And she was very keen on getting the Mondrian for the opening."

Harve shook his head. "It can't be 'er, right, Mont'. We 'ad the keys."

Monty shrugged but Riven could tell he wasn't convinced.

"Once the Mondrian were discovered missing," Harve continued, seemingly trying to be helpful, "we searched the place top ter bottom. We couldn't find any trace of the paintin'. And nuffink else appeared ter 'ave bin stolen."

"They wouldn't need to steal anything else, tho," Monty said. "That painting is worth more that the whole effin' gallery and everything in it, innit?" He shook his phone irritably. "There's no signal down here. Come Harve, give the keys to Riven and let's get out of here."

Harve pushed a keyring into Riven's hand and whispered in his ear, his voice suddenly full of threat. "You find it, Riven, you find that paintin' for Mont', uvverwise you'll 'ave me ter deal wiv, right?"

"I'll do my best," Riven replied, suitably chagrined.

"Come on, Harve. Leave the little oik alone." He grabbed his boyfriend's muscled arm and dragged him away. "I'm feeling sick innit? I'm gonna need a little pick-me-up… and a change of clothes. I feel so dreadfully grubby."

PRACTICALLY NOTHIN' LEFT

MONTY RAGED, A trapped whirling dervish of frustration struggling within the diminutive man. "I can't effin believe it! Sending an idiot to find that painting," he said, barging into his first-floor office, Harve patiently following him and closing the door. "What on earth was Landa thinking, tho? I thought that maybe, perhaps, Riven wasn't the fool I met all that time ago. But it appears I was wrong. This time Landa has really lost the plot, innit?" He threw himself theatrically onto his enormous office sofa and fretted.

"But per'aps, it's like a put-on-show? Yeah?" Harve replied, plonking himself next to Monty and draping a muscled arm around his thin, shaking shoulders. "Maybe this Riven fella is like Columbo or that uvver one… Monk? They always come across as right divs but still cop the bad guy, yeah? That could be it. Sure it could."

Monty removed his carpet-themed hat and threw it aside. It landed on the floor like a deflated cat. "But this isn't some dumb TV show, innit? There's a multi-million-pound painting missing, and I was the one who effin' lost it." He took out a small, elegant silver hip flask and unscrewed the lid.

"But Landa is yer best mate," Harve began uncertainly, "she won't let that 'appen. And besides, you can buy anuvver Mondrian if it comes ter that."

Monty sighed. "You're so good to me, Harve. I don't deserve you, but things are not that simple." He put the flask to his lips.

"You sure that's a good idea, Mont'?" Harve asked. "You've been hittin' the booze a bit heavily recently."

"Are you saying you don't want any?"

"I'm sayin' it's probably best ter keep yer wits about yer, that's all—and we've not eaten this mornin'. Empty stomach an' all that... But go on, why not? Yer brandy is the chuffin' best of the best."

They emptied the flask and sat back.

Monty so wanted to feel a buzz, to feel anything but misery, but the booze did nothing other than make him feel drowsy. The brandy was the last from his cellar that he'd been forced to sell off—he'd kept back a single bottle of Louis XIII de Remy Martin Rare Cask Grande Champagne Cognac. At a price tag of 35K per bottle, he should have sold it with the rest—money was tight—but couldn't quite do it. And now it was finished.

"We 'ave each uvver, right, don't we? Which means we can get through this," Harve said, his beautiful blue eyes sparkling.

"What you don't understand, Harve, is..." Monty's voice dried.

"You can tell me. You can tell me anyfink. It's just us two. Monty and Harve against the world! We can do anyfink we want! Anyfink! Can't we?"

Monty didn't answer for a few seconds, his empty stomach tightening after the hit of brandy. The booze was a bad idea, Monty realised, but he felt at peace now that it was all gone. It represented a turning point. The end of the life he'd had before. The start of something new, something different. "The truth is, Harve," he began, rubbing at his head, "the truth is that Landa put up all the money for this gallery. She helped me out, I'm indebted to her."

"She paid for this place, but I thought...?"

Monty sighed, the breath coming from somewhere deep

inside his body, filling the small room with the full force of his despair. "I lost it, Harve. My fortune. All of it. I got greedy and was ripped off. A scam. They took it all, innit!"

"Wot?!"

Monty sank even further into the sofa and into Harve's arms, a sad, shrunken figure. "It was my fault. And now I'm worth practically nothing."

"Nothin'?" The word hung on the air like a bad smell. "Didn't you go ter the rozzers? Didn't you get yer lawyers on it?"

"I couldn't. What they did was above board. Legal."

"But you said you were scammed? I reckon there's lots of fings yer can do ter get it back. Course there is. We just need ter sit dahn and work it out. There's a solution. I know it."

"I wish there was. I've been through this over and over. I'm finished. And there's nothing I can do about it. The suited sharks made it clear that there was a risk involved. I didn't listen, of course. I was too greedy. It was a deception of sorts, but I wasn't actually scammed. They took my millions, Harve, and it was all legal. The lawyers told me that. Told me to my face that I'd been stupid. That it was my fault to sign away all my money without reading the small print. It was malicious, and I'm pretty sure who was behind it."

"Who, Monty?" Harve spat, like he was ready to grab his Sword of Avenging and forever pledge himself to Monty's cause. "Who?"

Monty put a calming hand on Harve's arm. "Someone you don't want to get on the wrong side of."

"It doesn't matter who he is! We can bring him dahn. We just need a plan. A way of gettin' yer money back. Sure we do."

"That's the booze talking, Harve. Listen to me. It was Roo Osbourne. He's untouchable, innit?"

"But—"

"And now his Mondrian is missing, who do you think is gonna get the blame, Harve? Who do you think Roo effin'

Osbourne is gonna come down on like a ton of effin' bricks?"

Harve gave him a confused look.

"It's me innit? For eff's sake, Harve. Don't you understand the serious amount of poo I'm in?"

Harve nodded his head, realisation slowly starting to dawn.

"Trust me. I'm done for. The people he got to ruin me were very clever in their little scheme, giving me numerous chances to back out. Covering themselves in legalese. But no. I was insistent, I knew best, and lost the effin' lot."

"Then why not try and get even wiv this Roo Osbourne fella? Do sumfin to get back at 'im?" The cogs in Harve's booze-affected brain roughly banged and ground together. "Hang on, you didn't steal his paintin', did yer?"

Monty waved away the suggestion with a small, brown, beringed hand. "Listen to me, Harve. I'm skint. Brassic. Without cashola. Get it?"

The sparkle left Harve's eyes to be replaced by… Monty wasn't quite sure. Was it doubt?

"So yer not a millionaire anymore?" he said bluntly.

"Does that change things for you?"

Harve removed his arm from around Monty's shoulders and stood up, turning his back. If it was possible, Monty sagged even further into his enormous sofa.

"It's just a shock, right? I thought you were loaded."

"Well I'm not. I've just a measly few hundred grand to my name and a forty-nine percent stake in this gallery. Landa owns the rest and the building. Although she left it to me to run the thing. A lifeline. You didn't answer. Does it change things between us?"

Harve's shoulders sank, and he turned to face him. "Why should it? Luv conquers everyfink, sure it does."

Monty could see the sudden doubt in Harve's eyes. "But it's upset you, innit?"

"Yes and no, I'm just not—" Harve's phone rang. He looked at the number and hastily offed it.

"Who's that?"

"No one," Harve replied, guiltily, Monty thought. Despite how he felt about him, something had always been off about Harve. He was keyed into that sort of thing. Monty could spot gold-diggers a mile off—they were a constant problem in his world. Or had been. That's why he was so surprised about Jim Riven. He'd put him down as someone out to take Landa for a ride, but the man showed no interest in her lifestyle or her money. Indeed, he seemed rather to dislike it all. And when she'd grown bored of him, as she inevitably did with her beaus, he had taken the news with good grace and no pay-off.

Harve on the other hand? The annoying truth was that Monty loved him. He'd loved him from day one. Up to that point, the only person Monty had ever really loved was himself. And that was the problem. He was sure Harve was a conman. So sure, that he'd not had him investigated simply because he didn't want to discover the truth. He'd never thought it possible, but with his loss of money and prestige had come a huge slice of humility. Perhaps that's why he had fallen for Harve? All his so-called friends had ostracised him, until Landa made it known that he was to be treated no differently. But they did treat him differently, especially when her back was turned. He'd seen that world for what it was and had come to despise it. His old life had been a sham. Sure, he wanted it back again, he'd do anything for that. Anything. He'd learned his lesson and then some. But part of the new life he was making for himself involved sacrifices and one of them was Harve. He knew he'd had to tell him but had put it off time and time again. This admission hadn't been planned—it just came out. He had the world's most expensive brandy to thank for giving him the guts to do it. It was long overdue, but he was glad it was out there. He was skint and now Harve knew. The deed was done. He hoped beyond hope that Harve would stay. But if he didn't... sod him, innit? His heart fluttered. Harve couldn't go, he just couldn't. Perhaps I should tell him the full story, he thought to himself, but that was impossible.

Harve's phone rang again.

"Who is it?" Monty asked, irritated.

"I'm gonna 'ave ter take it. I'm sorry." Harve opened the door and gave Monty a wan smile. "I'll be back. Promise."

"And I've still got to get in touch with Landa."

A CUP OF OFFENDING TEA

LEFT ON HIS own, tea-less, and unsure what he should do, Riven awkwardly paced the main gallery room. The floor was old concrete that had recently been cleaned and buffed. There were a few more rat-holes, but the fresh plaster was still in place.

His eye was drawn to what looked like an old Colt revolver set into one of the side walls. At first, he thought it was an exhibit, but it was held in place by two ancient-looking screws and seemingly as old as the gallery itself. He could just make out the image of a flower supposedly coming out of the gun's rusty barrel. And above, also painted over in fresh white, were the words, Make Love Not War. Over half a century since the hippy 60s and that sentiment had still not been heeded. He tried the trigger, but it was fused solid. Shrugging, he took out his phone and took a photograph, sending it to his mate Dillon, who had an obsession for old guns. He shouldn't encourage him, but it'd be remiss not to pass it on.

He stepped onto the low stage and walked up to the back wall, tapping his knuckles on the hard bricks. He'd seen people on TV tapping walls and the suchlike and it seemed very much the appropriate thing to do, even if he didn't have any idea what he was doing. The wall was solid and still sticky with white paint. Dry enough to hang a painting, but Jen had told him the whole under-gallery had been recently refurbished—a rush job to get the gallery ready for opening night. Paint had even dripped onto the stage he noticed. It was a little shoddier than he was expecting, but he guessed all eyes would be on the Mondrian, not the floor. Two hooks at head height showed him where the Mondrian had been hung. He tested them with his fingers. Solid.

Riven shrugged. Nothing to see here. Perhaps I could just sneak away?

His phone rang in his pocket. He could tell who it was from the angry and insistent vibration and so wasn't in the least bit surprised to see the contact name:

Landa! No! Arrrrgggghhh! Run Away!

According to Monty, there was no signal down here, but then again, he surmised, that would be no barrier to someone like Landa. He checked the phone screen that registered a single signal bar and sighed.

When Riven bought his new smart phone a few months ago after much haranguing from Dillon to upgrade, he'd been particularly impressed with the vibration feature that gave a different type of buzz for every different person in his contacts list. For instance, Landa's vibration was sharp and jarring whereas Dillon's vibration was kind of wishy-washy and blurred. This was until Dillon informed him that no such function existed. And yet, the vibrations differed so much between his friends that he was sure Dillon had got it wrong. But after a visiting a self-styled phone guru in one of those peculiarly antiseptic phone stores run by tech-cultists stuffed with blank-eyed followers, it turned out Dillon was right. Which was perplexing on many levels.

He contemplated ignoring the call for a moment, but not for a long one. Landa would keep ringing and ringing until he answered. The girl was persistent, that much was for sure.

"Yeah, hi," Riven ventured, keeping the phone a good six inches from his ear.

"I let Monty talk to me!" Landa shouted. *"He may be my BFF, but he knows that it's over between us if my Mondrian isn't found! So we've not made up, okay? But he tells me you are acting less than professionally."*

"Oh."

"I don't like the sound of that, Riv, not one bit. You're supposed to be helping me out!" she shrieked. *"Leaving no stone unturned! And not accusing my friends. Monty had nothing to do with this, understand?"*

"Yes," he replied, his heart sinking. He'd been hoping to have a quick look around and then escape. But with Landa and Monty checking up on him, he'd have to actually look like he was doing something.

"I'm counting on you, Riv? Yeah? Really counting on you!"

"I know."

"So find my missing Mondrian. I know you can do it. I just know it! Don't let me down!"

The phone went dead and Riven replaced it in his pocket. "How do I get myself into such scrapes?" he moaned, his voice echoing off the gallery walls.

Sighing again, Riven left the main gallery and begrudgingly took a look around. I could still be in bed, he thought to himself, instead of being down here in this brightly lit hell. I'm going to have to go through the motions, otherwise I'll never get Landa off my back. She might even blame me for losing the painting. The thought, terrifying and long-reaching, galvanised him into action.

The place was a maze of rooms and unexpected spaces. It made for surprises and the feeling of discovery. He was impressed. It had obviously been designed by someone with a keen architectural understanding of gallery spaces.

In one of these rooms, he accidentally knocked over what

he guessed was a display of old 60s' tinned products including Vim, Kiwi Shoe Polish, Shell All Purpose Grease, Colman's English Mustard, Spam, Bird's Custard, Nesquick and more. The collapsing tins made a loud, rattling cacophony that echoed noisily. He quickly attempted to rebuild the display, getting grease on his hands from one of the tins that had sprung open, but somehow the display just didn't look right. He tried rebuilding it in various ways but lacked the artistic bent. In the end, he gave up and quickly snuck away.

Next, Riven entered a side gallery where stood a pair of double doors marked *Private*. He expected them to be locked but pushed through with no problem to find himself standing in a wide corridor at the end of which, steps led up to a sturdy pair of brand-new doors that were not only impressively locked, but also chained as Harve had described. This was where the larger gallery items were delivered, he surmised. Unless someone had the keys for both the chain locks and the doors, the Mondrian wasn't taken out this way. And Monty and Harve were the only ones with access to the keys. But then again, locks could be picked, and one or both of them could be lying.

Riven sighed. Is this what proper detectives had to deal with? Motive, opportunity, and um… some other stuff? It seemed dreadfully complicated.

He noticed a stack of white emulsion paint in large, plastic containers, as well as brushes and rollers—some of them needing a clean. He didn't know much about painting and decorating, but not washing your brushes afterwards was treated as something of a sin, wasn't it? They really must've been in a rush to open. He spotted some old rags and wiped his hands clean of the offending grease, noticing artworks stacked against the walls, various sad-looking sculptures, and a fire hydrant. He turned his attention back to the chained and locked outside doors. "If the Mondrian was taken out this way," he said to himself, "the doors must've been—"

"Locked from the inside after it was stolen," said a voice behind him, startling him. He turned to see the girl with the nice boots—Jen—holding a disappointing paper cup. "Your tea," she said, still annoyed, but her previous high-handed way of speaking to him was gone. Riven guessed that this was because he was no longer a pest exterminator and minion, but a friend of her employer and some sort of detective.

"No mug?"

"You think you deserve a mug?"

"Doesn't everybody? As a right?"

Jen tried to keep her face neutral but couldn't help a small smile. "So what's your connection with Landa?" she asked in a light-hearted way but Riven could see she was interested in his answer.

"She's an ex."

"An ex?" she repeated unbelievingly. "You went out with her?" Jen was either impressed or jealous. Or both. One thing was for sure though, she was mostly shocked.

Riven grimaced. "Yeah, please don't remind me."

"I thought you'd done some detective work for her. I didn't think that for one moment you were…"

"At it?" Riven answered for her, pleased to see how impressed Jen looked, even though she was trying to hide it. Perhaps there was hope for them yet.

"But she's so incredibly—"

"Rich?" Riven ventured.

"Well yes, but she's beautiful. I mean, well, stunning."

Riven shrugged as nonchalantly as he could muster. "I thought the same, especially when she wasn't awake. Which wasn't often enough for my liking."

"Yeah, she can be a stuck-up bit—!" Jen's pencil-thin eyebrows arched at her almost indiscretion. "I didn't mean to bad mouth her or anything, it's just that—"

Riven lifted a hand. "Don't beat yourself up about not liking Landa. To be honest, I'm not sure anyone does, apart from Monty. But, deep down, underneath all that utter, utter mess, there is a nice person trying to get out."

"Really?"

"Yeah," he admitted, like he too was surprised. "Really."

"But you and her?" Jen shook her head, long pencil-thin hair glancing her shoulders in a most agreeable way. "I'm gob-smacked. And now you're a detective, huh? That's a big step up from the local print shop. Wow!"

"I found one of Landa's missing Fabergé earrings, well her mother's earrings, and now she's sent me here to do the same for her Mondrian, well her father's Mondrian."

"Fabergé? So you must be working for an art insurance company, yeah?"

Jen was sounding him out, that was obvious. As to why, Riven didn't really care, he was just pleased that she seemed to like him again, and that she was sort of impressed. It may have taken over ten years, but that was still a result. "I'm more of a solo act, to be honest," he answered. "You know, doing my shaman thing."

"Riiight," Jen replied, extending the vowel in a slightly condescending way, the impressed look slipping from her face to fall heavily onto the concrete floor. "You're not an official investigator at all are you?"

"I'm not an official anything," Riven admitted. "Maybe a professional layabout perhaps? But no. Landa seems to think I'm going to help somehow. And Landa must be obeyed. So here I am. Obeying."

"All that stuff you said to Monty about not being a proper detective, was true then?"

"Pretty much."

"I thought you were just winding him up as part of your technique."

"Afraid not. Even so, I'm going to have to act like I am a proper investigator, just so I can appease Landa. And after I've done my bit—looking around, pondering, looking around some more—Monty can call the police."

"But didn't you find that earring?"

"It's complicated. You could say, the earring found me. As to how?" Riven shook his head, taking the cup from Jen and staring into its insipid milky depths. "Like I said, it's complicated."

The moment lingered.

Jen pursed her thin lips. "I suppose you'll want to know who had access to the gallery in the days before the painting went missing?"

"Will I?"

"Yes!" she replied more exasperatedly than Riven thought was necessary.

"Bill, the rat man, you remember him, yes?" she asked. "He had access to the gallery yesterday—the day of the opening. It was him who plastered over the rat holes as a quick fix. He was down in the main gallery room for hours. I left him to it. And besides, the man is a bit of a prick. He came in and out through the front door. I was very strict. Once the Mondrian was delivered, the back doors were to be kept locked and chained."

"That sounds…um …sound," Riven ventured.

Jen pointed to the brushes, rollers, and paint. "The painters and decorators finished the day before the opening. A rush job, but those guys work fast. They'll be finishing next week."

"Right," he replied, wondering why Jen was bombarding him with information.

"The Mondrian was left hanging down here in the under-gallery after the show. It wasn't moved. Monty phoned me at half past eight this morning to meet him here. We normally open at 10am. I say we, but it's usually me who opens up. Monty isn't a morning person, and the party went on till the early hours, so I was surprised when he called. It was out of the ordinary, but then again, there was a multi-million-pound artwork under his roof. That'd be enough to freak anyone out."

Riven sniffed at the cup of offending tea and grimaced, handing it back to Jen with an audible sigh. "The Mondrian?"

"Yes, the Mondrian." Jen's eyes widened as she spoke.

"You are a fan, I take it?"

"You've heard of Van Gogh?"

"Hasn't everybody?"

"Then imagine having one of his paintings, like *The Sunflowers*, in your possession, that you could go and have a look at any time. Just hanging on the wall. Would that move you?" Jen looked at him expectantly.

Riven was caught a little off guard. He searched around inside his brain for an appropriate answer before venturing a hesitant, "Yes?"

"That's what the Mondrian is like for me, and for other lovers of modern art. A Van Gogh all of our very own."

"I suppose that would be… um… cool?"

"Cool?!? That'd be amazing! It's a shame Monty doesn't appreciate art for art's sake, like I and others do. For him, it's the prestige and the value. Same for Roo Osbourne who owns it, although where he's concerned the Mondrian is just another asset. Philistine!"

"Quite."

"Monty came in so early today because of worry. I guess, even for a guy like him, having such an expensive artwork under his protection was screwing with his head. Which is odd, because as soon as we arrived, he sent me down here to check on it. You would've thought he'd have gone straight there himself."

"Would I?"

Jen paused a long time before answering, their eyes locked on one another. "You know what I mean. I went down into the under gallery and the Mondrian was gone. The wall was empty as you saw it, like some locked room mystery."

The phrase *locked room mystery* bounced around in Riven's head rather awkwardly and made no real impact on his cerebral cortex.

"Once I told Monty and Harve it was missing, and they were over the shock of it, we undertook an extensive search of the gallery, well, me and Harve did. Monty just sat and wailed. It's a deceptively large building, but it's mainly show rooms. There's no place to hide a painting the size of the Mondrian. And even cut out of its frame and rolled or folded, it would be difficult to conceal. No, if it was here, we would've found it." She turned her attention to the doors. "I suppose you will need to take a look outside."

"Will I?"

"That's why you're here isn't it?" she replied with poorly concealed exasperation.

"I suppose so."

"I'll go and get the keys off Monty."

Riven took out the keyring. "No need. Which ones do I need?"

Jen didn't even blink. "This one unlocks the padlock and this one is for the deadlocks," she said pointing. "The bolts and latches you can work out for yourself. I used to open up for Monty. Before the Mondrian arrived, they were my keys. But Monty became nervy and insisted on taking them himself soon after. I know what you're thinking…"

"Do you?"

"You're thinking I could've got the keys copied. But locksmiths are not allowed to copy keys for security doors and padlocks like these. They can only be requested from the manufacturer and there's a torturous paper chain to do even that."

"If you say so."

"I do say so. There's only one set of keys. Period. Only Monty or Harve could've gotten the Mondrian in or out this way."

Why Jen was protesting her innocence so forcefully was beyond him. He wished she'd showed this kind of passion when finding him a decent cup of tea.

"I'd take a close look at Harve," she continued in very much the same vein. "There's something dubious about the guy. He's been poisoning Monty about me, I'm sure of it."

"Really? He came across as your supporter earlier?"

"He's sly. After Monty's money is my guess. But Monty can't let me go. I pretty much run this place for him, even though he pays me a pittance."

"Monty said he was paying you a lot of money."

Jen shook her head. "That's just not true."

"Why would he lie about that?"

She shrugged and lowered her voice. "Well, you know Monty. He's away with the fairies. Every time I've asked for a raise, he says he's suffering from cash-flow problems or some other excuse."

"Then why work here?"

"Why? Have you not seen all the great art in this gallery? And I get to meet the artists. And Kowalski is exhibiting here next week."

"Kowalski?"

"It was quite some coup getting him to exhibit and paint here. Six months ago, no one had heard of him. Now, he's one of the biggest stars of the modern art world. And of course, it was me who also arranged last night's exhibition—helped enormously by the fact we had a Mondrian at our opening. Monty and Landa have their uses. They may be a little too young and more interested in the show of it, rather than the actual art, but they have connections. Before Monty managed to get the Mondrian, and before Kowalski confirmed, I was thinking of asking for a raise again and threatening to quit if I didn't get it. But a Mondrian can sure turn a girl's head." She lowered her voice again. "I've often wondered if there was a reason why Monty is so tight. Money worries perhaps? But then again, that ensemble he's wearing must've cost thousands. It's an original Santiago."

Riven invested in a knowing nod, guessing this Santiago must be some designer chap or chappess with an unhealthy interest in carpet off-cuts.

"Monty wowed as much with that outfit last night as he did with the Mondrian."

Riven's cerebral cortex, which had been struggling in neutral up to now, suddenly found a forward gear and lurched into motion. He'd met Monty more times than he'd liked. The man was always impeccably dressed and never wore the same article of clothing twice, never mind the same outfit. "You mean Monty is wearing the same clothes today as he did last night? Isn't that odd for someone so obsessed with their appearance?"

Jen shrugged. "Monty, Landa, their many hangers on and friends, live in a different world to me. Everything about them is odd." Jen gave him a pointed look, as if she was including him in her list.

Riven sighed. "Yeah. I've had first-hand experience of it."

They locked eyes for a moment. Dammit, Riven thought, Jen was, well, just lovely.

"Have fun," she said, walking away with something of a spring in her step, throwing the cup of offending tea into an old trash container.

Riven watched her go. His eyes slipping down to her waist and exquisite thighs and bum again, quelling a sudden stab of excitement. The chance of him asking her out after all this was over was high. However, the odds of her saying yes were a lot lower than he would've liked. Still, he thought to himself, you never know, I might just trip over the missing Mondrian and those odds would suddenly skyrocket. Unfortunately, as he approached the locked and chained doors, he didn't trip over the Mondrian or any other missing artwork. But what he did trip over was the blue ribbon of a discarded lanyard. An official *Outtasight!* VIP opening night gallery pass. A name was printed on the impressive-looking laminated card… *Kowalski.*

NOT QUITE AN EAST ENDER

JEN LEFT JIM Riven to do whatever it was he'd been brought here to do. Apart from annoy me, she thought to herself. The man was a full-on disaster area and yet, there was something about him. Niggling was the word. There was something niggling about the guy. He was irritatingly fascinating, or at least a subconscious part of her mind found him to be. The rest of her mind was pretty much in agreement that the man was an idiot of the first order. And it was this part of her mind that she decided to go with. The subconscious might be all mystical and way out there cool, but at best it was wish-washy and at worst, totally misleading. As such, Jen decided that Riven needed to be punished hard, and as often as she could manage given the limited timeframe.

The gallery had a makeshift kitchen that Jen used to make herself lovely, milky mugs of tea, just like the one Jim Riven had requested, so it had taken an effort to find an old nasty paper cup at the back of an abandoned cupboard, and comparatively easy to fill it with lukewarm, watery tea. Which was nothing more than he deserved after what he did to her.

Getting a Third when you'd worked for and expected a First, might not have knocked that many people back. To most, a degree was a degree no matter how well you did, but for Jen it'd been a body-blow that had taken years to get over. She'd worked menial office jobs and at one point found herself on the checkout at the local supermarket. She could've gone for more high-profile jobs, or at least jobs in the art sector, but her confidence had been wrecked. She'd only ever seen herself as a double-first graduate. Her future plans were all based upon that presumption. Everything relied upon her getting that grade. And the fact that she hadn't, had left her in a limbo she'd been unable to escape from.

Until a lucky coincidence that is.

She'd bumped into an old friend in a bar on holiday—what were the odds? And they'd spent the rest of the holiday together, resulting in a job offer working in the rarefied world of art evaluation—authentication, checking for forgeries, and investigative research—for the London Tate Gallery. And her friend wouldn't take no for an answer. Art evaluation was notoriously difficult, but such was the reputation of Jen's new team that if they said an artwork was the real deal then it *was the real deal*. Not that Jen made those decisions, but she was a member on the team that did.

She excelled from day one, also taking part in restoration projects at which she soon became an expert, whilst increasing her already wide knowledge of the modern art world—her single and most passionate passion. After another five years, she finally began to feel her old self again. The dreadful limbo finally went away, and the old Jen reasserted herself. She left the London Tate for a low paid but exciting new position working as the manager of a new en-vogue gallery. The wage was not up to much, but she was running the whole operation. Jen was on the up. And nothing would stop her.

She returned to the upper gallery, hearing the muffled tones of Monty talking on his phone in his first-floor office—one of the few places where there was a decent reception. His high-pitched whine could penetrate the blast-thickened walls of a nuclear bunker. She tried to focus in on his voice but could only hear the odd effin' this and effin' that. But then she became aware of another sound. A sort of hissing. She followed it, realising it was another voice, hushed and strangely familiar, coming from one of the gallery side-rooms.

"No Sheila, it's not like that, okay? …Aw come on! Look, I'm sorry for not picking up your call straightaway but I did tell you not to phone me on this number. What if Mont—"

A long pause. The hissing voice belonged to Harve, but his East End drawl had disappeared, in its place was something slightly posh and slightly annoyed.

"I told you, Hun, everything has hit the fan. Yeah, yeah—I know. But what am I supposed to do, just disappear? How suspicious would that be right now?—Of course I do. Of course. I'm doing this for us right?—No. No. I don't love Monty! Why would you say that? He's just a mark. A guy with more money than sense—You knew what I had to do before we started this. And don't forget this was your idea, yeah? You chose him—Don't say that. I didn't want to go through with it in the first place—No! I'm not being arsey. I'm just saying that it was—You can't be jealous, Sheila. Not now. Not after you forced me into this—Of course I like him. I couldn't do this if I didn't like him a little bit—Calm down. It's just a part I'm playing, so don't act all surprised if—That means nothing to me. Just sex. What?—The gallery manager? Of course not. She's not my type at all. All skin and bones, and you know how much I like something to grab a hold of—Yes, I'm sure. She's a stuck-up skinny cow with a thing for some artist or other—But you know me, I'm a one-woman man—Look, Hun, I've got to go. There's some investigator sniffing about—No, no, no! Don't get all hysterical, the man is an absolute idiot. A friend of that Landa woman I told you about. We'll be safe, okay? He's not going to find out anything. Look, Hun, I've really got to go—No, Monty isn't calling me, but even if he was, I need to be with him right now. He's in a mess, Hun, in a real hole—Please don't cry. We knew this wasn't going to be simple—Yeah, yeah—Just trust me, okay? And stay calm. We'll be okay, I promise. We've got to play the… um… long game, okay? Look, I've to go—I really have to—I'm going, okay—I love you too. But don't phone me on this number again. Bye."

Harve let out a long, world-weary sigh. "What are you doing, Harve?" he said to himself. "This is one hell of a mess."

Jen hung back as Harve walked past, hiding behind an impressive African fetish. I need to let Riven know about this asap, she thought to herself, and, of course, her boss. Although she guessed Monty wouldn't be that surprised. Harve was just about the most unconvincing East Ender she'd ever met.

£20 AND A BURGER

AFTER A GOOD ten minutes manhandling the doors—what Riven had been doing was less like manhandling and more like kicking and banging at the doors until they seemingly opened of their own accord—Riven emerged again into the cool spring morning, or what he assumed was the morning. He checked his watch.

Noon.

It was still way too early for him to be up and about, but the sooner he covered his bases, the sooner he could return to his warm, inviting and mostly safe flat.

He took out the lanyard and gave it another look.

Kowalski.

The artist that Jen had been so impressed with. There was also a photograph—obviously a promo shot—of a smiling, bearded, somewhat attractive man with his hair in a man-bun. Riven couldn't be one-hundred percent sure, but this Kowalski might be his competitor for the affections of the lovely Jen. He hoped not. He wrapped the ribbon around the pass and stuffed it into his jacket pocket, stepping into the alleyway.

It was wide enough for a truck to drive down and showed signs of being recently cleaned, although a ramshackle shack sat in one corner, backing onto the gallery wall. The makeshift home of a tramp, he guessed.

Attached to the shack was a washing line of sorts upon which was pinned a single, manky, and familiar-looking black tee-shirt. Perturbed, Riven went over to investigate. The tee-shirt was the same as the one he was wearing, with the same message printed in large white words: *Don't Mess With This Idiot!*. He checked the label. Written on the back in faded black ink was the name *James Aurelius Riven.*

Riven's mother had always made the young Jim Riven print his full name on the labels of his clothes—like she thought his school was a breeding ground for garment thieves. He'd resented this practice until his mother had suddenly died. He had only vague memories of what she looked like and, unfortunately, his eccentric and irritating father never kept any photographs of her. And so, as silly as it seemed, writing his name on the labels of his clothes, even his boxers, made him feel close to her, a way of keeping her alive in his mind. As for his awful middle name, he had his father to blame for that. That and his irritating nickname at school: Jarhead, imaginatively conjured up from his initials JAR and the terrible homemade back and sides haircut his dad inflicted upon him. To be honest, Jim Riven's dad had a helluva lot to answer for.

He stared at his name and shook his head. "How the—" he began but didn't bother finishing. Coincidences were something he actively tried to avoid, and yet coincidence was the only way he was going to find the Mondrian, so he decided to go along with it in the hope of something miraculous happening.

Back to the tee-shirt: He'd bought the only two ever made, or so he'd been told by the self-termed 'reputable trader' in the rather trendy and over-priced Camden Market. They were home-printed one-offs and expensive. How did it get here hanging next to a down-and-out's shack in the East End? He had an inkling. Landa again. It was one morning early on in their relationship when Riven had mistakenly felt himself very much taken by his new girlfriend—in that way someone who has recently been hit on the head feels a sudden lightness of being, before the headaches began in earnest. Landa had gotten up and put on his tee-shirt before wandering around his flat looking so fetching and all-round lovely that he'd said she could keep it. A few days later, Riven found the same tee-shirt stuffed down the back of his bin and covered in red wine stains. He'd tried to rescue it, but it was manky and stretched out of shape. He'd put it and some other old clothes in a bag and left it outside a charity shop. How it ended up on a tramp's washing line on the other side of London he could try and conjecture, but why bother? It was here, as was the girl with the nice boots. Maybe the Mondrian will also be lurking within easy reach?

"I hope so!"

He crouched down, pushed aside the plastic doorway, and peered inside the little shack. First off, there was no Mondrian lurking within easy reach inside. Bugger it! Secondly, Riven was surprised to find the place was almost liveable. Thirdly, and most importantly, there was no nasty stench other than the stale smell of a dried-up old kebab that appeared to have been nibbled at by rats. Otherwise, the shack was empty apart from an old bag of clothing. He recognised it at once. The same bag of clothing he'd left at the charity shop. He looked inside, poking at the contents. A few more of his tee-shirts, an old jacket, and a pair of much-loved turn-up jeans. He'd loved those jeans and had only stopped wearing them when his mate, Dillon, who was a fashion disaster area, had the audacity to tell him how unfashionable they were. He put the bag down and sighed, spotting a handwritten note on a makeshift table created from an upturned beer crate. He crawled inside and read it.

Mikey! It's Sam Smythe. Remember me? Where are you? I heard something happened to scare you away Thursday night. Was it those stuck-up gallery kids? There's £20 and a burger waiting for you if you get in touch.

I'll be here next Friday afternoon if I don't find you before then.

Mikey must be the down-and-out who lives in this shack, Riven surmised. Depending on the age of the note, it could be another week before this Sam—whoever he was—Smythe, would be back. Not that he cared either way. Something had possibly spooked Mikey the night before the gallery opening though. Could that have anything to do with the missing Mondrian?

Riven decided to root around inside the shack just in case the Mondrian was stashed here. It was a far-fetched hope, but why not? He could solve this whole thing and go back home, and perhaps get a date with Jen and her lovely boots. But the nasty shack held no hidden artistic surprises. Outside, he heard the sound of an approaching vehicle thundering down the alleyway.

He crawled out of the shelter just in time to see a large white van come to a screeching stop, its bumper nudging the makeshift shack so that the whole thing slid sideways and collapsed in on itself, forcing Riven to scramble out of the way.

HOMELESS CHIC

A SIGN ON the side of the van read:

SQUEAK-END PEST CONTROL -
No More Mr Mice Guy

Underneath was a smiling logo of a rather lugubrious bald man wearing a tee-shirt bearing the name 'Bill' and a speech bubble saying:

Rats gotta hurt!

A rather lugubrious bald man opened the van door and extricated himself from the vehicle to stand lugubriously on the pavement. It was the same Bill plastered on the side of the van.

Riven pushed himself up onto shaky legs. Bill towered over Riven by at least a foot. He was also twice as wide, his immense belly balancing against the laws of gravity to hang above an impressive tool belt. His head and face flushed red.

"Now wot do we have 'ere?" Bill said threateningly to Riven in a thick, South London accent. "I thought I'd got rid of the vermin problem. You're lucky I didn't run you over, you little prick."

Riven wasn't sure if he was scared, shocked, angry or a mixture of all three. "I beg… I beg your pardon?" he managed weakly.

"You beg my pardon, do you?" Bill bowed theatrically before straightening. "You can 'ave it, gladly. Now get lost! The people who own this gallery don't want another bleedin' vagrant living here and bringin' down the tone."

"Huh?"

"Look, if it was up to me, I would've picked up that Skanky Mike fella, thrown him in the back of my van and thrown him off London Bridge, but the local rag did that story on him, and he became untouchable… or so he thought."

"What?"

"Pest control. It's what I do. So hop it. That shack is now just a pile of ugly rubbish, which means, my son, you will not be living there. Unnerstand? It's a job for the council to clear up. I'll be in touch with them pronto, so don't think about rebuildin'."

"I hope you realise that you're not coming across as a very nice person?" Riven said feebly.

"Actually, I am a very nice person, especially to the people who matter in this life, but if you're vermin…" he tapped the side of the van with an immense, sausage-fingered hand, "you're gonna get pest-controlled." He took a step closer, the eyes in his large, red face glaring down at Riven. "This is your last warnin', get the fu—"

Riven pressed his index finger against Bill's lips. If it was possible, Bill's head went an even darker shade of crimson.

First Jen had thought he was working for Bill the rat man, and now Bill the rat man thought he was living out here as a tramp. What was wrong with people today? Sure, his black jeans, tee-shirt and jacket combo wasn't cutting edge designer wear, but it was a damn-fine look. There was nothing pest-exterminator or remotely vagrant-*esque* about it. But then he remembered the tee-shirt. Mikey must've been wearing it before, and Bill had come to the wrong conclusion. "You're working for Monty Fitzhugh, aren't you?" Riven said as Bill's mouth made a strange buzzing sound with Riven's finger pressed against his lips.

Bill pulled away, a confused look on his face. "Yeah, I am. I was told to clean the place of vermin. You know him?" he added guardedly.

Riven nodded. "Yes, I do as a matter of fact. I'm also working for him… sort of."

Bill straightened, the confused look turning to one of embarrassment. "Oh I see, you're into that homeless chic thing, yeah? You can see why I was confused. And you appearin' from that shack like that, well, I just put two and two together and made the obvious conclusion that you were also some skanky little shite. But I have to ask, why are you wearin' that down-and-out's tee-shirt?"

"This is not homeless chic!" Riven half-shouted. "It cost me… well, a lot of money. Just because Mikey was wearing its copy doesn't make me a down-and-out."

"You know that Skanky Mike loser? I thought you gallery fellas wanted rid of him? So don't give me any recriminations. That stuck up gallery manager bunged me two-fifty to do the job and that's what I did."

"Jen paid you off to scare away a tramp?"

Bill rapped the side of his van again. "I dispose of vermin, that's my job. She said Mr Fitzhugh wanted rid, but Skanky Mike had gotten himself into the local paper, making it difficult for the miserable little bugger to be moved on." He touched the side of his nose. "But I have my ways 'n' means," he said proudly, winking. "I gave him a little present to scare him away."

Riven's phone buzzed. He took it out to see a message from Landa...

Don't let me down, Riv! Don't let me

down! You can do it!

Followed by a series of incomprehensible emojis.

"Who's that from?" Bill said. "You look worried."

"It's the owner of a painting that went missing last night."

"What was that? A painting missin'? You mean the Mondrian?"

"You know of it?"

"Just because I'm the pest-control guy don't mean I don't have arty tastes. It was quite the paintin'. Money-wise, it's worth millions. I remember readin' about the thing when it was discovered a few months ago. The find of a lifetime."

Riven couldn't but help feel a little annoyed that this awful man seemed to know more about the painting than he did. It didn't seem right. Not right at all..

"And it's gone you say? Wow! That's big news. Very big news."

"Is it?" Riven replied, feeling very much like he'd said something he shouldn't have.

"Of course it is. You must remember all the furore after Edvard Munch's *Scream* was stolen? When was that? Nearly twenty years ago. It was front page news around the world, mate."

"Well, um, keep it under your hat for now, okay," Riven said, getting more annoyed with the man's art knowledge by the moment. "I'm here to try and find the thing, before news of it gets out."

"*You* are?" Bill said with a sneer. Adding an extra "You?" in a most derisive way.

Riven nodded. "Yes me!" he replied bullishly. "And everyone is a suspect."

"You don't suspect me, do you?" Bill said, taking a step forward and glaring at him. "I'm a rat man, through and through. That's all I care about."

A thought popped into Riven's mind. It entered so

unexpectedly, that it made all his other thoughts jump aside in impressed astonishment. "If the Mondrian had been taken through the back doors," Riven began, "Skanky Mike could've been a witness. And you were the one who got rid of him."

"Don't give me that nonsense. I told you, it was that stuck up manager girl who asked me to get rid of him. I'm tellin' you that now and I'll tell the police the same."

"The police have not yet been informed," Riven said, emphasising the yet in a way that he hoped sounded like a threat.

Bill pulled a disgusted face. "Good! If I were you, I'd keep the pigs out of it, unless you want to be fitted up for something you didn't do."

The pest exterminator's dislike of the police seemed personal, but judging by the guy's general demeanour, Riven wouldn't have been surprised to find out that the man had had dealings with them. "It's probably only a matter of time before they are called in. And you were here yesterday."

"Yeah, I was here. From early on. Are you not listenin'? They have a rat problem. And rats are my specialty as I told you. I planted poison and plastered up the holes before the show. I packed and went home and that was that. That paintin' was here when I left, as God is my witness."

Bill didn't seem the religious type. Although, Riven surmised, the kind of religion practiced by some churches these days wasn't as touchy-feely as perhaps the various prophets had hoped for all that time ago.

"And why would I come back if I had anythin' to do with it?" Bill continued.

Riven shrugged.

"Cos I ain't got anythin' to do with it, okay? That manager girl was very clear. She said to me that they've only got a few days before the next exhibition, and that they wanted their rat problem dealt with. That's why I'm here with Joey, to set traps and to lay down more poison, and to investigate inside the walls. But to be honest, rats these days are clever little bleeders. It's gonna take a few weeks to totally clear their infestation." Bill bashed the side of the van and a skinny teenager emerged, going to the back, and opening the doors.

Riven's eyes lingered on the kid for a few seconds. He looked familiar but he couldn't place him. He showed no similar signs of recognition… which was fine by Riven. He'd already had one uncomfortable encounter today. Another one would be just too much. Especially without tea.

"Say hello, Joey! Bill shouted at the skinny kid.

Joey walked forward and mumbled a hello while staring at the floor.

"This little toerag is working for me today. You know why?"

Riven had no interest in Joey, nor why he was working with Bill, and was rapidly losing interest in this conversation. Before he could answer, Bill carried on.

"I'm keepin' an eye on him. He's one of those bloody joyriders. Stealing cars, vans, trucks, whatever, and racing them. That's why I keep my keys with me at all times. He's a good kid at heart, but easily led. You listenin'?" Bill said to Joey, hitting him roughly about the head before turning his attention back to Riven who couldn't help flinching. "I'm sorry for nearly knockin' you down and I hope you find the thieves who took the paintin', but we need to get on. The rats won't kill themselves! More's the pity. Hey… what's that you've got there?" He pointed to Riven's pocket. "That's my Stanley Knife, what on earth are you doing with it?"

"I found it in front of the um… missing Mondrian."

"It was my dad's. I carry it with me as a keepsake to remind me what an all-round horror-show he was. I suppose I must've dropped it yesterday when I was workin'. Give it back."

Riven took out the knife and handed it to Bill, who snatched it off him.

"Thanks." He slid out the rusted blade and ran a rough finger over it. "See? It's blunt as anythin'. You couldn't cut nowt with it."

A second profound thought popped unexpectedly into Riven's mind, smugly rubbing shoulders with his first profound thought. "No, but it proves you were at some time standing in front of the Mondrian, doesn't it?"

Bill's lower jaw dropped.

Riven smiled. "Now, do you want me to leave the gallery doors open for you?"

Bill looked confused for a few moments before shaking his head. "Best lock up again. It was made very clear to me that I have to use the front entrance and the front entrance only." Bill's face twisted into a leer. "But either entrance with that stuck up tart of a gallery manager would be okay by me!"

"Quite."

Riven, despite being as red-blooded as the next man/woman/person/thing, had never properly learned how to deal with this kind of blokiness. It was always so unnecessarily crass. Of course, he understood the sentiment. He too would be very happy to enjoy the personal charms of Jen and her boots. Very, very happy in fact. And yet he didn't feel the urge to share this knowledge with Bill or anyone else. Not even Dillon. Although, if the actual event did happen, and if he was pressed by Dillon on the matter, he would of course make sure to let him know that things between him and Jen had progressed in a satisfactory fashion. Perhaps adding a Wahey! in a totally respectful manner that didn't degrade the experience or indeed pass any comment on Jen or her gender… mostly.

Smiling awkwardly, Riven made his way back inside the gallery, glad to be out of the presence of such an obnoxious man, feeling a sudden stab of hunger as he locked the impressive doors and padlocked the heavy chains.

He remembered last night's take home curry, half of which still nestled deliciously in his fridge. Riven always over-ordered, especially when he was hungry and even more especially when he'd been drinking. But there would be no warmed-up

Mushroom Jalfrezi for first and second breakfast today. He put his hand into his back pocket and discovered the wallet he found in the taxi earlier, reminding him he needed money. He decided to get out some cash, to sit down with a nice mug of tea, and try to forget about this whole business.

THE BOLLOCKS AND THE BRAINS

THERE WERE SIXTY-four species of rat in the world and Bill hated all of them with a burning, vengeful loathing that had fuelled his rise to become South London's premier go-to pest control service. Rats were his special speciality, his lifelong obsession, and, in his own words, "his bleedin' *raison detre*, innit!" And he reserved the majority of his venom for *Rattus Norvegicus*, known to non-rat-obsessed-folk as *The Brown* or *Sewer Rat*. These scum-covered bleeders—as he liked to call them amongst various other profane descriptions—grew up to 40cm in length, up to half a kilogram in weight, and were omnivorous, which meant they would quite happily nibble on a piece of discarded lettuce as they would quite happily nibble on one of your still-attached ears. Bill had made it his life-long mission to exterminate as many of the furry little buggers as was humanly, and inhumanely, possible. But more than that, he wanted them to suffer like he had.

He came from a long family of London rat killers stretching back into the eighteenth century. All of them one-man bands. They worked for themselves and only themselves. They lacked foresight, or what Bill called, *the bollocks*. Bill had the bollocks, all right, but he also had the brains. A winning combination. He had built up his pest control business from one-man-with-a-van to a franchising operation that covered most of south London. As such, it was unusual for him to work on the ground, but this job was one he had to do in person. The reason? Bill had a personal interest in the rat problem at the gallery that stretched back over twenty-five years.

Bill was angry and had been since the summer of 1995. Angry about the police, government, taxes, immigration, house prices, the cost of living, insurance hikes, Europe, what was called 'woke culture' in all those nasty papers he read, but most of all, he was angry about rats and the Outtasight! gallery.

Was it possible to hate a building? To feel rancour towards simple bricks and mortar? To despise the very area where that building stood? The answer for Bill was a resounding 'Yes!'. He hated the Outtasight! gallery. Not the name, that was new to him, but the building. It had been difficult to return here. To once again walk within its walls. But once he'd seen the address on the books, he'd been unable to ignore it.

Twenty-five years ago, the young Bill had no desire whatsoever to work in pest-extermination. He was young, he was cool, and he was horny. And none of the young ladies he expended a considerable amount of his time chasing would've been remotely interested in him if they knew he spent his days knee-deep in rodents, roaches, and rat poison, especially his then current squeeze who thought she was a vegetarian, wore an animal rights badge, and occasionally shared his late-night donor kebab. No, following in his father's footsteps was the last thing he had in mind for himself, although he was forced to help the old man out just to make some cash—and to show willing. His dad expected him to work for the family firm and Bill hadn't the guts to stand up to him. His father was a belligerent, violent, wife-beating drunk, who frittered away his money on gambling and drink. During one of his rare busy periods, his father had given Bill a job to do on his own, to learn the family business hands on—or so he told him. He just wanted the extra cash, while paying Bill a pittance. The job was at the Outtasight! Although, back in the summer of 1995, the building was being used as a warehouse for imported items from South America.

In those days Bill was, in his own words, *a cocky little bleeder* with, as it was often put to him, *far too much mouth and not enough trousers*. He'd been more than pleased to get the job. He needed all the money he could get to move out of what was jokingly referred to as *the family home* and to strike out on his own. He'd been saving money here and there for just this purpose, money he kept hidden under a clichéd loose floorboard in his bedroom. He managed to talk up his fee for his work at the gallery as a way of making a bit more money on the side. His useless father was incapable of marketing or salesmanship of any kind. As long as he got his cash in hand, he was happy as the day was long, which was usually the four or so hours between rolling hungover out of bed and going down the pub where he would stay until closing time.

The gallery was run by two odd-looking and odd-sounding rich guys in their late thirties who were using the space to catalogue and store artifacts from a South American archaeological dig on behalf of some weird London and elitist Piccadilly college. Some of these artifacts were particularly exquisite and expensive. Jewellery made from Mayan gold and inlaid with precious stones, as well as creepy stone carvings, figurines, scrolls, and other strange stuff that looked nothing more than so much junk. But it was the jewellery that took Bill's eye.

His first thought was to somehow pilfer the stuff. To break in one night and have away with it. The place had minimal security. They kept the sturdy back doors locked unless there was a delivery or pick up, but the front was a simple door with an external padlock that'd take seconds to access with a decent-sized crowbar and a bit of elbow grease. The only problem? The two guys who ran the place.

At first Bill had thought Cornelius and Darius were a pair of snobs and very possibly gay, but he couldn't have been anymore mistaken if he'd tried. They might've been older, possessed rather posh-sounding names, and dressed themselves in expensive tailored clothes—they also may have been very rich, coming from families that had given them an expensive classical upper-class education leading to expensive classical upper-class accents—and also, they may have hung out at more elitist drinking establishments, and spent far too much money on a night out than Bill thought was actually possible—but they were just a pair of lads like himself with dirty senses of humour and a similar outlook to life.

After the first week working for them, the guys took him to an upmarket strip club in Soho and paid for all his drinks and a lap dance. And, as their friendship bloomed, he'd had lunches at top-end, nobby restaurants and sometimes dined in the evenings at various elite members' clubs. These guys were seriously sleazy, but fun and loaded, and in the weeks that followed, he made a strong bond with them. Bill had never seen how the other half lived up close before, but he liked it, and wanted a slice of it for himself.

Their place did have a serious rat problem, however. A problem that he vowed to solve. Rats were getting into boxes, sometimes nesting in them, and living in the walls, and he'd been given free reign throughout the building to do what was needed to get rid of them—and the promise of a sizable bonus if he eradicated them for good.

Not only did Bill work hard to earn that extra bonus, but he also began to take a real interest in the items that were being catalogued—the guys even let him work on some of their acquisitions. There were artworks in stone, shells, bone, wood, obsidian, jade, clay, stucco, and textiles. As well as precious metals mostly found in items of jewellery, which Bill was the most fascinated by. His growing interest in Mayan art was genuine, and once the building was cleared of vermin, Cornelius and Darius told him a job was waiting for him if he wanted it. A job that paid considerably more than rat extermination. A job that he had gladly accepted. It was a no-brainer. There was money tied up with these guys and the college they worked for—a lot of it. But more than the opportunity and the cash, he enjoyed the work.

Bill was ecstatic and had gone out to celebrate with his mates. But that ecstasy didn't last very long. His dad was waiting for him when he came home. He'd been out to the gallery to see what was taking so long and had been told about the job offer Bill had accepted, and the extra money he'd charged them on the side. He'd gone ballistic, accusing Cornelius and Darius of stealing his son away and undermining his business. But not in those exact words. Bill went to the gallery the next day to apologise, but it turned out that not only words were exchanged between them and his father, but fists as well. And despite Bill's pleading, they withdrew the job offer and wanted nothing more to do with him, peeved with his violent father and even more peeved that Bill had been overcharging them, especially after all their generosity.

But it hadn't ended there. A few days later he was awoken by a visit from the police. His first thought was that his dad had been knocking his mum around again and had been surprised when they wanted to speak with him. Apparently, an expensive and irreplaceable artifact had gone missing from the gallery building. A gold ring of a feathered serpent god eating its own tail embedded with precious stones, a ring that had quite taken Bill's eye in the days before the incident with his idiot father. A ring like that would take anybody's eye. A ring with a sizable monetary value. And Cornelius and Darius were accusing him of sneaking into the building and stealing it.

More than the shock, the disbelief, and the shame was the thought that his new friends could accuse him like this. They were his mates, weren't they? The disgrace of being accused was too much to bear. He tried going back to the gallery to plead his innocence. "It was the rats!" he had shouted through the locked doors. "The rats took it!" But they wouldn't have anything to do with him. There was no other explanation that made sense. It wasn't a well-known fact, but rats were thieving bleeders. Even a heavy golden ring would be no problem for them to pick up and take into their nest.

Bill had thought that was the end of it, but it was just the beginning. He was arrested two weeks later on a charge of theft. Or as it was put to him, as a 'breach of a high degree of trust or responsibility'. The police had no hard evidence, it was all circumstantial, until they searched his house and unfortunately found his stash of cash that they took away as evidence. It was all they needed for *Probable Cause*. It made dreadful sense, no matter how wrong they were.

The case was circumstantial, which meant Bill's guilt could only be decided by a jury, and as such, he was put to trial. His defence that the rats had stolen the ring was almost laughed out of court. But Bill *knew* that's what had happened. He was sure of it. Things were touch and go until it came to the damning testimony from both Cornelius and Darius, who were seen as 'upstanding members of the community' just because they were posh and rich. Their statement was read out in court, outlining the events leading up to the theft that they believed had been opportunistic—Bill knew the layout of the building and had probably snuck inside during a delivery. It was the final and very real nail in a circumstantial coffin.

The jury had been convinced by it, especially when they were instructed to take into account the attack of a member of Bill's family upon the victims, the loss of Bill's job offer, and the resulting bad blood that arose from the incident. On top of this was the only real evidence—the money they found hidden in Bill's room. It was enough to convict him with no option for appeal. He was sent to prison for two and a half years.

In the end, Bill served ten months, earning an early parole for good behaviour. But those ten months changed him. Made him harder. Made him obsessed with proving everybody wrong. He wasn't sure who these people were, but they certainly involved the loudly accusing voices in his own head, voices that had stayed with him all his life. And there was one more thing… Bill left prison with a deep-seated, visceral hatred for rats.

Once out, he cobbled enough cash together to buy a cheap van and went back into the pest extermination business with a vengeance. And much to everyone's surprise, including Bill himself, it turned out that Bill had a real talent when it came to killing animals and making shedloads of money from it. Putting his dad out of work in months (his old man drank himself to death a few years ago and good riddance). In the next quarter of a century, Bill created a highly successful franchise that had made him a very wealthy man. He was proud of his achievements, but the stigma of the accusation and prison sentence had stayed with him. It was a personal pain that stabbed into him every time he thought about it, or whenever he was in the vicinity of the gallery. He came to feel a resentment for the building. Like it was somehow responsible for what had happened to him. He didn't care about Cornelius or Darius or any of the other details. No, his gripe was with the Outtasight! gallery itself and… *rats*. Always bleedin' rats.

Now he was working there again, he was hoping to redeem himself and, more importantly, hoping to redeem a significant profit. He'd suffered a lifetime of personal shame for something he hadn't done. To his mind, that gave him a helluva lot of credit. His plan was a simple one. He'd get his recompense—one way or another.

POSSIBLY POSSIBLE POSSIBILITIES

"I'M OFF OUT for a bit," Riven said to Jen after going back up to the ground floor gallery. He handed her the keys. "Everything is locked up downstairs, but don't worry, that's not a euphemism."

Jen smiled unencouragingly. "Monty and Harve left a few minutes ago. Said they would be back later on this afternoon. My guess is they're off out on a bender." She seemed almost relieved.

"He did seem a little stressed out."

"If that's what you'd like to call it… Where shall I tell Monty you've gone?"

Riven shrugged. "Tell him I'm following up on a hot clue."

"A clue? Sounds like you know what you're doing."

"Don't worry, it won't last. I'm actually off to find a decent mug of tea."

"You really are just doing nothing?" Jen asked, a confused look on her face. "Landa got you down here to do bugger all and somehow that's going to help us find the Mondrian?"

"Bugger all is about the size of it."

"But that makes no sense."

"You've met Landa?"

"Well, yeah."

"Doesn't that help explain things?"

"But the Mondrian is a multi-multi-*multi*-million-pound artwork. Why trust finding it to... well, sorry to be rude, to an irritating jerk like you?"

"My thoughts exactly."

"That's one helluva a lot of trust. Do you think you've any chance of finding it?"

"What I think or do not think does not make one blind bit of difference. I'm hoping to find it, but the only thing I've stumbled upon today is this." He took out the VIP pass belonging to Dan Kowalski and showed it to Jen.

"Where did you find that?"

"Tripped over it on the floor by the outer doors."

Jen flushed, although otherwise she seemed calm and in control. "What was he doing there?"

Riven shrugged. "Stealing a Mondrian perhaps?"

"He wouldn't need to. The last Kowalski painting sold for nearly ten thousand."

Riven attempted a whistle but it came out more like a raspberry. "Still, from what you've told me, wouldn't anyone who's anyone in the art world want a Mondrian on their wall?"

Jen nodded. "I see what you mean." She took a deep breath. "I've found something out. Something I think is important."

"You've discovered a deep and enduring love for me, perhaps?" Riven ventured hopefully.

"No. And from this point on I want you to properly understand that I have zero interest in you romantically. Yeah?"

"So you've thought about me in that way? That's a good start."

Jen shook her head emphatically but Riven was sure he could glean the tiniest amount of uncertainty.

"That Harve. He's not who he seems."

"Isn't he?"

"He has a girlfriend on the side, and that accent is put on. I overheard their conversation earlier. Sheila, Harve's girlfriend, was pushing him to get money out of Monty. And quite jealous.

Harve even had the audacity to call me a skinny cow!"

"Well, he's wrong there," Riven said. "You are, if anything, a finely proportioned and exquisitely dressed cow."

Jen's eyes narrowed at him in a way that told him she was singularly unimpressed with his last sentence, even if it did contain a compliment or two. "I thought Harve was gay, through and through."

"You think he's bi-sexual?"

"Must be."

Riven suspected there were more bipeople out there than let on. And yet, in this modern world of multi-partner-preference, Riven's sexuality was depressingly mundane. It was bad enough he was born Caucasian and middle-class, but nature had dictated there was to be nothing remarkable about Jim Riven, apart from his ability with serendipitous happenchance. He hated all that coincidence nonsense, but now, at barely past noon on a horribly bright, sunny, spring Saturday afternoon, he'd be very happy for the bloody buggering Mondrian to fall out of the bloody buggering sky and land on his bloody buggering head. He poked his head out of the door and looked up hopefully.

"What are you doing?" Jen asked.

"Sticking my head out of the door and looking hopefully at the bloody buggering sky."

"And that's helping how?"

Riven pulled his head back inside and sighed. "It was worth a try."

"What was?"

"Nothing."

"What are you going to do about Harve?"

"Huh?"

"I just gave you some useful information. Aren't you at least going to look into it?"

"Do you want me to?"

Jen gave him an exasperated look. "Don't you get it? If

Harve is not who he says he is, everything about him could be a lie. Maybe Harve drugged Monty or waited till he was asleep and returned here with the keys? He could've unlocked the doors, while his accomplice girlfriend waited for him outside. Harve could've given her the Mondrian, locked up, and returned to Monty."

"Is that what you think happened?"

"It's a possibility."

Riven attempted a sage nod. "The thing about possibilities is that they're all possibly possible."

"Um... what?"

"I mean, if you're inventive enough, you can make any theory fit."

"That kind of thinking will get you nowhere."

"But, just off the top of my head, this girlfriend of Harve... what was her name again?"

"Sheila."

"You say this Sheila wanted Harve to get money out of Monty?"

"Yeah. What of it?"

The gears in Riven's mind cranked awkwardly. "But if they'd just stolen a Mondrian, that's the last thing she'd be asking for."

"Unless Harve wanted me to overhear his conversation."

"You see, there are those possibilities again."

"We at least know one thing."

"And what's that?"

"You're impossible."

"Not impossible, just highly unlikely." This was all getting dreadfully complicated and Riven was gagging for a tea. "If you're suspicious of Harve," he began, "maybe when I'm out, perhaps you could, I dunno, possibly investigate him?"

"Isn't that your job?"

"Have you been listening to this conversation?"

Jen frowned in a most agreeable way. "Perhaps I should just

tell Monty. Let him deal with it."

Riven shrugged and opened the gallery front door. "If you want."

"Are you coming back?"

"Do you want me to come back?"

"Before today I never wanted to see you again. Unless it was in the news after being run over in a fatal hit and run."

"And now?"

"I would hope you survived but remained severely injured and in a coma."

"I see. Well at least that's a move in the right direction. Let's hope I don't get run over until I get my mug of tea. As to my return, don't hold your breath."

The doors burst open and in walked Bill lugging a large bag, closely followed by a sheepish looking Joey. "Right," Bill said, "if we're gonna make a dent in your rat problem, we're gonna have to get a shake on. I've been thinkin' about this all night and I'm sure I know where their nest is."

Jen ignored him and turned to Joey. "Who is this?"

"That's my sister's boy, helpin' me out. I told you yesterday that I'd be bringin' an assistant."

"Can you stop him staring at me like that?" Joey's eyes suddenly downturned, like he'd been caught out. "Dirty-minded little oik."

"Hey darlin', that ain't no way to talk to an employee."

"You what?"

"I was jus' sayin' that you shouldn't talk to the boy like that. I know he's a bit wayward but—"

"I'm not your darling, okay?"

"There's no need to get on your high horse. Look, we're sorry, okay. But we've got to get on."

Jen stepped in front of him. "No, actually. I've had enough of your mouth and your sneaky looks. Please leave."

"But we're half-way through the job, and I don't think you know what you're dealin' with, luv. I reckon the under gallery is rat city central for your whole problem."

She pointed to the door. "Go."

"But I can't! Not now! Didn't you hear me? I'm a gnat's wing away from finding the nest. That's why Joey is with me." He tapped his bulky and impressive tool bag. "I've brought in specialist equipment that he's gonna help me with. And besides, if we stop now, they'll come back in more numbers. You don't know what you're dealin' with. Rats are sneaky little bleeders."

"I've told you to go."

"What will Mr Fitzhugh say about this? It's 'im I'm working for. Not you."

"Then I suggest you contact him directly." Jen scribbled a number onto a gallery card and offered it to Bill.

Bill looked at Jen, at the card, and longingly into the gallery, his urgency deflating in the face of Jen's defiance. "Alright then. I'll phone him and come right back. Those rats won't exterminate themselves. C'mon Joey!" He barged past Riven and back out into the street, slamming the door so forcefully behind him that Riven was surprised the glass didn't shatter.

"I'm sorry about that," she said. "It's just that men like him… you understand?"

"You sure you don't want to share a mug of tea with me? Take your mind off all this?"

She smiled. "Thanks, but with Monty and Harve gone, I'll need to hold the fort."

"Perhaps another time then?"

"No."

Sighing, Riven closed the door behind him and walked out into the burgeoning afternoon.

YES AND NO

RIVEN'S PHONE MAP told him he was close to a shopping centre called Spitalfields Market. And, inspired, he strode down the street with a purpose that was at odds with his general sense of *what on earth is going on*, his eyes roving here and there, searching for a suitable café.

Suitable cafés were rare things these days. Coffee houses, on the other hand, were twenty-a-penny. Horrible, noisy, rattling places full of happening people on the go, or so they told themselves, overseen by self-important, bouffanted baristas obsessed with reading out vast lists of over-priced caffeine and expensive accoutrements, offering more choice and options than was healthy for a relaxed and ordered mind. Instead, Riven preferred the sanctuary of a traditional café. Sure, it was likely to be full of lower-class people with their lower-class opinions and lower-class dietary requirements—as many variants on bacon, egg, sausages, and beans as was possible—but at least they got the tea right. In a mug. Milky. And no fuss. And what was wrong with a traditional *All Day Full English Breakfast* anyway? Nothing. Nothing at all. His mouth watered at the prospect.

He was hoping Spitalfields Market would be crammed with such places but, as ever, hope was all he had. There was *Speedy Coffee*, *Espresso Mania*, *Artisan Coffee*, *The Just Coffee Company*,

Coffee! Coffee! Coffee!, *Coffee On The Go*, *Only Coffee*, etcetera, etcetera, etcetera, but no *Bert's Greasy Spoon* or similar. He was about to give up when he noticed a sign shaped like a teapot above a place called, *Misty's Tearoom*. A tearoom! Result! He walked towards the small shop front and was confronted with another sign that read, *Cash only*.

Bugger! Riven needed to get to a hole in the wall if he was going to be able to pay back the £85 he borrowed from that wallet and get a mug of tea. He spotted a group of people happily blocking the opposite pavement in front of a cash machine, and joined the queue, trying to be as patient as possible. Riven didn't particularly get on with queues. He always felt trapped by them. Atrocious things. Full of people who often wanted to engage him with the dreaded small talk. Queues were also the targets of beggars and loons of all kinds. Especially in London. He knew these people had been failed dreadfully by the state, and needed support and understanding, but it didn't mean he wanted to talk to them, especially when he was stuck in a queue and couldn't get away. It wasn't the best of attitudes, he realised, but unfortunates were usually smelly and could get aggressive. Then again, wasn't that the perception that everyone had? It was hardly compassionate. His mind drifted back to the note he'd found in Skanky Mike's now collapsed shack, written by, what was his name? "Sam Smythe?" he said out loud.

"Yes?" replied the woman standing in front of him in the queue. She turned to face him. A well-dressed petite woman of mixed Asian descent dressed in a beige trouser suit with an open-necked yellow shirt revealing more skin than was strictly necessary. An impressive tattoo of a snarling tiger squatted below her collar bones. Only its head was visible, the rest was hidden underneath her shirt. Riven guessed it must cover both breasts. "Um... what?" he mumbled, taken aback by her imposing smile and her even more imposing big cat.

The woman pushed back her long, voluminous, wavy brown hair. "You said my name, which means you know who I am, but I unfortunately have no idea who you are." Her voice was engaging, the words perfectly formed, like she was used to public speaking.

"You're Sam Smythe?" Riven asked, infused with the same uncomfortable feeling he always got when things like this happened.

She raised her professionally plucked eyebrows and curtsied. "That's still me, yes. Now, why are you blurting out my name in the middle of the street? Did you recognise me from behind?" She flashed him a cheeky grin.

"How could I …um …possibly recognise you," he stumbled. "I don't know who you are."

"You're not one of those awful stalkers, are you?"

"Yes and no."

"Yes, *and* no?"

Riven sighed. Trying to explain how things worked around him always gave him a headache. "I'm not intentionally stalking you, but it appears you may be caught up in a series of events."

"Sounds interesting… I think. Explain."

"Coincidences. Happenchance. That sort of thing."

"No, still no clearer. Do I need to call for your carer or something?"

"Let me start again," Riven said exasperated. "You left a note for the tramp living outside the Outtasight! gallery a couple of days ago, right? I found it this morning and was just thinking about it. I'm not following you, stalking you or anything else. But, of course, here you are."

"Here I am." Sam Smythe took a step closer to him, her impressive tattoo only inches away. "And you're saying this is a coincidence, yes?"

He nodded. "Part of what I'm going to call a string of serendipitous happenchances."

"Isn't all happenchance unlikely?"

"I suppose so, but I like the turn of phrase. I'm Jim Riven." He stepped backwards and stuck out his hand in the traditional manner.

Sam Smythe looked at the hand and then looked back at him. "You don't happen to work for that stuck-up gallery owner, Monty Fitzhugh, do you, Jim Riven?"

"…Yes and no."

"Again with the yes and no. Which is it?"

"Is the answer to this question important to you?"

Sam Smythe pursed her lips before answering, red lipstick bunching up into little ridges. "That note you found was for a local homeless celebrity, Skanky Mike, who Monty Fitzhugh is trying to evict from behind his premises. I spearheaded the campaign to keep him there. I'm a journalist working for the local rag."

"Ah yes, things are starting to make sense."

"I heard something spooked him a couple of nights ago and he's not been seen since. Do you know anything about that?"

"About what spooked that tramp?" Riven remembered Bill bragging that he'd somehow got rid of him. "I do actually, but it's nothing to do with me. To be honest, I don't like Monty. Or his gallery. Or being up this early."

"But you're involved with him?"

"Yes, but I certainly don't want to be."

Sam Smythe took a deep breath, straightened her jacket and nodded as if she'd come to a decision. "I find you very interesting, Jim Riven." She grabbed his hand and shook. "Do you like tea?"

CLOSED

"OH HI, MR Fitzhugh," Jen said, using the gallery landline to phone her boss. She had no idea where Monty and Harve had disappeared to, but she suspected that he would answer a call from the gallery seeing that she could have news about the Mondrian. And she needed to know where he was, just in case.

"Oh, it's you. I thought it was Landa. Now she's speaking to me again, she won't stop phoning. I can't keep putting her off. Did that awful Riven fellow find anything?" Monty asked boozily.

From what Jen could tell from the background sounds, Monty was in a bar of some kind. "What do you think? Jim Riven is more interested in getting a cup of tea than finding the painting."

"Figures."

"Where are you?"

"Out. For the foreseeable future, and drowning my sorrows innit?"

"You're not coming back today?"

"I don't want to set eyes on the place again. Not until Landa makes it official and gets the police involved. Or until that painting shows up, which I effin' doubt it ever will. Now what is this about? Has something else gone missing?"

"It's nothing to do with the gallery, Mr Fitzhugh. More of a personal matter. I've found out something. About Harve. And I thought you ought to know about it."

A long pause and the sound of a hand muffling the phone's speaker. *"Spill it."*

"I overheard Harve talking to…"

"Go on."

"Talking to his girlfriend. They're try and scam you."

Another long pause. *"I see."*

"I always guessed that accent of his was put on. Harve doesn't sound like any East Ender I'd recognise. I'm sorry, Mr Fitzhugh."

Another pause. This time, excruciatingly long.

"Are you still there?"

"Yes, yes. Thanks for your information. When did you find this out?"

"When? Today. You were upstairs in your office, Talking to Miss Osbourne, I think. Is when important?"

"I suppose not, innit?"

"I'll keep in touch with you about the, um, investigation. If anything comes up, you will be the first to know. In the meantime I'm going to be busy with the exhibition."

"The what, tho?"

"Dan Kowalski. His paintings have just arrived. I'll be hanging them this afternoon. The gallery will be locked until I'm done. I hope you don't mind?"

"If we don't find that missing Mondrian, there won't be an effin' exhibition, do you know that? But carry on, innit. What else is there to effin' do?"

"I'm really sorry Mr Fitzhugh. Honestly."

Monty offed the call.

That was less enjoyable than Jen had expected. Monty sounded genuinely sad at the news. Oh well, she had work to do. A lot of work if she was going to get Dan Kowalski's paintings hung in the way she had planned. At least the gallery would be empty which meant she wouldn't be disturbed. And after that bombshell, she doubted Monty would be back at all. She went over to the front door, twisted the CLOSED sign, smiled, and engaged the lock.

SERENDIPITOUS HAPPENCHANCE

MISTY'S TEAROOM WAS neatly sandwiched between an artisan gift shop that 'turned its back on mass-production in favour of the simple handmade and unique' which meant, as far as Riven could tell, that they could sell any amount of badly-made rubbish at extortionate prices, and an artisan beard emporium whose 'dedicated cutting specialists with no less than ten years of barbering experience were dedicated to serving the local area, enriching the community and creating life-long relationships with their clientele.' Their clientele in this instance appeared to be full-bearded men who were charged excessive amounts of money for what at best could only be a trim, by equally expansively bearded barbers.

Misty's Tearooms was a revelation, with not an artisan in sight. A glorious throwback to a forgotten age. The door opened with a tinkle of a small bell and not the squawk of some horrid electronic attention seeking device. Indeed, as the door closed behind him, he felt himself transported to a different world. A world that was quieter, more serene, and distinctly somewhere else. Judging by the décor, that somewhere else was probably in the early nineteen-thirties in the vicinity of Oxford. Small, elegant tables were dotted here and there. Old ladies, couples, and effete older gentlemen sat on elegant chairs in a calming quiet, the only sound the gentle patter of muted conversation and the occasional chink of cup on saucer. Riven had expected some resistance when he asked if they had mugs but was met with a smile and a selection of more-than-suitable tea-holding vessels. He chose a mug with a picture of a floppy-eared dog, while Sam Smythe went for something more feline orientated.

After they had poured, sipped and then sipped some more, they began to chat. Riven expected Sam Smythe to bombard him with a string of questions, but she kept the conversation to small talk, turning out to be somewhat of an inexpert flirt.

"I'm sure an attractive guy like yourself must've caught Monty's roving eye," she said, big eyes flashing seductively over the top of her mug, "although my guess is that you don't bend that way, correct?"

"Nope, I'm strictly butter-side up."

She took a gentle sip at her tea. "I bet the ladies are pleased to hear that."

"Yes, they are," he answered mechanically. "Once the news got out that I wasn't that way inclined, I had to hire a group of bouncers to drag them off me and a collection service for all the knickers they insisted on flinging in my general direction."

"Hahahaha! You're one funny guy, Jim Riven."

Her laugh was as false as her flirting. At least the tea was authentic. Riven didn't mind flirting per se, it cheered him up and occasionally led to something more fun, but Sam Smythe used it as a rather blunt weapon. And, as ridiculous as that was, Riven felt less than flattered. Did he expect every girl to swoon at his feet like he was some Lothario love god? Certainly not, but for her to use this technique on him felt slightly insulting, if not downright rude. "You know, you don't have to do… all this," Riven said, waving a hand in her general direction.

"All this what?"

"Pretending to like me. The obvious flirting. I get it. You're a journalist and trying to get me on side." He picked up his mug and sipped from it.

"Or maybe, my inexpert flirting is put on to make you think I'm not as sharp as I actually am? Lulling you into a false sense of security."

"Then why tell me that?"

"To perhaps lull you even further by taking you into my confidence as an equal."

"Um…" Riven said, feeling more than a little bit discombobulated.

The warm smile left Sam Smythe's face. "You think I believed that cock-and-bull story you gave me about Skanky Mike? You obviously wanted to talk to me, and that clumsy incident was the best you could come up with."

This 'new' Sam Smythe was more aggressive than he was expecting and more than suited the 'hard-nosed' journalist stereotype. Riven guessed this side of her was also fake and that getting to know the real Sam Smythe would be something of an achievement. Not that he was inclined to want to. "It's true about the note," he began, "what I told you. It *was* a coincidence."

Her lips pursed again. "I'm not believing that for one moment. No. You're involved with that Monty Fitzhugh, which you've already admitted. So I thought, let's soften the guy up, buy him some tea and pump him for information." She put down her mug, crossed her arms and leaned on the table, her head jutting towards him with an expectant look on her face.

A bit more of her tiger tattoo was revealed. It was kind of sexy, not that tattoos had ever done anything for Riven before. If it covered her chest and stomach, as it seemed, then it was quite some commitment to body art, and he mused, a little extreme. Nevertheless, the message was clear—she was a predator.

"So, what have you got to say to me? Out with it."

Sam Smythe knew he was hiding something from her, but

there was no way he could tell a journalist about the missing Mondrian, especially as one as wily as Sam Smythe. The faeces would properly hit the fan if he let that particular cat out of the bag. And then, inevitably, even more irritating clichés and adages were bound to follow. I shouldn't have come here with her, but the lure of tea was too strong to resist, he thought to himself glumly. In the meantime, Sam Smythe's expectant look didn't waver. If anything, it became more intense as the moments passed and Riven felt the need to say something. Anything. "What's your interest in Skanky Mike?"

"That's not exactly what I wanted to hear, but okay, I'll play," Sam Smythe said sitting back, flicking off her high-heeled slingbacks, and pulling one foot up onto her chair. She looked all coy innocence but Riven was reminded of the predator again. Coiled and ready to pounce.

"He's in the local hospital. Found out where he was yesterday," she continued. "They're assessing him before sending him off to the loony bin. Poor sod. But he'll be better off in there than on the street. I tried to see him for a face-to-face, but they don't like journos. Privacy and all that nonsense. But one of the nurses was more than happy to chat to me on the quiet for a square meal and a gin and tonic or two in the half hour they had off between shifts. Apparently, Mikey keeps hearing screaming. Someone who died a long time ago they reckon. Which is very interesting."

"It is? Why?"

"Because after Mikey disappeared, I knocked from door to door to see if anybody knew anything. Some of the locals also heard what sounded like screaming coming from the gallery."

"Screaming?"

"I know. Who knows what they were doing in there? Which is where I'm hoping you can help me."

"I'm not sure I can."

"We'll see about that." She leaned forward again and took another sip of her tea, her eyes narrowing. "What do you know about the Mondrian?"

Riven was taken aback. "You've heard of it?"

"You think I didn't go to Monty's big opening?"

Riven breathed a quiet sigh of relief. Sam Smythe had no idea the painting had been stolen. "But wasn't it VIP pass only?"

"Sure it was, but I'm an investigative journalist. Getting into the opening night was easy. The jumped-up gallery manager almost wet herself when I told her I was some big noise in the art world. I also had one of those artists fawning over me. You know the type? All big hair, big words, and a tiny… *personality*. Personally, I don't get modern art. All that fuss over that—I don't know what it was—but a kid could've painted it. Still, the insurance alone on having that thing hung there must've been through the roof."

"Insurance?"

"Yeah. There's no way that Mondrian was uninsured. The risk of it being stolen or damaged would be just too high. Not that insurance fraud isn't prevalent in the art world. Just another scam amongst many, like money laundering, underhand payments for authentication, and a host of other illegal activities that I'm going to expose when the time comes."

Riven was getting the sense that Sam Smythe was one dangerous biscuit.

"I'm sure there's more going on at the Outtasight! gallery than simple intimidation of down-and-outs," she continued, a manic look in her otherwise beguiling eyes. "That Monty Fitzhugh for instance. He was a big noise in Bitcoin. But my investigations reveal he's been cleaned out by a rogue investments and brokerage company. He's on his last legs financially. And yet he has enough money to not just buy a multi-million-pound East End property, but to totally renovate the place. Do you know anything about that?"

"Isn't this too big a story for a local paper?"

"You think I want to work on missing cat stories forever?"

"I suppose not."

"Certainly not. Sam Smythe is going places. But you're right. The local papers are no place for this story. You know why?" Sam sat back in her chair. "All the local rags are now run and owned centrally by that awful media baron blowhard, Roo Osbourne."

Riven choked on his tea. "He owns the local papers… your paper?"

Sam Smythe nodded. "Nearly all of them. You ever noticed how come election day the papers all have the same message plastered across their pages? You know the kind of thing? Getting the snails to vote for salt again. Well the same message is in all the local papers up and down the country. Usually word for word. And that's down to Roo Osbourne. You'd think the voters in this country would learn their lesson, but you know people?"

Riven shrugged.

"Thick as two short planks. In the meantime, from day to day, it makes it very hard to get any negative stories about rich folk in the press. Especially the dubious friend of that brat of a daughter of his."

Riven's mind made the obvious connection. "So why bother investigating Monty if your story won't get published?"

"Let's just say I'm building up a portfolio on Osbourne and everyone associated with him. One day, the other gits will turn on him, and when they do, I'll have something to sell. It'll get me where I want to go. The national papers and maybe even the telly."

"That's very ambitious."

"I'm an ambitious woman." Her hand subconsciously stroked the head of her tiger tattoo, long-nailed fingers gently circling like a feline claw. "Something is going on with that gallery. Roo and his daughter are close, but he certainly won't be leaving his media empire to her, that's for sure. She's a loose cannon. So why was Roo Osbourne's Mondrian at Monty

Fitzhugh's gallery?"

"You know Roo Osbourne owns the Mondrian then?"

She nodded impatiently. "I told you, I'm an investigative journalist. That's how we work. Start with a small story about rich kids trying to evict a tramp and turn it into a national story of fraud and money-laundering." She took another sip of tea. "Now what have you got to tell me about Monty? Do you know how he was financing his more than little enterprise or not?"

Would it hurt to tell Sam Smythe about Landa, seeing that he was sure it'd never get published? He made the wise decision. "Yeah, I'm going to have to plead client confidentiality and all that. Not that I want to, but you've sort of put me on the spot."

"Client confidentially?" Her fingers stopped their circling and pointed at him threateningly. "So you're playing it like that are you, James Aurelius Riven?" She spoke the words loudly, and heads in the little tearoom turned in their direction.

Riven was taken aback. "How do you know my full name?"

"Duh," she said pointing at herself. "I did a quick search on you when I popped to the toilet. Not that I found out much. You're the son of a London professor of antiquities who's as much a mystery as you are."

"So I'm a mystery. Cool, I think."

"Just tell me what you're doing for Monty, and I'll make sure you remain anonymous, which evidenced by your lack of any social media profile, you seem pretty good at doing already."

"All I can really tell you is that I went to the gallery as sort of a favour."

"Go on…"

"It's to do with that serendipitous happenchance thing I mentioned earlier."

"You're still sticking to that story, huh?"

"It's the only one I've got."

"And you want me to believe that?"

Riven was beginning to get annoyed. "You can believe it or not believe it. It makes no difference to me."

"There's no need to get snotty."

"Sorry. It's been a long day and I've not had my normal ten hours sleep."

"Sure. I understand. I also like to have my regular snoozes. I can get catty without them." She fixed him with her big eyes again. "How do you feel about a little test?"

"A what?"

"A test of trust that I find very useful in situations like this one."

"Go on."

"I want you to empty your pockets and put the contents on the table."

"Huh?"

"It's a simple enough request. If you are who you say you are, a victim of coincidence and nothing else, then you will have nothing to worry about. But if you are hiding something or possess something that points to you not being who you say you are, you won't want me to see it."

"That's not great logic, is it? What if I have something embarrassing on my person? I certainly wouldn't want to take that out in front of anybody, never mind in front of a well-to-do tearoom."

"Are you carrying something embarrassing on your person?"

"Well no, but that's not the point."

"Then you won't mind emptying your pockets."

"Will you be doing the same?"

She shook her head. "I'm not the possible creep in this equation."

Riven sighed. When it came down to it, there was no reason for him to do anything. He didn't need any more from her—she'd already bought him the tea she'd promised but the fact she thought he was working for Monty irked him. Of course, he was sort of working for him, and secondhandedly for Roo Osbourne—finding his missing Mondrian for his nutjob daughter—but it was very much against his better judgment. "Okay," he groaned inwardly at the content of his next sentence. "I'll show you mine if you show me yours."

"Ooh, I've not played this game for a long time. But go on then. And to show willing, I'll go first." She opened her purse and inelegantly emptied its contents onto the table. There was a bank card, tissues, lipstick, Lillete's, a condom, some loose change, money in a clip, a biro and notebook, and a old, battered looking and very familiar hand-painted flash-drive.

THE VERY LARGE LIZARD

"EFF OFF HARVE!"

"But why? Wot've I done?"

"And you can lose that ridiculous accent, innit? I always knew it was fake."

"That's just not true, Monty," Harve replied, his East End accent even thicker than before.

"Just effin' stop it, okay! Just stop it!"

Harve sighed. "Alright," Harve said, his accent now gone. "But I only did it to please you."

"Yeah, well that doesn't matter anymore. I want you to eff off and I want you to eff off now!"

The other punters in the small and cosy *The Very Large Lizard* bar watched with a mixture of amusement and naked self-interest. Harve was quite a catch, and many had been envious of Monty's beau when they had loudly entered the bar a short while ago.

The Very Large Lizard had been gay since the early 70s, as evidenced by a photo-wall of gay activism featuring marches, Stonewall, rainbow flags and Pride. As well as its fair share of sequins, glitter and feathers. Back in the day, it had been seen as a den of iniquity and drug-taking, and had been raided by the police many times, but by today's standards, the bar had been nothing more than a very tame meeting and drinking place for like-minded individuals. The place had a slightly run down and a vaguely sad air, like a deflated, tinsel covered party balloon.

"I've been suckered once by an S.O.B," Monty spat. "I won't be suckered a second time, especially by a two-bit conman like you."

"But Mont', let me explain."

"Explain what? About why you've got a girlfriend?"

This raised a few intakes of breath and a chorus of oohs from the audience of punters.

"I was going to tell you, Mont'. I promise. It was all her idea. I didn't want to go through with it. I hated every moment of it."

"I bet you did!"

"You know what I mean. And look, I'm still here with you, even though I know you've lost everything. Why else would I stay if I didn't have feelings for you? If I was really such a bad-hat, why would I do that? Why would I stay with a loser?"

"A what? Innit? You're calling me a an effin' loser? How dare you, Harve! How dare you! Just eff off. Eff off out of my effin' sight!"

"But Mont'!"

Monty grabbed his gin and tonic that he'd hardly taken a sip of since they arrived and threw it in Harve's face, causing a chorus of gasps from the audience at the bar.

Harve wiped his face, grabbed his coat, and left.

"What are you all looking at? You never seen a loser before!" Monty said.

The audience at the bar hastily turned back to their drinks.

PROFESSIONAL HABIT

RIVEN POINTED TO the flash-drive. "What's that?" he asked as nonchalantly as he could muster, although his heart was running the 100 Meters Hurdles Olympic final.

"This thing? I should've thrown it away. Skanky Mike found it. Said it fell out of the turn-up of some jeans a well-wisher had given him. I think it must've been in the wash or something… there's nothing on it. I checked. The thing is corrupted, unreadable. He still charged me twenty quid to get it off him though, the tight git. I thought it might've had some connection to the gallery but no."

Riven couldn't quite believe it. The flash-drive was Jen's. Sam Smythe obviously hadn't noticed, but the flash-drive had been hand-painted in blocks of red, yellow, and black, in a trellis of horizontal and vertical black lines in the style of Piet Mondrian, although most of it had been chipped or worn away. He'd been wearing his favourite turn-up jeans when the flash-drive went missing in the local printers all those years ago. It must've fallen into them. And was there all this time until he sent them to the charity shop with his other old clothes. Somehow, the bag and the flash-drive ended up with Skanky Mike. Riven felt a sudden hotness under his collar. He liked to joke about the coincidences that sometimes ruled his life, but to be honest, they scared him silly.

"You okay?"

"Yeah, sure," he replied, trying to compose himself.

"Good, because it's now your turn."

"My turn for what?"

"Hey, I showed you mine, it's time to show me what you've got."

"Oh right. Yeah, sure." Riven stood up onto shaky feet and pulled a used hankie from his jeans pocket. There was also his credit card, his phone, and the VIP pass for Dan Kowalski he'd found in the gallery in his jacket pocket.

Sam Smythe picked up the pass and grimaced at the photo. "This is that idiot who tried to chat me up last night. Kept banging on about chiaroscuro like it was a magic word that would get my knickers off. My guess is that his big words were making up for something less than average. She pointed to Riven's back pocket. What's that? You're not supposed to keep anything back, them's the rules."

"Oh yeah, I forgot," he said, producing the wallet he'd picked up in the back of the taxi.

Sam Smythe stared at the wallet open-mouthed. "Where on earth did you get that?"

The hotness under Riven's collar burned with extra heat and he felt dizzy. "This isn't your wallet?" Riven asked. "Is it?"

"No."

"…Oh."

"But I know who it belongs to."

"…Ah."

"Where did you get it?"

Riven took a long, steadying breath. "Well, that's a bit of a long story, actually. Another one of those serendipitous happenchances I mentioned. Let me try and explain. I took a taxi to the Outtasight! this morning. But the only problem? I had no money when I arrived, and the taxi driver was demanding cash. Eighty-five quid to be exact." He pointed to the wallet. "And then I saw the corner of this weird alligator-skin wallet sticking out from under the seat I was lying on. I picked it up, opened it, and inside I found exactly eighty-five pounds." He took a deep breath. "Coincidence, you see?"

"But this belongs to my Great Uncle Sebastian… I'd know it anywhere. That clasp has his initial on it, although it's nearly been rubbed off."

Riven studied the clasp and could make out a single initial 'G'.

"That single letter is his signature. Unmistakable."

"G?"

"For Grosvenor."

Riven took a steadying breath. "I think I passed your test and then some, yeah?"

Sam Smythe wasn't listening. She picked up the wallet, flicked the catch and opened it gingerly.

"I'd very much like to meet him, this Sebastian," Riven said, realising that the only way out of this mess was to go with the flow. To let whatever was happening to run its course. And as much as he wasn't keen on the coincidences that occasionally messed with his life, Riven was doubly relieved. He'd managed to convince Sam Smythe of his integrity and perhaps, just perhaps, here was a link that might lead to the missing Mondrian. The hot feeling disappeared, leaving him feeling a little lightheaded and silly.

"I'd seriously advise against that," Sam Smythe said with more than a hint of anger.

"You sound like you don't like him very much."

"And him me. Despises me to be honest. We don't talk anymore."

"Why not?"

She shrugged, her eyes unfocused, the hard-nosed reporter suddenly gone. "That's for me to know."

"Well look. Here's the problem. I sort of borrowed his money. I should've told the driver, but, I dunno, sometimes I think there's other forces at work. He paused, adding in a jokey voice, "Forces about which we know nothing."

Sam Smythe didn't smile. Instead, a frown creased her face.

"I would really appreciate you giving me his number," Riven continued. "I'm not happy being in debt to him. It wasn't exactly stealing. Of course, when I return the wallet, I'll return it with the money replaced." And maybe find the Mondrian hung on his wall, he thought to himself.

"You're saying that you found this by accident?"

He nodded.

"In the back of a taxi?"

"Yeah."

"Because of your serendipitous happenchance thing?"

"Yeah."

"And now I'm supposed to believe that this is another coincidence?"

Riven nodded again, this time vigorously.

"But that's mental."

"I'm not sure that's the PC way of putting it, but yes, it is. And it was your suggestion for me to empty my pockets, remember?"

Sam Smythe was obviously finding this a struggle.

"It's a mind-bender, I know, but it is what it is."

"You're not trying to mess with my mind?"

"No."

"And you're not going to tell me your connection to the gallery and Monty Fitzhugh?"

"I can't really. I wish I could, but it's a long story. A story that I don't want to get into."

"That's very convenient."

"Not as convenient as you might think. But right now, I'm interested in this wallet and its owner. It might have more significance than I realised. Perhaps you could tell me more about your great uncle. What does he do?"

"You mean what did he do? He was a photographer. Very famous in the 60s. A friend of the pop and rock bands, as well as royalty. And a real player. He practically knobbed anyone and everyone that moved. He's a vile, selfish, despicable person. Now he just sits in his rambling London mansion and rots. Which is good by me."

"Do you have his number?"

"No, just his address. I'm not sure if I should give it to you."

"I thought I passed your little trust exercise?"

"I suppose you did." She shrugged and took out a phone from the breast pocket of her jacket. Riven noticed a large microphone icon. She'd been recording the entire conversation.

Sam Smythe shrugged again. "Sorry, professional habit."

"You realise everything I've told you about the coincidence thing is off-the-record, yeah?"

"You think there's a story in this nonsense you've been telling me?"

"I dunno. But my life is not my own because of it, and to make the thing public, well, things would get properly, um, mental."

"What's your phone number? I'll send you over his contact details."

Riven was unsure about giving it to her but his need to find the Mondrian was weighing heavily on his mind. Out of everything that had happened today, this felt like the most tangible lead, and so he acquiesced. A few moments later, he received a contact for Sebastian Grosvenor. "Thanks."

"Make sure you don't give him my regards," Sam Smythe said, standing up.

"You're going?"

"I'm not sure what game you're playing—or even if it is a game," she said, "but I can see this is a waste of my valuable time." She scooped her things off the table and back into her purse. "Goodbye James Aurelius Riven." She slid out of the startled little tea shop like a cat eager to evade its owner's new dog.

Riven shrugged. Sam Smythe was a bit of a loon but

dangerous all the same. Nevertheless, she had left him with at least another mug of tea in the pot, a sizable jug of milk, and a new lead—the owner of the wallet, Sebastian Grosvenor. Oh, and one more thing.

He opened his palm and stared at the flash-drive he'd purloined.

THE SCOOP

SAM SMYTHE LEFT *Misty's Tearoom* feeling perplexed. The meeting with Jim Riven hadn't been as productive as she had hoped. But whatever he wasn't telling her, she would find out soon, she was absolutely sure of it. There was a bigger story at the Outtasight! And she had the determination, skills and the balls to—

Her phone rang. A number she was unfamiliar with.

"Hello…?"

She offed the call a minute later and stared back at the teashop. The person phoning had told her exactly what she wanted to know about the Outtasight! and what was going on in there, which, she realised, was quite the coincidence. Especially after the conversation she had just had and the remarkable appearance of her vile uncle's wallet.

She shook her head. Coincidence or not, the upshot of the conversation was that Media tycoon Roo Osbourne's Mondrian had been stolen from the Outtasight! gallery after last night's show and Jim Riven was investigating its disappearance. The informant didn't want any money for this information, just anonymity. The story was the biggest scoop of her career by a distance and then some. To be the journalist who broke this story to the world would certainly put her on the map. And yet, there were more angles to work here than just publication…

TEA, CAKES & NO EARACHE!

RIVEN TURNED THE flash-drive over in his hands. Could it have any bearing on the missing Mondrian? he wondered. A ten-year-old broken flash-drive? It seemed unlikely, but he knew of someone who could help in this department—his daft mate Dillon. He was a no hoper in most aspects of his life, but at computers, he was an absolute whizz.

He picked up his phone and rang him.

"Yo!" Dillon replied in his usual cheerful manner. *"Isn't it a bit early for you to be dragging your conscious carcass about?"*

"Yeah. Landa."

"Landa? No?"

"Yeah."

"Yeah?"

"Yeah!"

"Ouch! So what do you want? I'm kinda busy."

"I've got a corrupt ten-year-old flash-drive that needs your attention."

"Oh yeah?"

"Yeah."

"What's on it? Important stuff?"

"Dunno. But it sort of came my way, yeah?"

"Came your way? Is it happenin' again? The thing?"

"Yeah."

"No!"

"Yeah. Can I drop it off?"

"Yeah, sure. I'll do my magic on it, but I can't promise anythin'. Yeah?"

"Yeah."

"See ya laters."

Riven put the phone down and only then noticed the patrons of this quiet little teashop were staring at him. An old woman in a blue pastel dress and even bluer rinsed hair pointed aggressively at a sign on the opposite wall with a blue-veined hand:

TEA, CAKES, AND NO EARACHE!

Riven raised his hands, mouthing 'sorry' before slipping the offending phone into his back pocket. He'd need to go straight to Dillon's. He hated waiting around more than anything, but there was still tea in the pot and to leave it would be some awful kind of heresy, especially in this chintz-themed shrine to the magical leaf. He poured himself a fresh mug, sat back in his chair and pondered, becoming aware of someone approaching and standing next to his table. A person in a rather snazzy waistcoat and tailored trousers.

He looked up to see an effete gentleman in his 60s staring at him from a rounded face dominated by a pair of over-plucked eyebrows.

"I wondered, dear boy, did I hear correctly just then?" he asked in voice far too posh for the East End, or for any end of London for that matter. "That your lovely young lady referred to you as James Riven?"

"Yes," Riven replied, finishing his mug of tea with a resigned sigh. It was certainly turning into one of those days. "But she's not actually my young lady. That position is free at the moment. Some might say very free."

"I'm terribly sorry to hear that. Love at any age is a

complicated beast. But when two souls, however unlikely, are meant for each other, they will one day find a way to meet. I truly believe that."

"Okay," Riven replied bemusedly, hoping that this man didn't think it was their souls that were meant for one another. "What is that you want exactly?"

"Let me please apologise for barging in on you like this, especially when you are so obviously savouring your tea but Riven is somewhat of a singular and unusual surname. And I was thinking that one of my professors has a boy called James. You wouldn't happen to be him, would you?"

"If you're talking about Professor Cornelius Gaius Riven, my father, then yes. He works for some very peculiar college in the poshest part of Piccadilly. I take it you must be something to do with that?"

"Yes, very much so. I'm Sefton Quayle, Master of College Ouroboros." He bowed. "I must say, I have been wanting to meet Professor Riven's boy for long time. A long time indeed. And here you are. Just popping up out of nowhere so to speak. And so idiosyncratically dressed."

"What is wrong with the way I'm dressed?" Riven replied indignantly. "Because I've been receiving some odd comments today." Riven's style, mostly black clothes with the occasional less-than-black tee-shirt, had never generated so much comment before. It was a simple look that managed to do two jobs at once —or so he thought. He didn't fit in with the common herd—he had his own style—but neither did he look so outlandish as to raise comment. "I like black, thank you very much. It happens to be my favourite colour."

"You do realise black is not really a colour?"

"It isn't?"

"No, although there is some debate on the matter."

"Is there?"

"Oh yes. But we do know that black results from the absence or complete absorption of visible light. Indeed, black ink and dyes are not intrinsically black but are instead made from a mixture of the darkest available pigments."

"And you know this how?"

"I've always been fascinated by black. Call it a life's obsession. But I digress. I did not wish to be insulting, so permit me to rephrase. I very much approve of your look, James Riven. It is very becoming." Quayle gave him a little bow. "Pleased to make your acquaintance."

"Well now you've met me," Riven replied wondering where the effete old duffer was going with this. "What of it?"

"Your father has been very valuable to me—to the college—over the years. And you never know, an opening might open up at any time."

Riven replayed the man's sentence again in his mind, but there could be no doubt about it. "You're offering me a job?"

"Work is an ugly word don't you think? But the answer to your question is *yes*."

"Oh, right. Thank you, I think. But I'm afraid the idea is a non-starter. I'm hardly academic. The last book I read was about speed reading… it's still overdue!"

Sefton Quayle clapped his hands together in delight. "How very droll. I can see you are quite the jester. Your father on the other hand? Not so much."

"Truth is, I'm not the college type. Nor do I have any interest in all that Mayan stuff my father is obsessed with. I'm just not designed for working. Jobs and me don't get on. Never have. But more than that, I don't excel in any area, other than annoying people, especially my father who often told me that I irritated the heck out of him."

"Please don't let an errant father put you off, dear boy. You'll find a lot of people suffer from exactly the same malady. And do not concern yourself about your lack of scholarly ways, College Ouroboros isn't exactly high on academia, which you would soon discover if you paid us a visit." He nodded his head vigorously. "Yes, yes. You must come and see us and let me and the other professors sound you out."

"There's no way my father would want me working with him," Riven replied. "And besides, I don't want to work with him either. He always treated me like I was some kind of dreadful failure. And still does."

"Well yes. Of course. To be honest the man is an awful, awful bore, but then again, he's also been awfully useful. And the college has a tradition of suffering the most eccentric of personalities in its pursuits. You'd fit right in."

"Doesn't that sound like a bit of an insult?"

"Does it? I'm afraid being the master of such an important college can also lead to its own set of eccentricities. But I must get on. I'm sorry to have intruded upon you, James. Here's my card." He passed Riven a gold embossed calling card. "Think on my offer and get back to me."

Riven flipped it over in his hand. It was heavy and expensive looking. And had an embossed image of a very stylised, Aztec feathered serpent, seemingly eating its own tail—the Ouroboros—a symbol he very much associated with his father. There was no phone, email, or website, just the address in Jermyn Street, Piccadilly. What century did this old duffer live in?

Sefton Quayle doffed his hat, smiled, and left the little teashop.

A college in the middle of Piccadilly? Riven thought. What a preposterous idea, but the place was supposedly ancient, standing there for hundreds of years. Paid for by a hoard of Mayan antiquities stolen in the early part of the last century. Or so he'd discovered. Not that he'd been remotely interested in his father's work. He picked up the wallet and his handkerchief, and headed to the door, hoping beyond hope that the growing list of today's coincidences wouldn't involve his father. That would be worse than two hundred Landas.

SUCK MY DUCK

JIM RIVEN DREADED the London Underground. He'd never had a single pleasant journey on the tube in his whole life. Did anybody? He despised the thing. Full of all those people he didn't want to meet. He remembered reading a travel quote from way back:

> *Trains are beautiful. They take people to places they've never been, faster than they could ever go themselves. Everyone who works on trains knows they have personalities, they're like people. They have their own mysteries…*

Riven supposed this was very probably true when trains were new and exciting. The steam, the travel, the romance, and the thick choking, climate-altering smoke of it. Getting away from the cities to the countryside and the resorts, would've been quite the thing. But humanity, with its over-riding desire to ruin everything remotely nice or fun, couldn't possibly allow this to continue. People enjoying carefree and fun travel? No way! Now, the only mysteries trains held involved:

Why did they break down all the time?

Why were they never on time?

Why did they cost so much?

And why was nearly everyone forced to stand for most of their journey?

However, the biggest mystery for most travellers involved the source of the persistent and bitter smell of urine that never seemed to be adequately dealt with. Hopefully not from the warm seat they finally managed to park their eager backsides onto.

Tube trains were similar to the above, but worse by a factor of *are you kidding me?*

Riven pushed his way into a packed carriage, grabbed a handhold—there were no seats at this time of the day—put his head down, and took out his phone to play *Suck My Duck*, the creation of Dillon, who was gainfully employed by a games' company as some kind of coder. The *Suck My Duck* app was a side project of his, although it had received more complaints than downloads. Nevertheless, Riven had become addicted to abducting the little yellow birds with the suction gun shaped like an erect knobbly penis. The fleeing ducks made a pleasing *Flup* sound as they were sucked down by the bell-ended nozzle into the twin testicle-like hairy sacks that swelled satisfyingly. The trick, Dillon told him, was to not suck too many ducks. "If your sacks become overfilled," he explained patiently after he'd installed the game against Riven's will, "then they're gonna explode everywhere and you'll have to start all over again." Dillon was a strange, twisted, but on the whole, reliable kind of messed up guy.

Riven lifted his head to leave the train at Wood Green and found himself staring at a young woman who was herself staring at Riven's phone. Shrugging, he extricated himself from the lunchtime crush of Tube humanity and stumbled onto the greasy station platform. Even after a short journey, Riven felt like a change of clothes was needed but that was another luxury denied him today.

Ten minutes later, he was standing outside Dillon's

tenement building. An old five-storey house converted by greedy landlords into a series of depressingly tiny flats. He rang the doorbell and was buzzed in, climbing the four or five flights of stairs to the top floor attic. The grubby door was open, and he pushed inside.

Dillon's flat consisted of a small living area, come bedroom and kitchen, and an even smaller toilet and shower room. The slanted attic roof underneath which Dillon's unmade bed had been awkwardly placed, was covered in printouts of technical drawings of various antique pistols, posters of moustachioed heroes and busty heroines from a number of 70s action TV shows and a montage of James Bonds striding across his ceiling like the Ascent of Man with shaken-not-stirred Martinis and a Beretta. On the opposite wall stood a single rack of clothes on which were hung three identical brown corduroy suits and ten identical *Suck My Duck* tee shirts, the colours going from bright yellow to a washed-out vanilla depending on the number of times they'd been in the laundry. There was also a makeshift shelf-come-workbench covered in bits of cobbled together motherboard, computer chips and wires. A small area was taken up with what only an estate agent might describe as a 'kitchen', although, they would be stretching incredulity further than was comfortable for even their profession. Here sat a small sink, a small microwave, and a rather large mess. Dillon sprawled himself on a gaming chair that, in another life, would've been found in a super-secret, high-tech jet fighter. He lazed in front of a desk containing a breath-taking array of computer equipment including various and impressive PCs and laptops, monitors, backlit, multicoloured keyboards, and flashing mice. Dillon's room, its décor, and the man himself, had an air of accomplishment and of hopelessness about it. The place smelled of week-old fast food—as evidenced by a Leaning Tower of Pizza boxes stacked against the wall—and the faint aroma of stale sweat and sadness.

As for Dillon's bathroom and toilet—a tight rectangle

containing a small toilet and a tiny shower cubicle—the less said the better. Riven had learned the hard way to give the narrow room a wide berth. He shuddered at the memory of his first and last ever visit. Riven wasn't the tidiest or cleanest of people, however, next to Dillon's place, Riven's unkempt flat was a relative crime lab clean room.

"You have it?" Dillon said, his hypnotic stare leaving a bank of impressive-looking monitors full of lines of squiggly blue and green Sanskrit, like what you see in all those heist and hacking movies. He swivelled around on his chair and sat forward, sticking out one chubby hand, his long shaggy hair tangled into his voluminous beard, his eyes magnified by his beer bottle bottom glasses. He wore his customary beige corduroy trousers—the top button undone due to a longstanding button phobia—and a tight-fitting bright yellow *Suck My Duck* tee-shirt stretched over his round belly. Riven was reliably informed that over five-hundred others were stuffed in various boxes under Dillon's bed.

Riven gave him the flash-drive.

Dillon plugged it into one of his computers and clacked away at an important and unusual looking keyboard, various windows opening on the monitor before him. "Yeah," he said, staring at the screens. "It's shagged, alright."

"Can you get anything from it?"

Dillon shrugged, finishing a Coca-Cola can, and throwing it at his overflowing bin. It bounced off the side, joining many other empty Coca-Cola cans on the floor. "Maybe. I have my ways and my means."

"Cool."

"Don't hold your breath. Sometimes, when a piece of technology is shagged, that piece of technology is properly shagged. Yeah?"

Riven sighed and sat down on the bed. "Yeah."

"Jus' the way it is."

"No worries if you can't do anything with it. But there

should be a dissertation on there."

"Yeah? A university thing?"

"Yeah."

"What's it about?"

"Modern Art, I think."

"Cool."

"You know anything about that?"

Dillon shook his shaggy head. "Nah."

"Me neither."

"If I can fix it, when do you want a copy?"

"Asap."

"Right. On it." Dillon clacked away busily.

Dillon was a great mate and an all-around good guy. But there was one aspect about him that Riven loved. It made Dillon special and put him above everyone else he knew.

Nothing weird ever happened when he was with him.

The man acted like a terrific dampening force, or at least, that's what Riven believed. In his presence, there were no coincidences, no serendipitous happenchance, and no weird nonsense—other than the weird nonsense that Dillon brought with him as standard. Whatever skill Riven possessed, Dillon was immune. It meant that he was one of the very few people—if not the only person—he could be relaxed around. Sitting here, on Dillon's unmade bed, in his tiny and untidy bijou flatlet, Riven was the most relaxed he'd been all day. He sighed heavily and stood up. "I've got to go."

"Sure thing, Riv. We out for beers later?"

"Unlikely."

"No Saturday night beers? Sounds serious." He stopped his clacking and turned to fix Riven with a hard stare. "You're not back with Landa, are you?"

"No."

"Good to hear. She's one fine looking lady though. You did well there. But…"

"Yeah."

"Yeah. So you gonna spill?"

Riven sat back on the bed and sighed. "I'm in a bit of a state to be honest and it's all about a missing painting." He retold the day's events so far, Landa turning up, the missing Mondrian, the threat of Roo Osbourne and the rest, embellishing his own bits to make him look a lot cooler than he really was, and afterwards, felt purged.

"Woooow!" Dillon said.

"Yeah," Riven replied. "That's pretty much my interpretation of today. What did you think of that antique gun I found at the gallery?"

"The antique what now?"

"A Colt revolver. I sent you the photo hours ago."

"No you didn't."

"I did." Riven took out his phone.

Media not sent. Retry?

"It didn't send. Sending it now."

Dillon's phone beeped almost immediately.

"I'll take a look at that later." Dillon turned back to his monitors. "First, I'll crack on with this."

Riven left Dillon to it, checking the address of Sebastian Grosvenor. He too lived in North London, in a place not too far away from Riven's flat.

GROSVENOR

THE WEATHER, WHICH had started off the day in a bright and cheery mood, had pretty much decided to keep the whole sunny thing going into the afternoon. As such, after leaving Dillon's, Riven decided to walk to his next destination. Sure, it would be faster to take the tube, but there was something about walking alone with just his thoughts that appealed to him. The morning had been a full-on affair. He'd been pushed out of his comfort zone, pushed into a posh, East End gallery, and pushed into solving a mystery he had no interest in, other than his self-interested need of appeasing Landa. The injustice of it all was almost too much to bear. A surge of anger blasted through him like an electric shock. He wanted to shout, to shriek, and to scream at the complicated mess his life had become. But didn't, his rage a sneeze that never quite happened. If anything, it made him even angrier.

Camden wasn't that far away, and the thought of returning home, locking his front door, and crawling back under his duvet, was a compelling one. And so, with a considerable and growing resentment, he headed towards the address Sam Smythe had sent to his phone, pausing only to take out a hundred pounds from the hole-in-the-wall and to buy himself what turned out to be a dry and unappetising gourmet cheese sandwich. Riven often wondered why food retailers felt the need to add the word *gourmet* in front of their most uninspiring products. But he knew the answer. It was the same reason why meat producers were allowed to use *premium* for cheap sausages or bits of pig gristle coated in lard. Or for other companies to use *quality, fancy*, or *select* for their similarly nasty product ranges. It was due to a total lack of accountability when it came to using adjectives. If anyone should be reported to the grammar police, it was these gits.

Sighing, and still working his tongue at the remnants of plastic-like cheese and whatever else was trapped between his teeth, he wondered what this visit would bring. Normally, he'd run away from this kind of thing. This was the first time he'd actively been chasing down the annoying coincidences that had tainted his life ever since he was old enough to realise that his life was irreparably damaged. He needed this over and done with and soon.

Grosvenor lived in an area of Islington that poor people would occasionally wander through, marvelling at how the 'other half' lived, without realising just how badly they had miscalculated their fractions. Riven entered a square of houses around which were parked large and weighty, dark-coloured, four-by-four vehicles like a ring of well-maintained and expensive, gas-guzzling guard dogs. In the centre of the square sat a small but nicely maintained, tree-lined park. Grey squirrels cavorted with one another amongst the well-trimmed boughs, whilst the occasional well-trimmed nanny watched over various well-trimmed offspring.

Grosvenor's mansion was an impressive six storey building nestled between two other impressive six storey buildings. An impressive porch, supported by two impressive columns framed an impressive door. Feeling nervous—he wasn't sure why—he rang the impressive doorbell and stepped back.

No reply.

He rang again with the same result.

He was about to leave when an impressive, raspy voice

sounded over an intercom. *"What do you want?"*

"Oh, hi," Riven began, feeling singularly unimpressive amongst all this impressiveness. "I think I found your wallet." A long pause.

"What?

"Your wallet, I found it." He took out the wallet and held it up. Another long pause. "Hello?"

"Wait."

The door cracked open and an old man with collar-length, white hair slicked behind his ears, and a proud, stern face dominated by a powerful nose, stuck out an arm. Riven guessed he must be Sebastian Grosvenor. "Give it to me."

Riven lifted up the wallet. "It's all there," he said. "The eighty-five pounds."

"I said give it to me." He snatched the wallet off him, and the door slammed shut.

Riven stood there for a moment or two. This wasn't the way he had expected this to go. He'd been hoping for a polite thank you and detailed directions to where the Mondrian could be found. Or at least a hint or three. Or something. Anything. A complicated set of coincidences had brought him here, and this was it? Sighing, he turned to walk away.

"What's this doing in my wallet?"

Riven span to see Sebastian Grosvenor filling the doorway. A tall, wide-shouldered gentleman in a well-fitting cream suit and a wide-open frilly shirt revealing gorilla-like grey chest hair in which a gold medallion nestled cheesily. He was old, slightly bent and a bit haggard, but still a grandiose figure of a man, possessing the air of an aged and venerated 70s movie star brought out of retirement to win a Supporting Actor Oscar in his very last movie. He held out Monty's Outtasight! gallery card Landa had given Riven this morning, leaning his weight on an ornate and sturdy cane.

"Sorry, yeah, I um, put it there for safe keeping and promptly forgot about it."

"Forgot about it? What do you mean by that?" he barked.

Riven had obviously said the wrong thing but he wasn't sure what. "Are you Sebastian Grosvenor?" he ventured.

"That's *Grosvenor* to you, boy," he replied as if the name meant something.

"Hello. My name's Jim Riv—"

"Come here!" the man barked, his voice sounding like he'd been giving orders all his life.

"Excuse me… what?"

"I said come here. I want to look at you."

"Um… okay." Riven approached Grosvenor and was hit by the overpowering smell of aftershave and whisky.

Grosvenor grabbed Riven's jaw with a large hand, looking down at him intently, angling Riven's head this way and that. "I may be losing my marbles, or at least that's what they've been telling me, but I never forget a bone structure. And yours is… familiar. Come in." He let Riven go and walked into the house.

Riven followed the intimidating man inside, closing the door behind him with a feeling of unease. The hallway was not lit, but remarkable all the same, full of framed black and white photographs. Even in the gloom, he recognised some of the faces. Frank Sinatra, Oliver Reed, a young and stunning Diana Rigg, The Beatles, The Rolling Stones, Jimi Hendrix, Mick Jagger, Bowie, and a lot of other people from the 60s and 70s who he didn't recognise. Men and women captured by the camera in the prime of their lives. Young, sexy, vibrant and vital, and now mostly dead.

Grosvenor stalked off purposely on long, sturdy legs, but with a slightly lost air. As if he wasn't exactly sure where he was going—until he noticed a new looking elevator with open glass doors. He stepped deliberately inside and Riven attempted to follow him. "No!" Grosvenor said forcefully, rapping his cane painfully against Riven's arm. The thing was thick and heavy with a bulbous end and quite lethal. "The elevator is for

Grosvenor only. Meet me on the sixth floor." He closed the door with a bang and the elevator jerked and began to ascend.

Riven found the stairs and made his way up, rubbing at his arm. The contrast from Dillon's place to this massive mansion was immense. The cheapest houses in Islington were priced at around 900K, this mansion must be worth… he did the calculation in his head… gazillions. Riven passed the first, second and the other floors, marvelling at more photographs, paintings, sculptures and Art Deco features and fittings. By the time he reached the sixth floor, he was out of breath.

"Hello," he ventured,

"Who's that?" It was Grosvenor speaking from an open doorway.

"Erm, it's me remember? Jim Riven. I bought your wallet back."

"Of course! I know that! Now get in here!"

Riven entered a gallery-like room, with more photographs—prints the size of paintings, one taking up half the length of the wall. The room had the feeling of an Egyptian tomb that had not been disturbed for thousands of years, except for when the cleaner gave it an occasional dusting. And as he scanned the pictures, some of them erotic, almost pornographic nudes, and others, portraits and studies, he realised they were of the same model. A beautiful, long-limbed young woman with wide eyes, full lips, and even fuller breasts. One photo had her standing outside the Outtasight! gallery, the smiley winking face peeking out from behind her.

Grosvenor held a large tumbler of whisky that, from time to time, he gulped from. "I never forget a face," he said, his eyes narrowing in Riven's direction. "Did I already tell you that?" he added, less confidently.

Riven nodded.

"Do you recognise the subject of this collection?"

The woman in the photos was beautiful. Mesmerising in fact. And yes, there was something familiar about her, but he couldn't put his finger on it. "Was she famous?"

A flicker of confusion crossed Grosvenor's features. "This wallet, where did you find it?"

"In the back of a taxi. Under the seat. I only noticed it because I was having a little nap."

He nodded. "It started with napping and losing things."

"What started?"

"This…" Grosvenor couldn't find the word and waved a big hand irritably before him. "This thing. Forgetting stuff."

Riven knew what he meant. Alzheimer's was not a good way to go for anybody, but Grosvenor was a proud man, he could tell that much from what little he'd seen of him.

Grosvenor went through the wallet looking for something he couldn't seem to find. "There's no address, so how did you know to come here?" he barked.

"I bumped into your great niece, Sam Smythe. She recognised your wallet and gave me your address."

"You know her?"

"In passing. It was a bit of a coincidence to be honest."

"She's ashamed of me. Did she tell you that?"

"Only that you didn't meet eye to eye."

"That's an understatement. She even changed her surname. Her surname! But then again, *Grosvenor* is a swear word these days. But not back in the day. Then I was a young man surrounded by beautiful available women. And of course I did what young men do. What young people do." Grosvenor's eyes glittered like two lascivious disco balls reflecting his many conquests, and to Riven, it seemed, the long years fell away from him. "When you get older, get to a certain age," Grosvenor continued, "you're not allowed to do the same things, not without allegations of impropriety." The glitter in his eyes winked out, and the years returned to haunt his face again. "How can making love be improper when its consensual? Answer me that?"

Riven didn't know what to say so said nothing.

"And all my liaisons were consensual," Grosvenor continued. "Not that Sam saw it that way. I thought she was interviewing me about my life, about my triumphs, about my legacy. But the little witch was after a different story altogether. Most of it made up from hearsay and gossip, and she sold it to one of those nasty magazines. Accusing me of all manner of indiscretions. And now look at me. I've spent the last five years as a prisoner in my own home. I'm fading. I'm fading away, Rosie."

"Who's Rosie?"

"Rosie? You know her?" He waved at the photographs. "My muse."

"You wanted to show me something, remember?" Riven ventured, feeling his heart sink. Grosvenor was more far gone than he'd realised. He was getting nowhere. "Something to do with these photographs, perhaps?"

"They're not just photographs, they are portraits!" He bashed his heavy cane onto a wooden table sitting next to the wall, making the table, the ornate silver-tipped decanter of whisky that sat upon it, and Riven jump. "But unlike the contrivance of a painter, my work is the art of observation. About finding beauty in the everyday. An unexpected look in the eyes, a gentle curl of a lip, a certain quality of light playing across naked breasts, nipples, and hair. Or the angle of an arm or leg or chin, or the curve of a buttock or spine. I have the eye to spot those moments and to preserve them forever."

Grosvenor finished his whisky and replenished it from the decanter. "I don't give a jot what anyone thinks. My photographs are all I care about. I capture fleeting moments like a thief stealing from the universe itself... can you understand that? For when a moment has gone, nothing can bring it back. Nothing! Look at these photos again, properly this time, and tell me if any one of them is anything but the highest art..."

Riven was out of his depth and Grosvenor rambling. But it was obvious this man was once an important person back in the day. He knew nothing about him or his indiscretions, but then again, Riven never really followed the news that much. But he was right about the photographic prints in this room. There was nothing tawdry about any of them. They may have included nudes and erotica, but this was art. Even Riven, with his limited understanding of the subject could see that.

"Without my camera," Grosvenor continued, "I don't know what I would've become. It's always been my guide. It allowed me to see things the average person would never even notice. Using my intuition to flick open the shutter, to freeze a moment in time. To make people care about those moments. It's what made me. I wanted to preserve them, you see? Those girls. In celluloid. In black and white. Preserve them for all time. I don't care what Sam wrote. Art transcends the muck and mire of human life and goes beyond it. Creating something special and untouchable. This is why I have this room set out like it is. To remind me that amongst all the false glamour and all the manure, I was able to produce pure art, my life's best work." Grosvenor stopped speaking to stare teary-eyed at one of the large, framed prints.

Riven took the chance to ask a question, although it felt like a total stab in the dark. "Look," he began, do you know anything about a Mondrian?"

"Piet Mondrian?" Grosvenor replied coming back to himself. "Of course. Never loved his use of colour though. Black and white is my game but I understood his ethos. Why?"

"One of his paintings was stolen from the Outtasight! gallery last night, that's all."

"Stolen?" He chuckled. "The art world loves nothing more than a high-profile art theft. Gets everyone talking about art again, but most importantly, it boosts prices!" He gave Riven a sideways look. "You're not a reporter, are you?"

"Me? No way."

Grosvenor shook his immense head. "No, you're not. I can smell their stench a mile away. A particularly nasty ordure.

Who did you say you were again? You have a very familiar bone structure…"

"Jim Riven."

He shook his head as if trying to clear a fog. "So, a robbery you say? At the Outtasight! Was it Tarquin? He was always a shifty little bugger."

"We don't know who stole it. That's what I'm trying to find out. Who's Tarquin?"

"Tarquin!" Grosvenor rapped his cane onto the table a second time, before raising it above his head threateningly. "Don't mention his name to me, not if you value your life!"

Riven took a step back. "Right… I should probably go." The poor sod is all over the place, he thought to himself. He had a feeling Grosvenor could be dangerous, especially with that heavy stick of his. "I think I perhaps have upset you."

"Upset me? Don't be foolish, boy!" Grosvenor took a gulp of whisky and swilled it around his gums before speaking. "I know the gallery. Of course I do," he said, suddenly lucid again. "I exhibited there countless times back in the day." His old eyes flicked back in time. "I have many fond memories of the place."

"You do?" Instead of a cold stab of discomfort at this revelation, Riven felt a twinge of excitement. Maybe this old duffer would be of use after all.

Grosvenor lifted his whisky glass at a large portrait of the stunning model this room was a shrine to. "The Outtasight! is where I met Rosie. They've reopened it, huh? And used its original name?"

Riven nodded.

"You're the first person to set foot in my house apart from the cleaner and my nurse in years. You want to know why?"

Riven groaned inside. Grosvenor's erratic mind couldn't focus on one thing for more than a moment.

"It's your face, boy. I never forget a face."

"But we've never met before," Riven said trying not to show

the exasperation he was feeling.

Grosvenor shook his head. "No, but your bone structure, the dimensions. Your skin tone and the way the light catches your jawline. There can be no mistaking it. You're related to my greatest model. A descendant. You must be."

Riven shook his head. The man was clearly off his rocker.

Grosvenor swept his arm around the room and gulped at the whisky, tears forming in his eyes. "This is Rosalind *Rosie* Ruskin."

Riven experienced another of those moments—one of those moments that he was having far too many of today—and another shiver ran down his spine to join all the other shivers that were huddling down there. Rosalind Ruskin was his grandmother on his father's side. She'd died when he was a teenager. He remembered seeing her once or twice. She was a typical nan and nothing like the beauty in these photographs. Although the likeness was there. From the little of what he knew of her, she was supposed to have been a society girl when she was younger, which he now guessed must've been olden times slang for enjoying your youth with as many beaus and as many drinks as you could manage. And now it turned out she was the mostly naked muse for Grosvenor, an old, letchy, 60s photographer whose grip on reality had somewhat slipped. "Wow... she was beautiful," was all that Riven could muster at the news.

"She was indeed. But what are you doing here? Did Tarquin send you?"

Yet another shiver launched down Riven's spine, changed its mind, shivered up again and then, as if realising its mistake, shivered back down. "Tarquin, the guy that you hate so much, was my grandfather," he whispered, feeling overwhelmed, backing away from Grosvenor and his dangerous cane. "I knew the name was familiar—it's not a name you easily forget. Not that I ever met him. He went to India and disappeared before I was born."

Grosvenor took his attention away from the portrait of Riven's grandmother and stared at him with a most peculiar expression on his face, his cane thankfully held loosely at his side. "But what a series of coincidences. You finding my wallet, you knowing about the *Outtasight!* gallery, you meeting that disaster of a grandniece of mine and, to top it off, you being related to my life's greatest muse and my greatest enemy."

Grosvenor's lucid moments were intense. And even though the man was clearly troubled, he deserved to be treated with respect. Riven walked over to the decanter and, with a nod from Grosvenor, poured himself a whisky and sat down. "You're right. It is quite a series of coincidences, that much is for sure. I'm bedevilled by them. They've cursed my life. Indeed, I've never really felt like my life is my own. More like I'm a puppet in some dumb TV show. A puppet with too many interconnected and tangled strings. Hell, my life is one big tangle." He sipped at the whisky and coughed. He wasn't used to hard liquor, but he really needed it and took another. He looked up to see Grosvenor holding a small, pocket-sized camera, taking photographs of him.

"What are you doing?"

"Force of habit. I always carry a camera around with me. Even now. Not that I have much to photograph these days. Nor can I remember taking the photographs when I print them. But just then, when you were speaking about those interconnected tangled strings, there was something in your face—a unique quality I've never seen before—and I wanted to capture it." The wistful look on his face twisted into one of sudden anger. "I loved Rosie and I guess she loved me. But that was until Tarquin came along and took her away from me!"

"I'm sorry, I really am."

Grosvenor's anger disappeared as quickly as it arrived. "How… how is she? How is Rosie these days?"

"She died nearly twenty years ago."

The old man took in the news with a pained smile. "Oh…

I thought that maybe… but of course. We are all so old! Photography can only capture the now. Once the photograph is taken, the subject becomes part of the past. And yet we hold onto that moment, don't we? We want to keep it forever. For me, Rosie is still the vivacious girl in these portraits." He held up Monty's card. "I met her there you know. Rosie. At the Outtasight! I'll never forget her standing at the end of the long under-gallery, eyeing some painting or other, a vision in white. And as you can see, she was… absolutely Outtasight."

"You should visit. It's been refurbished."

"Me and Rosie made out there many times in the under-gallery," Grosvenor continued, ignoring him. "Me a roaring lion, she a delicate gazelle. We often used to snatch an intimate moment or two, the sound of voices chatting close by. But then again, the risk of getting caught was something that exhilarated Rosie." His gaze drifted off into the distance, his proud face contemplative. "I exhibited these very photographs there. Out of everything I've ever done, that was the pinnacle." He sat back and laughed darkly, necking an almost full glass of whisky and refilling it. "Was Sam right about me?" He asked, his voice slurring with the booze, his tone suddenly maudlin. "Was I the guy she portrayed in that awful story? I don't know. I can't remember. I'm so confused by it all. Not that it matters anymore. My life is done. Finished." Grosvenor suddenly sagged and Riven jumped up to help him.

"Rosie dead… I always thought that perhaps someday we'd… I don't know. Be together again." He lifted his glass to toast the room and nodded. "To Rosie!" He downed the whisky in one and Riven did the same, coughing and spluttering.

THE STICK MAN

TWENTY MINUTES LATER, Riven found himself glad to back on the square outside Grosvenor's mansion. The man was a maudlin mess and had tried to make him stay. He had to promise to return, which Riven had done, begrudgingly. He was still processing what had been revealed to him. Those wondrous and beautiful photographs of his nan. To see her in this new light was startling, but he was glad to have found out about her. She'd lived an interesting life, until she'd given birth to his father that is. He couldn't imagine that was anything less than a major downer for her. Riven's dad was a class one jerk and even had a certificate to prove it. Perhaps those traits came from his grandfather Tarquin? Especially if Grosvenor was right about him.

Grosvenor had promised to send a tasteful series of prints to Riven's flat and so he had given him his address. "You're not far away," he'd said. "I may just bring the prints over myself, if you don't mind? And a bottle of whisky. I used to hang out in Camden back in the day. I loved that place."

Riven had nodded, saying, "Just make sure to turn up at a civilised hour, after 2pm, at least. And please don't use the buzzer!"

Back out in the fresh afternoon air that was just starting to cool down, Riven was feeling lightheaded and more than a little woozy. He'd drank too much whisky and decided to go home for a lie down. And there was something else, despite the all the convoluted happenchance, the serendipitous findings, and coincidental meetings, he'd come up with a blank. Grosvenor knew nothing about the missing Mondrian. Nothing at all.

Very soon, Riven was back in Camden Town, making his way to the safety of his flat. He loved the place. It was a vibrant, happening, leafy borough, where the main leaf of choice was determinedly marijuana. Indeed, it was impossible to walk down any Camden street, road or back alley without smelling its rich, pungent tell-tale aroma. So much so, that Riven firmly believed anyone living in Camden Town—or just passing through—was more than likely to fail a drugs test, just because of the very air they breathed.

Back in the 80s and 90s, the place had had a run-down vibe, and still did. But now that run-down vibe had become particularly desirable. House prices had skyrocketed. These days it was full of skankily-dressed but prosperous residents, skankily-dressed but affluent students, and skankily-dressed but still decidedly comfortably off drug dealers.

The mixed-up mess that was all humankind could be found in Camden Town, from immigrants and students of all nationalities to celebrities and pretentious literati—how these writers managed word one with so much distraction on offer, was beyond Riven. Added to this mix, was the newer addition of bourgeois bohemians—youngsters with wealthy mummies and daddies pretending to be destitute, known to some of the more resentful residents as Bo Hoes. As for visitors, Camden Town was also popular with punks, goths, indie kids, and those of any age looking to have a great night out and meet people, and to be found later on—either slumped over in an alleyway, slumped over in Camden Town tube station or slumped over a member of the opposite sex, the same sex, or of an indiscriminate sex, in any of the previous locations.

The buildings were as disparate as their occupants. Old

but respectable terraced housing sat next to newer council estates, many of which had been turned into private flats. And despite the general affluence of its residents, Camden Town had long been associated with criminal activity of all types. Mainly drug dealers, who amongst all these wealthy people, felt that the place had gone downhill a bit recently. And if the drug dealers are thinking like this, it wasn't a good sign for the neighbourhood.

Riven wasn't put off in the slightest. He loved Camden Town. It was always busy and bustling no matter the time of day or night. And it had many venues in which him and Dillon could drink the night away. Most bars were brash, loud, and borderline illegal, but more recently mixed in with these were quieter places where blokes with voluminous beards could stroke them in the comparative quiet of a real ale establishment. Real ale could only ever be drunk in silence due to deeply held religious beery beliefs. There were also drag bars, music venues and nightclubs as well as a multitude of take-aways mixed in with restaurants serving diverse food from around the planet, as long as you liked your vegan falafels very, very spicy, that is.

He was just breathing in the heady cocktail of diesel fumes and dope when his phone rang, buzzing with that same jarring sensation that he recognised far too easily. Landa. And she wasn't going to be happy.

"Where on earth do you think you're going?" she shrieked at him.

"Er… um… what?"

"You're on your way back home, aren't you?"

"No," Riven blurted guiltily. He looked around him. Had Landa had him followed?

"You better have found my Mondrian!"

"Not exactly."

"Not what? I'm relying on you, you know that? You've just got to find it, Riv, you've got to!"

"I'm trying my best. It's just that everything hasn't quite

come together in the way that I'd hoped it would come together."

"I'm at the gallery now. The place is locked up! I've been banging on the door for ten minutes."

"You're at the gallery? It was open when I left. Jen should be there to let you in."

"Jen? Who on earth is Jen?"

"The gallery manager."

"That stuck up skinny minx with the boots? I remember her alright. She had the audacity to explain to me about Mondrian. To tell me that his art 'was utopian and reflected nature's spirituality'."

Her impersonation of Jen, although exaggerated, was spot on.

"She said it to my face! In front of my painting! As if I hadn't already read that on Wikipedia! Well, I own it, I told her. What the hell do you own apart from last years' A-line and no titties? That wiped the smile off her thin lips, I can tell you."

"Maybe she popped out for lunch?" Riven ventured, his ear ringing, even with his phone held at a distance.

"With the Mondrian missing? How dare she! I thought I was going to break the glass I was knocking so hard. I almost felt like throwing a brick through the window. I paid for that place, you know? Paid for it with my own money and Monty..." Her voice turned into a squeak and became inaudible.

"What about Monty?"

"He's taken my money, got my Mondrian stolen, and now he's disappeared."

"Disappeared?" Riven said, wondering why he felt the need to repeat her words. He was only prolonging the awkward conversation.

"He's not answering his phone, and everyone answers when I ring. He, of all people, knows that!"

"Oh. I heard he'd popped out for a drink with that Harve chap. I'm sure he'll be back soon."

"Harve? That little gold-digger?"

"Yeah, I've heard that as well."

"He's got his claws into Monty like no other. D'ya think he has anything to do with the Mondrian being taken?"

Before he could attempt an answer, Landa spoke again.

"I want you to come here now, okay?"

Riven was in sight of his flat's front door and longed to go inside. "Of course. Sure."

"I'm banking on you, Riv. Don't you dare let me down. You won't will you?"

"I'll be there as soon as I can."

"And what do you expect me to do in the meantime? Wait out here on the street?"

"There' a nice tea shop not far away. You could go there."

"Don't be ridiculous! I'll expect you here ASAP!"

Riven turned dejectedly away from his flat and made his way back to Camden Town tube station, before walking absentmindedly down onto the platforms and jumping on a waiting train. The carriage was empty, and he had a choice of seats. He sat down by the doors and almost immediately closed his eyes, letting the carriage gently rock him. He could feel the whisky warm inside, a warmth that he sank willingly into…

…A thin, effete-looking, balding middle-aged man with a Hitler moustache and wire-rimmed glasses stood in front of him, staring with intense, intelligent eyes. He wore a long, blue paint-stained coat and carried a smoking cigarette in one delicate hand. Behind him, in a large factory-like room, were hung various paintings of vertical and horizontal black lines filled with blue, yellow, and red blocks. Other, similar paintings leaned against the walls. A word flitted into his mind.

Mondrian.

"Huh?" Riven mumbled.

The man was standing next to a painting that seemed out of place amongst the others. A large canvas, white, except for a stick man painted crudely in black. As he stared, the stick man came alive and rushed straight at him.

A sudden rush of air and the bang of a passing train. "Aaarrgh!"

Riven opened his eyes to find himself in a packed carriage, people giving him strange looks. He rubbed at sore temples, feeling more than a little nauseous. Swallowing a mouthful of saliva, he got off the train at the next stop and exited the tube station, thankful for the now colder afternoon air. The day had seemingly given up on its sunny vibe and was settling into something far gloomier and in keeping with the season. Leaning against a nearby wall, he took out his phone, searched for Piet Mondrian and was met by multiple images of a thin, effete-looking, balding middle-aged man with a Hitler moustache and wire-rimmed glasses.

"Bloody hell!"

A DETOUR

ROO OSBOURNE WAS sitting in the back of his electric blue, custom-made Rolls Royce Ghost on the way to his place in Kensington when his phone trilled. The number came up as *Unknown*. Intrigued, he answered, waiting for the other person to speak.

"Hello, is that Roo… Roo Osbourne?" The voice belonged to a young woman.

"Speakin'. And who on earth are you? This is a restricted number… or it's supposed to be."

"I'm Sam Smythe."

Roo smiled to himself, impressed and a little taken aback. "I know you, Miss Smythe. You're that annoying journo who's been tryin' to investigate me. You're not the first to try and you won't be the last. But you're the first one to get a hold of my personal number and have the guts to use it. I'll give you that. Now what do you want?"

"A job would be great, and maybe a nice town apartment."

"Don't you work for me already?"

"You know what I mean."

"You think this is how this works? You dig around in my dingo-droppings enough times to get my attention and then ask me for a promotion and a slice of real estate? You've got another think comin'. You know I can ruin you as easily as I can discredit a left-wing government?"

"I'm well aware of your reputation. It's... it's terrifying. But I have some information that you might want kept quiet. And I thought you could help me out with a quid-pro-quo."

"Well that all depends on the information, doesn't it? What is it?"

"Will I get that job?"

"Listen to me young lady. You'll tell me what you know and after that, we'll see what happens to you, unnerstand?"

"It's about your daughter."

"Yolanda?" Roo shook his head. "Go on."

"From what I've managed to find out, she borrowed your Mondrian to exhibit at her friend's gallery. Owned by a young man by the name of Monty Fitzhugh. You know him?"

"Of course I do. But so what? She may have not asked my permission to show the thing, but that's hardly newsworthy."

"But here's the rub... it's been stolen. If news gets out about it... well, it'd be an international story, too big for even you to bury, with you and Yolanda at the centre of it. Especially after you paid a record sum for the same Mondrian only a few months ago."

"Strewth!"

"Yeah. And I know how you like to keep your face out of the papers. I just saw your daughter outside Monty Fitzhugh's East End gallery in Spitalfields a few minutes ago. She did not look happy."

"And how did you find this out?"

"An informant. I checked the info with the gallery manager. She denied it, of course, but was lying through her teeth. She seemed half scared to death to be honest. And who wouldn't be? As soon as the press find out, her life won't be worth living."

Roo sighed.

"I had this number and decided I had to use it," Sam Smythe continued. *"Good enough for that job and a North London apartment?"*

"Let me talk to Yolanda and I'll get back to you."

"I'll send you my number."

"Don't worry, we already have it." Roo offed the phone and threw it down. Ever since Yolanda had met that idiot Monty, she'd hardly been out of trouble. Even bankrupting the little toerag made no difference, although he'd been amused by how easy it had been to take him down. If he's somehow involved, I'll kill the little beggar! he thought to himself.

"Stephen," he said over the intercom to his chauffeur, "we're making a detour. Take me to Spitalfields in the East End."

He tapped at his phone and waited while it rang.

A GRUBBY HANDKERCHIEF

HALF AN HOUR later Riven was standing outside the Outtasight! Gallery feeling dazed. Coincidences were one thing—visions were something else altogether. Just what had Grosvenor put in the whisky?

"Jim Riven? Is that you?"

He glanced in the direction of the strangely familiar voice and saw Harve lurching drunkenly and happily towards him, like Riven was some long-lost friend. He looked dishevelled and distraught—his perfect mess of his hair now just a mess. And judging by his red-rimmed blue eyes, his earlier cockiness had been blubbed out of him.

"Hi Harve. You, um, alright?"

Harve grabbed Riven by the shoulders and attempted a hug, but Riven was too quick and sidestepped him, pushing him away.

"No! I'm not alright," Harve blurted, crumbling like a beach sandcastle against the tide. "It's Monty, he's dumped me."

"I'm sorry to hear that," Riven said, trying his best to sound supportive while looking around for Landa who was conspicuous by her absence. "You two seemed, I dunno, right together, until I found out what a lying, gold-digging little git you were." Riven was surprised by his words, Grosvenor's whisky had made him rather loose tongued.

"What?" Harve said incredulously. "Was it you who told him?"

Riven shook his head irritably. "No. That honour goes to Jen. She heard you talking to your girlfriend."

"Sheila! I should've never listened to her. But then I suppose, I would never have met Monty."

"I thought that accent was put on."

"I read somewhere that Monty found the cockney accent sexy. I did it for him."

"Because you were trying to hustle him. No wonder he dumped you. That's a horrible thing to do."

"I know!" Harve burst into sudden tears, pulling out a grubby handkerchief from his pocket. Loose change fell on the floor, which he scrabbled around to pick up, as well as an old tissue and a screwed-up bit of paper that rolled away into the gutter. Riven grabbed at it and handed it back to him. "What's that?" Harve asked, dabbing at his eyes.

"Dunno," Riven replied irritably. "You dropped it." Where on earth was Landa?

Harve took the paper off him, unravelled it, shrugged, and stuffed it back into his pocket, before wiping away his tears and blowing his nose. "Look, if you see Monty, will you tell him I'm sorry? Will you do that for me? I know I don't deserve him, I loved him, you know? Really loved the guy."

"Yeah, sure," Riven said non-committedly. Monty could be a pompous ass sometimes, but he didn't deserve to be treated like this. No one did. He hadn't realised what a problem gold-diggers were in Monty's and Landa's world. To have such horrible creeps leeching off them was appalling. The man did seem genuinely upset though. Then again, if you're going to mess with people's emotions just to get a payday, it's your own fault.

Harve blew his nose again and stumbled away.

"And good riddance," Riven said under his breath, putting

Harve to the back of his mind. He had more important matters to deal with. Landa had been insistent that he come to the gallery, but she was nowhere to be seen, and there were no missed calls from her. He pushed at the gallery door, and it opened. If it had been locked when Landa was here, it certainly wasn't now. He walked in, wincing again at the bright lights, calling "Hello?" in that particularly English fashion that was embedded into every English person's DNA, next to other important English chromosomal sequences that dealt with tea, saying sorry when it wasn't your fault, and feeling guilty anyway.

He heard voices below and made his way downstairs to the under gallery. At the bottom, he bumped into Bill and Joey who were busy with what appeared to be a camera scope that Bill was using to peer inside the walls. "You're back?" Riven ventured. Stepping over wires and other equipment and whatnot.

Bill looked up from the apparatus's small screen and gave him a wan smile. "Yeah, I got Joey to apologise." He flicked a thumb in the direction of his nephew who kept his gaze on the floor. "Not that he had anythin' to apologise for. That gallery manager is not his type at all. Said that girl didn't have much up top to ogle at. Then again, he doesn't share such sophisticated tastes as you an' me!" he added with a wink. "No. Joey here prefers skanky and tattooed slags, ain't that right?"

Joey shrugged.

"So what you looking for?" Riven ventured, impressed with the technical machinery Bill was using, and less impressed with the sudden mental image of Joey's skanky and tattooed slags.

"Rats, innit. I reckon this entire wall is gonna need to come down. It's rat city central in there. The source of all the gallery's infestation in my considered opinion."

"But won't that mess up the next show?"

"Nah, nah, nah! Course not. We'll have the wall down and back up again in a jiffy." Bill sounded almost manic. "I know the trades. Drink with 'em all the time. By this time tomorrow, you won't see any difference. I'm just doing a final check before poppin' off to get the jackhammer."

"Jackhammer? You've cleared this with Jen, with the gallery?"

Bill shrugged his massive shoulders. "They were very clear about this job. They told me to do what was needed to end this rat infestation once and for all. And I take my job very seriously." He pulled the probe free of the wall and turned to Joey. "C'mon. Let's pack all this up and get out of here. The sooner we've gone, the sooner we can get back."

Riven left them to it and headed towards the under-gallery where he found Jen laughing with a familiar face. Dan Kowalski from the VIP pass he'd found. Dan was annoyingly tall and irritatingly attractive. He wore a pair of rainbow pantaloons tied with a knotted white cord, open-toed sandals, and a big, flouncy white shirt. His long hair sat in a tight bun atop his head, and his immense beard was tied with gold tinsel. To Riven, he looked like a new age, vegan genie/djinn. Dan stood over a large canvas laid flat upon one of the abandoned launch party tables and was busily applying white acrylic to its surface with more attention than was required. Suddenly, in one of those filmic pull-out zoom moments that modern directors are so unimaginatively fond of, Riven's eye was taken by the far wall, the wall where the Mondrian had been hung before it had been stolen. In its place was a large white canvas with a clumsy stick man painted in black in the foreground.

THE DIPTYCH

THERE COULD BE no doubt about it. It was the same stick man painting Riven had seen in his vision! He stared at it for long moments, wondering how he'd let his life get so out of control, when all he'd wanted was a lie in, to drink more mugs of tea than was probably healthy, and to have a warmed up Jalfrezi for first afternoon breakfast. Next to the painting was a smaller, scrappier canvas of the same scene. Hints of green poking from the edges. But they were similar to one another.

Riven's eyes spread quickly around the room, like Covid at a Texas prayer meeting. The gallery side walls had similar paintings of various shapes and sizes, but all very much following the stick man theme. It was all too much. Riven felt suddenly dizzy, disorientated and discombobulated. Felt like the world was crashing down upon him. Felt like... he couldn't put his finger on it. But he didn't care for the sensation, that much was for sure. And then... nothing happened. Nothing at all. He gave it a few more moments, but still nothing. And slowly, he came back to himself, back to the gallery full of weird paintings, back to Dan and his self-assured, cocky voice, and back to Jen listening to him with rapt attention.

He took a long, deep breath, his heart slowing down and moving from the region of his mouth to return once again to its proper place within his chest. He focused himself on the main painting again. He'd never seen it or Piet Mondrian before today and both had featured in his London Underground hallucination. Why? Did it have some importance? Some relevance to the missing Mondrian? If it did, he had no idea what. And there was one more thing… the hot feeling at the back of his neck had suddenly turned to ice and now an Arctic blizzard was blowing back there.

Riven decided to forget about what had just happened. To try and get back to normality as fast as he could. He put all his attention on Dan and Jen's conversation, listening to their words. Using them to pull himself back to whatever reality it was he'd left behind.

"I know you've a trained eye, yeah?" Dan said to Jen, sagely stroking his beard and adjusting his topknot, oblivious to Riven trembling behind him, "so you'll understand just how crucial this stage is. The right thickness of the paint, the brush's direction and line, and the length of strokes. There's a will behind it, but also an element of pure dis-cov-ery. And you may not know this, Jen, but the beginning of knowledge, is the discovery of, you know, the stuff we don't yet understand, yeah?"

Dan's voice was one of those hippy voices with over-pronounced vowels containing a nasal quality that made you want to blow your nose. It was trying so desperately to sound serious and considered but came across as over-bearing and more than a little pretentious. It was a voice that shouted, 'Punch me!' very loudly. Or at least that was Riven's take on it.

Jen nodded, seemingly mesmerised, unable to take her eyes off Dan's canvas.

"Behind the paint is, of course, one of my earlier colourful daubs, and here and there, I let that colour leak through, yeah? The magic being where and how I do that and, of course, where I don't. You see, Jen, my use of white isn't just a sort of absence of colour but an attitude all of itself."

Jen's smile turned into a full-on beam.

An unusual but welcome emotion entered Riven's mind. *Jealousy*. To be honest, he was thankful for anything remotely normal after his recent experience, and so he centred on the emotion and let it fill him, until he felt quite, quite put out. Jen had only recently been re-added to his list of affections, and of course, there was that mix-up with her dissertation, but he'd been hoping that, well maybe, they could put all that behind them and start again. And despite everything, he was sure she liked him. But here she was, smiling like a doped-up hyena at this artist fellow. Then again, Jen loved art and Dan was an artist… well, sort of.

"Hi there," Riven ventured over Jen's shoulder, his voice a lot louder than he was intending, making both her and Dan jump.

"Oh, it's you again, is it?" Jen said turning to him, sounding unimpressed, although he was sure he'd seen the beginnings of a twinkle in her eye.

"Apparently…"

"Who is this?" Dan said, giving Riven and his tee-shirt the once over.

"Dan Kowalski, meet Jim Riven," Jen replied. "He's a shaman," she added derisorily.

"Oh hi," Dan said. "Have we met before? You seem familiar."

"Very possibly," Riven replied. "I get a lot of that. More than is generally comfortable to live with."

Dan Kowalski stared at him for a little longer than Riven thought was necessary. "So, you're a shaman… Cool!"

"Not exactly," Riven replied, feeling the need to show he was a real and very possible contender for Jen's affections. That machismo thing rearing its ugly head again. He really should've learned his lesson from his experience with Landa, but machismo, especially when it was twinned with his libido, became a powerful force that worked overtime to make his life unnecessarily complicated. "I'm a private investigator," he added pompously.

Jen made a sound like a strangled wasp.

"I'm here because of the Mondrian that was stolen last night, by special request of the owner."

"Yeah, I was just talking to Jen about that," Dan said, his paintbrush hovering over his canvas like a bird about to expertly defecate on a car. "It's gonna be like big news for sure. Big, big news. The biggest." Dan seemed very excited at the possibility. "But yeah, what a truly awful thing to happen. Do you have any clues as to who took it and how the deed was done?"

"I'm afraid I can't reveal the details of an active investigation."

"Are you sure about that?" Jen asked.

"What does that mean?"

"I mean, have you been talking to a certain Sam Smythe by any chance?"

"Well, um, yes as a matter of fact. Why?"

"She was here earlier, asking me for a comment regarding the theft of the Mondrian. Of course, I told her nothing, but Monty won't be pleased that you've involved the press. It's going to turn into one hell of a freak show."

Riven raised his hands. Sam Smythe was more of a journalist than he'd realised. "I also told her nothing. Not one word. Scout's honour. Although I've never been in the scouts, so that doesn't mean that much. But if I had been, I'd have easily earned my 'Keeping Schtum' badge. No mistake."

"Huh?"

"I kept quiet. Of course, I did. For Landa and unfortunately for that fascist father of hers."

"Then she must've heard it from someone else. But who? And why would they want to get the press involved? Unless they wanted to embarrass Roo Osbourne. He has a lot of enemies. And him losing the Mondrian will be one major embarrassment."

"But there's no bad publicity, surely? Yeah?" Dan said, beaming.

"The art world will go nuts over this," Jen replied. "You wait and see."

Riven shrugged. "Anyway, Dan," he said, finding it hard to remove the sarcasm from behind his words. "Jen told me all about you. I'm very pleased to meet you and your spectacular pantaloons in person."

Dan beamed again, capped white teeth appearing suddenly from within his voluminous beard. "It's always a boon to make a new acquaintance. I'm blessed to meet you," he said, putting the palms of his hands together and bowing. "Every new day gives me a reason to smile. And you've added to my smile. For that I'm forever grateful."

"Um, thanks." Riven gave Jen a sideways look, but she appeared oblivious to these dreadful platitudes.

"I hope we will create wonderful memories today, yeah?"

"Me too," Riven replied with mock seriousness, giving Jen another look. Surely, she'd give a grimace at least. But no. Nothing.

Dan raised his head and his smile, if possible, became even wider. "You know what they say? It takes forty-three muscles to frown and only seventeen to smile…" He nodded encouragingly.

Riven wondered what he was getting at for a few moments before it dawned on him. Jen might not be grimacing, but the frown that inhabited Riven's face more than made up for it. Dan wanted him to smile, but Riven had not been having a smiley day today. Rather the opposite in fact. A fact that needed to be alluded to, especially now he was forced to deal with Dan's passive aggressive claptrap. "Thank you, Dan, for such an interesting fact," he began charmingly. "I have one of my own. Did you know that it takes absolutely no facial muscles to… *not give a damn?*"

A look of confusion crossed Dan's face.

"Shush, Riven!" Jen said. "Ignore him Dan, Riven has a peculiar sense of humour."

"No, no, no," Dan said waving her away. "It is the ability to take a joke, that proves we have a sense of humour, for sure. And I can take a joke. Certainly, I can." He gave a forced chuckle. "It takes no muscles to not give a damn… nice. Very funny. I get it. I really do."

"I believe this belongs to you," Riven said, taking out Dan's VIP pass, very much playing the hard-nosed investigator. Jen raised her thin eyebrows and frowned at him.

"Where did you find that?" Dan asked, seemingly oblivious to his tone.

"By the under-gallery outer doors. What were you doing there last night?" he asked aggressively.

"I must've dropped it when Jen gave me the tour," Dan replied without a beat, giving Jen a wink. "You don't think I had anything to do with the robbery, do you?"

"I'm afraid everyone is a suspect at the moment." Riven pocketed the pass again. "I'll keep this as evidence."

"Do that. It may be worth something someday. But I'm not your man, okay? Sure, I'd love my own personal Mondrian, who wouldn't? But even if I had somehow purloined it, what would I do with the thing? What would anyone do with it?"

"What do you mean?"

"I mean that nearly every Mondrian is accounted for, yeah? Logged and catalogued. For sure. You couldn't sell it. Not unless you had a buyer lined up who was willing to pay the cashola for a stolen painting—which is possible. But that's some risk, man. Particularly when it belongs to Roo Osbourne. We know he's a bulldog, yeah? A bulldog who will bite you hard. He's not the type to let anyone steal from him and get away with it. No, he'd find the Mondrian and punish the thief, and anyone associated with them, to the end of their days and then, very probably, into their next life."

"What do you want down here, anyway?" Jen said to Riven, her frown certainly not turning upside down. It seemed she was less than impressed with his investigator performance.

"You've not seen Landa, have you?" Riven asked, wondering where she'd gotten to. "It's just that she was trying to get in a short while ago and locking her out is perhaps, maybe, possibly, not the best of ideas."

"I've not seen or heard from her," Jen replied. "But, as you can see, I've been very busy down here."

Riven breathed a sigh of relief. Landa had disappeared for the time being and that could only be a positive. He had other things on his mind. Things he'd been trying to ignore. He turned to the far wall and the twin paintings hanging there. "What can you tell me about those paintings?" he asked Jen, knowing he couldn't mention the vision. She thought him enough of a fruit-loop as it was already and adding 'seeing things' to her list of reasons not to go out with him, didn't seem like a good idea at all.

Jen drew breath to answer, but it was Dan who spoke.

"It's my diptych," he said proudly, waving his brush like he was conducting his own words. "*The Stick Man*, two paintings as one, and my masterpiece. I've never exhibited it before, so it was a shock to come down here and see it hung so spectacularly in this fantastic space."

"Dan's paintings arrived soon after you left," Jen said. "I had them brought in and I've spent the afternoon down here unwrapping and hanging. That's why I wasn't around to let that Landa woman in. I was so engrossed. Dan is such a talent, it's easy to get lost in his work."

Dan bowed at the compliment.

Riven stepped onto the small stage and examined the larger of the two canvases. Even up close, it did nothing for him. But it wasn't his inability to understand modern art that was perplexing him, but the reason why he'd had a vision about it. If it was a vision. But it must've been. He'd never seen Dan's diptych or Piet Mondrian before. Unless he was going, quite, quite mad.

"My work," Dan began enthusiastically, "signifies precisely

the non-being of what it represents."

"Okay," Riven ventured. "I'll bite. What's that exactly?"

"The universality of the landscape and our place amongst it, yeah? Combined with the collective sense of the mag-nificent."

"Of course… And the stick man?"

"Yes, the stick man. *The Stick Man*. The anti-motif. A black figure amongst a sea of white that obscures most of the colour. It is neither the object of objecthood nor the art-object. It is rather the indirect object of meaning."

Jen nodded at his side, like she understood what Dan was saying. Riven didn't. So far, it just sounded like a series of impressive words that didn't match up to anything or each other. And if Riven knew anything, he knew words. He was annoyed, the same question stabbing at him again. Why have a vision about Dan's artwork? It made no sense. "What does it mean?" he whispered to himself.

"Ah, the ultimate question," Dan answered, stroking his impressive beard. "What does anything mean… intrinsically? But perhaps I can elucidate, yeah? Perhaps I can throw some light on your understanding? The piece represents the zeitgeist between upward modality and our impact on nature as a consequence. Its perceptions are crafted from both rural and urban dialogues, yeah? When one experiences the first moment of inception, when our eyes rove over the work, what at first appears to be simple chaos is soon replaced with a sense of the newness of order. In, like, an endless oscillation of a familiar but an ultimately neo-zeitgeist, yeah?"

There was no doubt that Dan was highly intelligent, but it was in that stupid way that sometimes affected those born with too many brain cells. "How much is it worth?" Riven asked, having switched off halfway through.

"I don't put any value on art, other than my own personal preference. This diptych is my masterpiece and as such, priceless."

"I reckon, sixty to eighty thousand pounds," Jen said.

"I won't sell. This is what started it all. *The Stick Man* will stay with me forever."

"What if someone offered you a million pounds for it?"

"Don't you understand? Dan can't sell this piece," Jen said knowingly. "That would devalue his zeitgeist. Make a mockery of it."

Dan beamed. "Right on, Jen. Right on." He placed his hands on his heart and smiled at her. "You totally get me."

Riven felt like he may throw up. "But you're selling the others?" he said caustically, casting his eye over similar versions of the painting on the other walls."

"Well, yes," Dan replied sheepishly. "The neo-zeitgeist must be appeased after all."

The larger of the diptych, that Dan was never going to sell, was roughly the same size as the Mondrian, Riven thought to himself. That was suspicious… wasn't it? "You say this only arrived this afternoon?"

Dan nodded. "I shipped the collection myself earlier today and then made my way over here. And I'm also painting a new piece just for this exhibition." He nodded back at the canvas in progress on the table.

"Including your, um, diptych?"

"Until this morning, it was hung on my studio wall, in pride of place."

Riven reached out to the larger of the two paintings, letting his hand run up the edge of the canvas, his fingers sliding over the metal pins holding it in place on the wooden frame.

"Please… do not touch," Dan said. "I only let Jen hang these as she is an expert art handler."

Jen smiled and made a heart shape with her hands. "I thank you from the bottom of my heart." She fluttered her fingers as if throwing the heart to Dan, who caught it and held it close to him.

"I will treasure it forever."

What was wrong with Jen? Riven thought. She was a snarky, intelligent, no-nonsense girl. This was nothing like her. Unless…? He swallowed heavily. Unless she'd fallen for him. Dan was an idiot, that much was for sure, but a successful and very possibly, soon to be very rich, idiot. "Bugger it!" he whispered under his breath. There was a distinct possibility that he was now not only trying to find the stolen Mondrian to appease Landa and save his bacon, but to also impress Jen. The question was… how on earth was he going to do that?

As his brain struggled to come up with any useful or relevant answers, his phone rang. Landa again. Although the phone's buzzing seemed more restrained.

"Hello," he said. "Where did you get to? I came to the gallery, and you were not here."

"No. I'm at a bar about a twenty-minute walk away. I thought perhaps, you could come and maybe have a drink with me?"

Landa didn't sound herself at all. What was wrong with the girl. "Is everything alright? Are you okay?"

"Yes, yes, I'm fine. But you need to get here as soon as, okay? Will you promise me?"

"Yeah. Sure. Of course. You ring and I jump. I know the drill."

"Now don't be like that. I'll see you soon."

She gave him the name of the bar and offed the phone.

"Who was that?" said Jen.

"Landa. She wanted me to go and have a drink with her."

"I still can't believe that you and her…"

"You're not jealous, are you?"

"Don't be ridiculous."

"I'd better be off. I'll see you later perhaps?"

Jen said nothing, turning back to Dan and his new painting.

When Riven arrived at the bar a short time later, he was met by a burly looking bouncer. "Sorry mate, the bar is temporarily closed to punters. Okay?"

"Oh," but I was supposed to meet someone in here. You

can't miss her. A stunning girl all in red."

"You Mr Riven?"

"My father is Mr Riven, but I suppose in this instance, yes, he is me."

"Huh?"

"Yes, I'm Mr Riven."

"Good, you're expected. They're sitting in the back."

"They?"

The man said nothing and opened the door for him to enter.

The place was a typical London pub, cheesily decorated, and smelling of stale lager and hopelessness. He stumbled inside, his eyes adjusting to the dark and made his way to the back where there was a raised area and inbuilt seating. Here sat Landa, looking very demure in her latest crimson-themed ensemble. Sitting next to her, was the complete opposite. A weird-looking crumple of a man in a very expensive suit that somehow didn't suit him. He did a double take. The man was Roo Osbourne.

PLAYING FOR TIME

"**HELLO MR RIVEN,** we meet at last," Roo Osbourne said, standing up to shake his hand. Riven tried not to stare at the man's famously tiny hands but couldn't stop himself.

"Please sit down," Roo said. "And close your mouth, mate. It's hanging open."

"Sorry, um, yeah, okay," Riven replied, sitting opposite. He was a table's width away from Roo Osbourne, and it felt dreadfully too close for any human being to be.

"I've brought you here to thank you in person," Roo began. "My lovely daughter tells me you've been helping her retrieve my stolen Mondrian."

Riven blushed. "Yeah, I've been doing that, yeah."

"And that congratulations are in order?"

Riven was confused. He looked at Landa for a clue and could see that she was willing him to answer, but what should he say? "We're not engaged… are we?" he joked, regretting it immediately.

"No, silly," Yolanda said. "I told you he was funny, Daddy. Always playing the fool. Daddy wants to congratulate you on finding his stolen painting. Congratulations!"

Riven played the sentence through his mind. Once, twice, three times. What the what?

"Are you feeling okay, Mr Riven?" Roo Osbourne asked with a smile so vicious that it probably carried a flick-knife.

Time slowed. What on earth was Landa playing at? She might be able to lie to Roo Osbourne and get away with it but Riven surely couldn't. Could he? And what was with Landa anyway? She was acting all girlie and weird. This wasn't the Landa he knew. Not at all.

"Daddy is very busy, so I've volunteered to look after the return of the Mondrian. To get everything sorted and shipped," she continued gallantly.

Landa was obviously playing for time. But this was a very dangerous game. Roo gave him a threatening look. A look that said you better tell the truth otherwise you're in a heap of dingo droppings, mate, a heap of dingo droppings I'm going to personally ensure you are forced to eat.

Landa on the other hand was beautiful, beguiling and wanting Riven to lie through his teeth to one of the most dangerous men on the planet. Her face pleaded with him. She had faith that he wouldn't let her down, faith that he would lie to her father, but more than that, she had absolute faith in him, in Jim Riven. It shocked him to his core. No one had ever had this much belief in him at any part of his life whatsoever and yet, Landa, the girl he'd been so pleased to get out of his life, absolutely did. That meant something, even if she was loopier than the world's most loopiest rollercoaster ride. And for reasons only known to the machinations of his chronically undernourished psyche, Riven made very much the wrong decision.

"Thank you," he heard himself saying. "I'm not what you call a traditional investigator, but it all came right in the end. Glad to have been of help."

Landa clapped her hands together in front of her face like a devout nun happily squashing a series of heretic insects. "You see, Daddy, I told you Riven sorted it out. There's nothing to worry about. Panic over."

"That painting represents a considerable financial investment," Roo said, his small, eyes focused very much on Riven. "The thought that it was stolen annoys me. And I hope you can understand how much I do not like to be annoyed."

"Everything is under control honestly, Daddy. You don't need to worry about it. I'm sorry for taking your painting in the first place. That was so stoopid of me. And that's stoopid, with two Os. I shouldn't have done it, but, phew, thanks to Riv, it's back at the gallery and everything is now sorted."

Roo wasn't convinced. Not in the slightest and Riven felt a chill not so much as enter his bones, but repeatedly stab into them.

"You understand that this is my daughter, and I will forgive her anything? Even lying," Roo said, leaning aggressively towards him.

"But I'm not lying, Daddy."

Roo ignored her heartfelt plea. "But I will not suffer lies from anyone else. No matter their relationship with anyone from my family. I trust my daughter to the ends of the Earth, but I will not have her made a fool of or used by others for financial gain. So, James Aurelius Riven, I will ask you again, has my Mondrian been found?"

Landa's eyes were like stalks, her impressive bosom heaving.

"Yes." Riven replied.

"Will you tell me who stole it?"

Now he'd started, Riven found himself lying like it was out of fashion. "I'm afraid I can't do that. My investigations led to the return of the painting unexpectedly. I am trying my best to find out who was responsible. I succeeded partly because of your daughter's persistence but mainly because of my own investigations. Your Mondrian is back in the gallery. And…," he added realising almost immediately that Roy Osborne was a player of the very first order and trying to fool him was one of the most stupidest things he'd ever done in his short life, "…I call that a result."

"I told you, Daddy," Landa said, "Riven is absolutely brilliant, isn't he? Absolutely. He's the very, very, *very* best." She sounded like she believed it, which was more than Roo Osbourne did.

"You may think that, my love," Roo said with a hint of resignation, "but you are far more trusting than is good for you. I have a different view on the world. I've shielded you. Kept you away from the reality of it. The real world is full of predators. And predators come in many different guises."

"Riven isn't a predator, Daddy. He just isn't."

"You need to become aware that—because of who you are—you will attract freeloaders and chancers. Like that Monty you are wasting money on. He lost his fortune through greed and arrogance, and yet you are squandering your allowance on him."

"Monty is my bestest. I love him Daddy. If you only got to know him, you'd—"

Roo lifted a hand and Landa stopped speaking immediately.

More than anything else Riven had seen tonight, or read about the man previously, that one gesture convinced him of the man's singular and absolute power.

"Let me tell you what we're going to do, Mr Riven," Roo said. "We are going to get up, go outside and get into my very expensive custom built Rolls Royce Ghost. Then we are going to drive in absolute hand-crafted comfort to Monty's gallery, where you will show me my returned Mondrian. You understand me?"

Riven gulped. Of course, Roo Osbourne would want to see his painting. Of course, he would! What had he been thinking?

Roo's gaze fixed upon Riven, and it was a not a gaze that anyone anywhere in any life, on any planet of the solar system, in any galaxy or anywhere else in the universe should ever have to endure. "And if for any reason my painting is not where you say it is, and I find that you have been lying to me, to my actual face, things will not go very well for you. Do we understand each other, Mr Riven?"

Riven nodded.

"Good. Now when are you going to close your mouth?"

THWACK!

GROSVENOR PAID THE driver, got out of the taxi, and found himself standing outside the Outtasight! gallery.

The last time he'd been here was in a different century. And yet, the place was no different, paying homage to the gallery as it was in the 60s. Every detail of the frontage was as he remembered it. Down to the Outtasight! logo and the yellow winking smiley face.

A shiver passed through him and for a few moments he was back there. Back in his youth, back outside the gallery. The moment evaporated as soon as it had arrived and, shaking his head as if to rid it of a troublesome strand of hair, Grosvenor pushed open the gallery door. Inside, all similarity ended. The interior followed the same design as he remembered but the so-called artworks were very different. He was from a less pretentious time and what he saw here was overblown and ostentatious. But it mattered not. This was not what he'd come here for. The visit from the grandchild of his greatest muse had brought back many memories and he fancied seeing the old place again, before he lost any more marbles. The bag was already half-empty as it was…

"Hello!" he shouted, his voice still pleasantly booming.

No answer. He rapped his heavy cane on the counter.

"Hello!"

Shrugging, he made his way inside, marvelling that his intimate knowledge of this building hadn't deserted him. His nurse had had the audacity to tell him he was going nowhere today. That he was having one of his bad days. What did she know? If I was that far gone, I wouldn't have been able to sneak out so easily.

He found his way to the steps that led down to the under-gallery. Was that jazz he could hear playing? And the chatter of voices? The music faded in and out on the edge of his hearing.

I'm late for the party, he thought. He stood still for a few moments. Is there a party? No. I'm daydreaming again. "Get a grip, Grosvenor!"

He made his way down the steps, hoping to meet Rosie. She loved a party and jazz was her thing. Not all this modern rock an' roll.

As he reached the bottom of the stairs, the music stopped, and he came back to himself again. "There is no Rosie," he whispered. "Not anymore. She's dead." He cursed his malfunctioning brain, but for a few moments she was alive again and waiting for him. That was better than now. Than this.

Perhaps the nurse had been right. Perhaps this was a mistake. But I'm here now and Rosie will be disappointed if I leave.

He made quick progress walking past the smaller gallery rooms, his heavy cane clicking on the concrete floor until he arrived in the under-gallery. Tables and chairs were laid out, balloons and bottles of Champagne. But where was everyone? Had he arrived early? He was sure he had heard music and voices.

"Rosie!" he called. "Rosie where are you."

"Ooh, hello," a voice said behind him.

Grosvenor turned towards the voice and immediately bristled. "Tarquin! What are you doing here?"

“No, no,” Dan said. “I’m Dan.” He offered his hand. “Dan Kowalski, and you are…”

Grosvenor took a step back. He was frightened, confused. “Where’s Rosie, Tarquin? What have you done with her?”

“Hang on… I think I know you. You’re Grosvenor! Wow! I’ve always been such a great fan of your work. Until, well, all that stuff that came out. What are you doing here? You haven’t come for a sneak preview of my exhibition, have you? I suppose to come in person to the opening night would be awkward for you. But I’m wittering—”

Thwack! Grosvenor hit Dan with his cane.

“Ow! What the hell!” Dan shouted.

“I won’t let you take her, Tarquin! Not again!”

“Get off me you old—”

THWACK!

THE THROWBACK

THE TRIP TO the gallery in Roo's custom built Rolls Royce Ghost was a depressingly slow one. Traffic in London was such that cars had become climate altering, slow-moving prisons. The Rolls was a showy, decadent, ostentatious gas-guzzler, but Riven couldn't fault the engineering. It was beautiful. A real shame that he was riding in it under these circumstances, with the weight of the world and Roo Osbourne on his shoulders. They could've walked to the gallery and back again a few times at the rate they were going. But it was the silence that was doing Riven's head in. The horrible silence of it.

Riven sat behind the driver, facing the impassive, yet still somehow condescending and threatening face of Roo Osbourne and the sometimes frightened, sometimes hopeful face of Landa. She was a beauty, there could be no mistake. How she came from the loins of the man sitting next to her was beyond him. Riven had never seen Roo Osbourne up close before. There was something off about him. Suddenly, the phrase, 'The throwback from the Outback' jumped into his mind and he had to stifle a nervous giggle. But Roo *was* a throwback, he was sure of it. A long-lost primeval ancestor who was bred out of existence by the more successful Homo-Sapiens. He suspected that the man was the result of all those non-dominant genes suddenly getting a one-in-a-billion evolutionary chance. Obviously, those same genes were no match to the dominant genes of Landa's also absolutely stunning mother. Which was good news for Riven's ex-girlfriend.

He texted Jen to tell them they were coming, with Roo's approval of course, after which Riven had tried the dreaded small talk. But it seemed Roo was as much in love with the concept as Riven usually was. He gave Riven the barest shakes of his head, and they were forced to sit in a stern, overbearing quiet. Like one of those awful silences you occasionally endured at school when the headmistress gathered everyone into the main hall and wouldn't let you go home until someone owned up. The man was a brute. No doubt about it.

Time rushed by with a dreadful sluggishness before, finally, the magnificent vehicle pulled up outside the Outtasight! gallery.

Electric doors opened automatically and Roo and Landa got out. Riven wanted to stay where he was. He wanted the doors to close and for the fantastic automobile to power away. To the airport perhaps. A trip to a faraway land seemed like a good idea just now. And perhaps a change of identity.

"No shilly-shallying Mr Riven," Roo said, and he was forced to extricate himself from the fabulous vehicle.

"Circle the block, Stephen," Roo ordered the chauffeur. "I've got a feelin' this won't take very long. After you, Mr Riven."

There was nothing else for it. He had to face the music. "Let's get this over with." Riven lifted his head high, stuck out his chest and marched into the gallery like he was on a mission.

The entrance area was still too bright, but he paid it no attention. Jen was nowhere to be seen. Good, he didn't want her to witness his humiliation. They arrived at the steps to the under gallery and were met with shouting voices from below. Two men in an argument. Dan and someone else, someone familiar, although Riven couldn't place him. Suddenly everything became quiet. Riven jogged down the stairs, Roo and Landa following.

This is it, he thought to himself. This is what your machismo led you into, Jim Riven. If you'd just ignored Landa at that party, none of this would've happened. A strange feeling washed over him. What was going to happen in a few moments time was going to be a total disaster, no doubt about it, but the fear and the horror left him. The lack of doubt and the absolute certainty of catastrophe suddenly freed his mind. Perhaps this is how people felt when they knew their time was up, that they were going to die? It was a maudlin thought granted, but he found that he didn't care. What would certainly happen, would certainly happen. And that was that.

They walked past the outer rooms and turned into the under-gallery.

This was it. This was actually it…

He heard a gasp of surprise from Landa and looked up. Framed on the far wall, in pride of place, was Roo Osbourne's missing Mondrian.

JUMBLING

MINUTES BEFORE THE entrance of Roo Osbourne and the soon-to-be astounded Riven, Grosvenor found himself lost, confused, but ecstatic and elated. Tarquin lay unconscious on the gallery floor. All he needed now was to find Rosie.

The sound of approaching footsteps. He looked down at Tarquin. A large purple bruise swelled on his forehead. But it wasn't Tarquin, was it? Everything was so mixed up. What on earth have I done? They'll put me away in a home… or a prison. I'll never get to see Rosie again.

Thoughts fought with one another, jumbling around his skull, until one thought became louder than all others.

GOLD-DIGGERS

AN EXPRESSION OF disappointment crossed Roo's face to be replaced by one of grudging admiration, the unused muscles straining awkwardly like an over-thirty-something's back when reaching for the remote they've dropped behind the sofa.

"He did it Daddy! Riven did it! I knew he would. I just knew it. Just like he found Mummy's missing Fabergé earring!"

"Her what?"

"Nothing Daddy, nothing. Oh Riven!" Landa was literally jumping for joy.

"Now, now, Landy," Roo said. "Don't make me think you're surprised by this. You assured me it would be here, remember?"

"Of course, Daddy, of course. But to see it again. I'm just so thrilled!"

Roo wasn't convinced, but he knew when he'd been outplayed. "You astound me, Mr Riven," he said, glancing at the Mondrian and its trellis of black lines and blocks of yellow, red, and blue. "And that is a rare experience for me. Well done, mate. Well done indeed." He turned to leave. "I'll get someone to come and pick up my property within the hour. The Mondrian's going back to my vault and staying there. Goodbye Landy."

"Goodbye Daddy!" she hugged him, and even though the

man looked and sounded like a brute, Riven could see the love he had for his daughter. It was probably why she'd turned out the way she had. He was sure she'd had everything and anything she'd wanted as a child. Landa had taken his priceless Mondrian, got it stolen and embroiled him in tonight's events, and yet he'd already forgiven her. That much was obvious.

"You will be hearing from me very soon, Mr Riven." Roo said after Landa had disentangled herself from him. And for the first time this evening, Roo Osbourne was not threatening him.

After Roo had left the under-gallery, Riven was hit by a wave of shock. His legs went wobbly, and his stomach felt like a swarm of very angry bees had set up home in it, had a wild housewarming party, drank a lot, danced a lot, had a few fights, and then suddenly all went to bed for a much needed lie down. The last thing he had expected was for the Mondrian to be back in the gallery, just like Landa had told her father it would be. Like he had told him. Landa had trusted Riven. In fact, when he thought about it, all the way through this, she'd been in no doubt whatsoever that he'd come through for her. This made him love her that tiny little bit more. Not enough to want to go out with her again, God forbid. She was a special person… but in her own special way that required quite a sizable distance to enjoy.

Nevertheless, he'd done absolutely nothing and yet the Mondrian had returned as if by magic. He was elated. The painting was back, Landa was off his back, and he could go back home and have a special treat. Curry in bed!

Riven went over to the Mondrian and touched the canvas. It was definitely the real deal. Up this close, it was kinda magnificent. He knew nothing about the artist or his influence on twentieth-century art when he was forcibly woken this morning, but now, it spoke to him. It really was something special.

"I told you it was a beaut!" Landa said, hugging him again,

her girlie voice now gone and back to its more raucous adult tones. "If I wasn't already spoken for, then I'd show you my thanks in that very special way that I know you like."

Riven blushed. "But you are spoken for. Is he a good guy?"

"He's rich. So not a gold-digger."

"But is he a good guy?"

"Yeah, I think he is."

"Good for you."

"And he's got such a lovely fat—"

The rest of this conversation was thankfully cut short by a loud exclamation. "Effin' hell! It's back, innit!"

Monty stood at the back of the gallery. He looked a bedraggled figure, still wearing his carpet-off cut clothing, although it looked like a dog had slept on it and then used it as a chew toy. The hat had also been lost somewhere on the way. He stepped forward, staring in disbelief at the Mondrian, his eyebrows jumping up and down like two elegantly styled trampolining caterpillars.

"Riven did it!" Landa squawked proudly. "He found it!"

"Riven?" he said incredulously, his gaze not leaving the painting. "Where on earth was it, tho?"

"Um, well, that would be um telling," Riven replied.

"I suppose I should thank you," he said, his eyes finally finding him.

"He'll be thanked alright!" Landa blurted. "Daddy was very impressed."

Monty sat down on a chair and rubbed his head in his hands. "Thank the effin' eff."

Landa went over to him. "Daddy also talked about you and the Outtasight! He was very strict with me about it. I'm going to have to sell my share of the gallery."

Monty freed his head from his hands and nodded. "Yeah, I guessed as much, innit?"

"And he won't let me help you anymore. He's kind of blaming you for the whole thing. But I made him promise. No lawyers. You're off the hook but I can't do anything else. He's tied my hands"

Monty shrugged. "I knew he'd win in the end, innit?"

"What does that mean?" Landa said, confused.

"Nothin'. It's all over. Effin' everythin'."

"What will you do?" Landa asked, and Riven could see she had genuine affection for the guy. The fact she couldn't help him was crucifying her. "Maybe you can go and stop at Harve's? I never trusted the guy but—"

"I'm afraid not. That's over, innit."

"Oh no, but you loved him. Didn't you?"

Monty nodded his head, tears in his eyes. "He was a gold-digger. Jen told me. A conman. But I knew it anyway tho. The guy was so effin' useless at it that it kinda endeared him to me. I was just fooling myself, like I have been since I lost everything. He didn't know I was a loser. It was fun keeping him around while he thought I was still somebody. Until I found out the lying git had an effin' girlfriend. That was too much to bear."

"I saw Harve a while ago," Riven said. "He was a bit of a mess and did seem genuinely cut up about your split. I think the guy loved you. That's what he said anyway. Not that he deserves you."

"No way. He just loves himself."

"That's where you're wrong, Monty. I do love you. I love you very much."

Riven was startled to see Harve standing behind them. He seemed somehow taller. Confident. Like a cat who had not only got the cream, but who had also bought the local dairy.

"Get out of my sight!" Monty snapped. "I've lost everything. There's nothing left for you to take."

"It doesn't matter. I came back to ask you something."

"Just go, innit!"

"No, Monty." Harve took out a ring case and opened it, revealing an impressive diamond. "I bought this with all my money. Everything I've been saving. I cashed it all in and left

Sheila. I told her the reason why. I've fallen in love with you, Monty, and I want to be with you forever." He went down on one knee. "Monty Fitzhugh… will you… will you marry me?"

Monty was confused. "You're asking me what? Innit?"

"I want you to be my husband."

"But I don't have a penny to rub together. I'm skint, Harve. Have you lost your mind? I'm no use to you or anybody, innit?"

"I don't care that you have no money. It doesn't matter to me. Nothing does. Only how I feel about you. How we feel about each other. I can't fake that, and you know it."

"But—"

"But nothing. Now, what do you say?"

"Yes," Monty whispered. "Yes," he repeated, his voice getting stronger. "Of course, I effin' will. I love you, innit!" He flung himself into Harve's arms and they hugged and kissed.

If Landa had been excited by the return of the Mondrian, she now went into ballistic overdrive. "Daddy said I couldn't help with Monty or the gallery, but nothing will stop me organising and paying for your wedding. Nothing! You're going to have the best day ever. And for the honeymoon, I'll fly you anywhere in the world."

Harve shook his head. "I'm afraid I can't let you do that, Landa," he said, standing up and pulling Monty up with him.

"Why not?" Monty replied, a little crestfallen.

"Don't let pride get in the way," Landa said. "I don't want to be rude, but you were a gold-digger, out for what you could get, so I don't understand why you would turn down my offer now."

Monty's face revealed he was thinking the same.

"I have a confession." Harve said, smiling. "It's… well, it's a big one." He took a deep breath. "It was me."

"It was you what?" Monty replied. "You didn't steal the Mondrian… did you?"

"Is this true?" Landa said, her voice suddenly accusing.

Harve raised his hands. "No. I didn't steal your painting.

That kind of thing is way out of my league. I mean look at what I was doing. Fleecing money out of nice guys like Monty. I'm was a small-time idiot."

"Then what?" Landa asked and Riven was also intrigued to hear his answer.

"It's been in the news all week," Harve said.

"What has?" Monty asked.

"The missing lottery ticket for the largest jackpot in Lotto history. All those millions. It was me! I had it in my jacket pocket all this time and didn't know it was there. I nearly lost the thing. But Riven saw me drop it, picked it up and gave it back to me, for which I can never thank him enough. If he hadn't… it doesn't bear thinking about. But I'm now a multi-multi-millionaire!"

"Whaaat!" both Landa and Monty intoned.

"Yep. I'm just back from verification and emptying my savings account, and of course, buying this ring. I can't believe it. But don't you see Monty? You're back in the bigtime. I don't want any pre-nup. When we're married half that money is yours and we can do what we want with it. And I want you to help me move into this new life of money. But no investing, okay?"

After that the conversation turned into screams, shouts, and tears. Riven was also stunned. Harve, a millionaire! It was a nice move to ask Monty to marry him before revealing that news.

"We're all going out to celebrate!" Landa announced at the top of her voice. My treat! Come on Riv. We'll even go to a place where they'll make your much-loved Jalfrezi."

"No."

"Riven you have to come with us."

"No."

"You're coming and that's that. We have so much to celebrate."

"No, Landa."

Landa had always had trouble with this particular word, and Riven was forced to use it a few more times for it to properly sink in. "I'm not going anywhere. I'm staying here with the Mondrian. I'm not letting it out of my sight until it has been picked up by your father. You can understand why, yeah?"

"I should never have let you get away—you know that?" Landa said, leaning over to kiss him on the cheek. "But of course, stay and guard the Mondrian. You are my little soldier, aren't you?" And with that, and a helluva lot of squealing, shouting, and singing, they left Riven on his own with the returned Mondrian.

REVOLVER

RIVEN HAD NOT been lying when he told Landa that he wanted to stay and keep an eye on the Mondrian. Someone had to step up and show a bit of sense, but more than that, he was totally perplexed by its reappearance. It had been, well, almost too perfect. He'd been hoping for some miracle all the time he sat in the back of Roo's Rolls, and the last thing he'd expected was for that miracle to actually be delivered. Things didn't normally happen like that for him. The coincidence thing never worked in his favour, or nearly always didn't. Sure, he found out his nan had had a racy past and that wasn't a negative coincidence, but it was neither particularly positive either. The Mondrian being returned as he had fervently hoped for was uber-positive and it worried him. These things tended to come with a balancing negative. He put that thought at the back of his mind and concentrated on the Mondrian.

Recent events had somewhat blurred his memory, but he was sure that he'd heard two voices arguing, one of them Dan Kowalski and another familiar voice, before he, Roo and Landa descended into the under gallery. If so, where were they and, for the matter, where was Dan's diptych?

He gave the whole under gallery a quick search. Dan wasn't here and the outer doors were still locked and chained. It seemed to him that one mystery had been solved and another created.

And where was Jen? He really wanted to see her to show off his success with the Mondrian, and to use that success to ask her out. Unless she was the one who had found and re-hung the painting? But if she had done, the first person she would've called was Monty, so that was unlikely.

He wondered where Jen had gotten to. He'd expected to find her waiting for them when Roo arrived. But on second thoughts, a tactical withdrawal was probably the better move. Especially when it came to Roo Osbourne. He took out his phone to text her about the return of the Mondrian when his phone buzzed. A message from Dillon.

You in the gallery mate?

Yeah

I'm outside

You're here?

Yeah? Can I come in. I saw that Roo Osbourne fella leave in that posh motor of his, and then Landa and Monty. I thought I'd check you were here before barging inside

I am here

Yeah

Yeah

A few minutes later he heard Dillon's dulcet tones above. "Riven, where are you?"

"Down here."

Dillon finally appeared. "Oh, there you are. This place is a bleeding maze. And why is it so bright?" His eyes found the far wall and the Mondrian. "Is that what I think it is?"

"Yeah."

"You only bloody found it then?"

"Not really. Although I'm trying my best to take the credit."

"And it's worth millions?"

"Yeah, many of them and then some."

"It ain't up to much."

"I used to think the same, but it's grown on me. I think it's kind of brilliant. Now what are you doing here, Dillon? You do realise this is well south of the Thames. I hope you brought your passport?"

"It's that antique revolver, the photo you sent me."

"What about it?"

"I really wanted to take a look at it myself."

"Why's that?"

"Well," he began excitedly, "it looked like one of the missing Navy Colt 44s on the photo you sent. And if that is the case, it'll be a find and a half."

Riven drew breath to speak, but Dillon cut him off.

"It's the one with the five-cartridge chamber, and the bevelled barrel that is half an inch longer than other models. Sure, it had a bigger failure rate, but it was one of the most accurate handguns Colt ever produced. There was a problem with the production line that, by the time it was solved, Colt had moved on to the more popular and iconic, 45 pistol. But it's the 44s that collectors like me go nuts for, mainly because they're so rare. I just need a looksee at the serial number. Where is it?"

Riven hardly ever got annoyed with Dillon, but he'd had a long day and his obsession with guns was something he just couldn't connect with. He thought he may have found a clue or something. Not this nonsense. "You've come all this way just for that?" he blurted testily.

"Well, not just that," Dillon answered a little defensively. "But, yeah, mainly. I also rescued that dissertation thingy for you." He stuck out a chubby hand in which was Jen's missing flash-drive. "Did you want this back? It still dun't work. Totally knackered. But I've emailed the fixed Word file to you. Should be on your phone."

Riven took the flash-drive and the anger and irritation left him. He couldn't be annoyed with Dillon. He'd do anything for Riven, and had stopped everything to fix a file that, in the scheme of things, wasn't that important, although it might help mend the rift between him and Jen. Ten years too late, but even so.

"I didn't read it but it's all about Mondrian. Lots of photos of his paintings but too much writing. A case of TLDR;"

Riven had no idea what his mate was on about but nodded like he understood the acronym.

"So where is this lovely old Colt?"

"Over there."

Riven showed him the revolver screwed into the gallery wall.

"Oh yeah, wow!" Dillon exclaimed. "That's a Navy 44 alright. I knew it! And the five-cartridge chamber is still intact—it was replaced with the six chamber on a lot of them. Amazing!"

"It's worth a lot then?"

Dillon nodded vigorously. "Yeah, five, maybe six-hundred pounds."

Riven was less than impressed. "Is that all?"

"You don't understand, do you? It's not about the value, it's about the find. There's a list of missing serial numbers for all the Navy Colt 44s ever produced, if I could find one of the missing ones, I'd be a living legend in the community. And hang on, there's a number!" He got in closer to the revolver. "I can see it, but it's—"

Two things happened at once. The revolver attached to the wall depressed, trapping Dillon's finger. He yelled loudly. But Riven didn't notice. The wall where the Mondrian was hung rotated a hundred-and eighty-degrees revealing Dan Kowalski's diptych and the man himself propped up underneath it, a bruise on his head the size of a golf ball.

DISSERTATION

DILLON FREED HIS finger and jumped into action, going over to Dan. "You okay, mate?"

"Um, yeah, sure," he said. "Cool," he added in a sort of a dazed afterthought. "Where am I, man?"

"In the Outtasight! gallery."

"Of course, yeah. Some old bloke with a stick attacked me. Kept calling me Tarquin. Said I'd taken Rosie off him."

Grosvenor! Riven realised. Of course, the other voice.

"And then I passed out I think, or all the lights went out."

Dillon dragged Dan over to one of the chairs and tried to revive him by pouring him day-old, flat champagne.

Riven went over to the revolver and pushed it. The gun sank into the recess and popped back up again, meanwhile the wall silently rotated again, returning the Mondrian.

"Wow," Dillon said. "That's so cool."

"Yeah."

"Yeah."

Dillon left Dan for a moment and clambered up onto the stage. "Try it now, Riv."

Riven depressed the revolver and the wall spun again. A few seconds later, the revolver depressed all on its own and Dillon and the Mondrian reappeared.

"There's a lever on the inside," Dillon proclaimed. "And

the fully exposed mechanism. It's a cool piece of engineering, expertly balanced. It's also been greased, which means someone has been behind there recently. And something else came to me while I was back there…"

"What?"

"Outtasight! Don't you get it?"

Riven did get it. Outtasight! the name of the gallery was the biggest clue of them all! There was no doubt about it, the revolving wall was designed in the 60s to keep the main artwork out of sight until it was ready to be revealed by revolving the wall. And the mechanism? A revolver. It was so obvious.

So that's how they stole the Mondrian, Riven thought to himself. Although it wasn't stolen at all. Just hidden. And that was why the wall was still sticky with paint and why the brushes hadn't been cleaned. Someone had quickly painted the inner wall to match the outer.

Whoever that was.

That someone knew about the wall and flipped it sometime between the gallery closing and when it opened Saturday morning, when it was found 'missing' by Jen. They could even have been hiding in the secret room. And that someone had probably used that old tin of grease he'd knocked over earlier in the day to lubricate the mechanism.

It also appeared Grosvenor knew about the revolving wall as well, seeing that he used it to hide Dan after he was knocked unconscious. It was probably where he and Riven's randy nan used to make out. He said they could hear people nearby.

"The Mondrian was here all the time," Riven said, "it was just hidden from view."

"Was a good plan," Dillon said. "Whoever it was who hid the Mondrian, were onto a good thing."

"Whatdyamean?"

"Well, all they did was hide it. It wasn't stolen, per se," Dillon said, like he was performing a complex Agatha Christie-esque dénouement in a very posh dining room of uppermiddleclass suspects who probably all did it. "All they'd have to do was hope it wasn't discovered and then, at some undisclosed time in the future, pop down, revolve the wall and properly steal the Mondrian. In the meantime, they've no connection to the disappearance. No evidence linking them to it. Nothing."

"But who?"

"I suppose we won't find out who that is now the cat's out of the bag."

"I suppose not." Riven sat down and sighed. The Mondrian was back, Riven was in Roo Osbourne's good books and even Monty was back on his feet with Harve. But nothing felt resolved. There was more to this than just a simple revolving wall but… what?

After Dillon had insisted on taking Dan to the local Accident & Emergency hospital, Riven had stayed behind, dutifully waiting for Roo Osbourne's men to pick up the Mondrian. When they arrived, they were led by a short fat man dressed in an impressive suit with bowtie and tails.

"Are you Jim Riven?" he asked in a broad Birmingham accent.

"I suppose I am," Riven replied. "You been sent by Roo Osbourne?"

"You guess correctly," the man replied.

"You are looking very dandy," Riven added. "Is this in honour of Piet Mondrian or something?"

"Not quite, but when Roo Osbourne calls, you answer. No matter what you had planned. Even if you had promised your wife an evening at the opera and a romantic dinner afterwards. I'm Colin Artman, his in-house art expert."

"Artman?"

"A Scottish surname and, yes, it is rather apt. Although I do tire of having to talk about it every time I meet someone new. I can get a bit sketchy."

It took Riven a few moments for his beleaguered brain to register the pun. "Oh, right. Very funny."

"Thanks. It can take a while for some people to get the picture."

"Well, there's the Mondrian," Riven said, feeling the need to point it out, hoping that Colin wouldn't hit him with any more of his awful jokes.

Colin Artman stood back and admired the painting for a few moments. "Wow. Just wow. I advised Mr Osbourne to purchase this piece when it came up for auction a few months ago. It is a masterwork. I know it intimately. And how wonderful to see it displayed in this amazing room." He went over to the far wall and examined the Mondrian. "Yes, yes," he muttered. "There can be no doubt. This is Mr Osbourne's painting. A superb example of the master at his best. Is it to your tastes?"

"I didn't think it would be, but it's very much grown on me."

"This particular piece had been missing for nearly half a century until it turned up in an old, abandoned gallery storage room. That was quite some find I can tell you. I advised Mr Osbourne not to wait around and to make an offer and to buy it immediately, which to his credit, is exactly what he did. I wanted him to exhibit it, but he was only interested in its value as an investment and so, sadly, it was put into storage." He lowered his voice. "I have to give his daughter credit for her audacious move, she at least knows her art, although I heard that the painting had been involved in some sort of heist?"

"Sort of," Riven replied.

"Roo Osbourne has a fabulous collection of artworks. I keep trying to get him to loan it to galleries or even take it on the road, but no." He signalled to the two men who accompanied him to take down the painting, which they duly did, wrapping it in plastic and carting it away. "Such a shame," Colin said. "It's back off into storage. But it's been a pleasure to see it so excellently mounted." He extended a white-gloved hand and bowed. "Goodbye, Mr Riven."

"Um… goodbye."

He turned and left.

And that, Riven thought to himself was that.

Once back on his own again, Riven revolved the wall one last time, Dan's diptych taking its place at the centre of the under gallery which now seemed an empty, lacklustre place with the Mondrian taken away.

He texted Jen.

> The Mondrian was found and has been returned to Roo Osbourne!!!

No reply.

> I've closed the gallery and switched off all the lights. That took a while I can tell you! I've pulled down the front auto-locking shutter, so the gallery is safe

Still no reply.

> In other news Dan was taken to A&E with a bump to the head, but I think he'll be okay. He was lucid. Well, as lucid as he can be

Nothing.

> Jen!!! I've not heard from you since I texted about Roo Osbourne's visit. Let me know you are okay. I'm worried

He waited outside for a few moments, staring at the screen,

relieved to finally see the interim message *Jen is typing* before a reply landed.

All okay

Was that it? He waited for a clarification. Nothing. Sighing, he made his way to the tube.

By the time he arrived back at his Camden flat, he was knackered. His plan of curry in bed went out of the window. He was too tired. Instead, he made himself a slice of toast and almost fell asleep eating it in the kitchen.

He awoke with a start early Sunday morning. He was sure his phone had buzzed with an important message from someone. Jen, he was hoping. But nothing. Instead, was yesterday's unopened email from Dillon. Attached to it was Jen's dissertation entitled *The Missing Mondrian*: *Fantasy or theory?* He looked at the time. It wasn't even 7am. Not even close to bloody 7am. Yesterday had really buggered up his biorhythms, and Riven's biorhythms were sacrosanct. As a result, he couldn't get back to sleep. What he needed was something boring to watch or to read. He lay back on his pillows, tapped at his phone, and opened Jen's dissertation. I may learn something, he mused, scanning through the introduction and sitting bolt upright.

IN THE HALLS OF VALHALLA

RIVEN HAD SPENT his time after reading Jen's dissertation lying wide awake in bed and thinking things through. Thinking things through had never been one of Riven's strong points. He was of the opinion that going with his gut was the better option. And despite how going with his gut had never really worked out for him, he always went with his gut anyway. Indeed, when he had a choice of going with his gut or not going with his gut, Riven very much went with his gut. Today would be no different, but going with his gut meant he really, really, *really* needed to think things through for a change.

That is why, at 11am Monday morning, a long time before his normal waking time, he found himself sitting in the outer office of one Roo Osbourne on the fifty-third floor of the ostentatious Central London Roo Corps Tower. It was one of those hermetically sealed, glass and aluminium outer offices you could build a sizable house in. Not that you'd want to live there. It was nearly sixty floors above ground level, which meant that popping out to the shops was a six-act drama with far too many intermissions. And just how would he get a curry delivered? Impossible. No, the Roo Corps Tower wasn't the most touchy-feely place. Then again, it suited Roo Osbourne down to the ground. Fifty-three floors down to the ground to be exact.

The doors to Roo's London office were two immense wedges of burnished oak. The kind of doors that wouldn't have been out of place in the Halls of Valhalla, although these were excellently veneered, varnished, and polished to a dazzling sheen, and not covered in blood, vomit, beer and the odd axe, which was the traditional decor for Viking afterlife get-togethers. Riven knew that Roo Osbourne was overcompensating for something, but he wasn't sure what it was. If Riven wanted to impress anybody, huge doors would be well down Riven's list, at the very bottom below owning a red Ferrari, a football team, and building a penis-shaped spaceship. At the top would be employing his own personal curry chef, a Shiraz sommelier, and having a doorman to deal with any unwanted doorbell issues and denying entrance to certain loopy ex-girlfriends.

The vast doors opened and out stepped Sam Smythe. She was surprised to see him, as was he to see her, and came over. Riven shuffled on his seat while she made the long, awkward approach.

"So, you're after your pound of flesh as well, huh?" she said when reaching hearing distance, her tiger tattoo hidden behind a smart business suit.

"I suppose I am," he replied. "I thought things through. Properly. Weighed all the pros and cons and came up with the nuclear option. And you?"

"I'm now working in the media department of Roo Corps. I finally made it."

"You don't think you'd prefer to work for someone else, like, I dunno, Genghis Khan, Pol Pot or Richard Branson? Last time we spoke you were trying to bring Roo Osbourne down?"

Sam Smythe lowered her voice. "He won't live forever, and I'm finally on my way." She held up a keyring. "And I've got myself a brand-new North London pad. Goodbye Jim Riven and good luck."

The door opened and he was ushered forwards by one

of those impossibly attractive women Roo liked to surround himself with. What on earth am I doing? Riven thought, knowing it was far too late to back out now.

He entered the equally impressive office of Roo Osbourne. It sat on the building's corner, floor to ceiling windows giving fantastic views of the Thames, Tower Bridge, the Shard and all those relatively poor people he no doubt loved to lord it over.

The man himself sat at an impressive desk. Riven had seen a lot of *impressive* recently, but he had to admit that on his recent scale of impressiveness, the desk was pretty impressive, and when it came to a more detailed description, he was happy to leave it at that. He was gestured over and took a seat.

"I'm surprised to see you so soon, mate. Very surprised," Roo Osbourne said with a smile.

"That makes two of us."

"Fair play. Yolanda likes you, Mr Riven, she likes you very much. And, apart from the way you dress and generally live your life, you are a not a bad guy."

"You had me investigated?"

"Of course, I had you investigated. When you and Yolanda were, shall we put it, at it like knives."

"Oh."

"Yes, her little girl act doesn't fool me. She's a healthy young woman and healthy young women have healthy young women needs. I'm no prude, Mr Riven. I'm many other things, but you don't get where I am today without having an innate understanding of human nature. Now, before we start, Yolanda is seeing someone, and I believe you know who. I want you to tell me who they are as a sign of trust."

"I don't know them, or their name but I know of them."

A pause.

"Well go on then. Tell me."

All Riven knew was that Landa's new lover was an architect friend of her father's, but he wasn't about to divulge that to the man himself. Landa had shown real faith in him earlier and besides, to do so would be bad form. Then again, he'd come here for a favour and annoying Roo Osbourne before they'd even started was not the way he wanted this to go. He took a deep breath. "No."

"No?"

"Landa's my friend. We didn't make it as, ahem, a couple, but you don't rat out friends. Even to Roo Osbourne. But you know that because you know exactly who she's going out with, don't you?"

"That's astute, but yeah, of course I do. That was a little test that you passed. Well done."

"She likes him," Riven said.

Roo shrugged.

"She does. Don't interfere."

"I'm afraid you're not in a position to tell me what I can or can't do to the lover of my daughter, no matter how much I may be in your debt."

"Leave them be.'

"I'm my own boss, Mr Riven. And I'll take my own advice. Now, why are you here?"

"Yesterday and this morning, I did a lot of thinking."

Roo raised his eyebrows.

"A lot of things fell into place. Like how it was you who bankrupted Monty."

"So, what if I did?"

"He's learned his lesson, I'm sure of it."

"But the man is still an idiot!"

"You will not find me in disagreement with your assessment, but he's harmless."

"Again, I'll take my own advice on that. Now stop stalling and get down to it. I owe you a favour, but don't push your luck. What do you want?"

"It's something that you will find particularly beneficial."

"What is it? I don't have all bleedin' day."

Riven took a deep breath and told him.

Roo sat back in his chair. “Bloody hell!”

BEAUTIFUL MOMENTS TOGETHER

AFTER TALKING TO Roo Osbourne, Riven stayed in the city, taking in a few sights and inspecting various gourmet, choice, and supreme range sandwiches, waiting for a text from Monty Fitzroy which finally arrived in the afternoon.

> *Landa wtd me 2 tel u wen Dan wl B bk @ d Outtasight. he'll bthere n 30 innit! u effng IckE wnkr!*

Followed by a line of incomprehensible emojis. Monty seemed to be back to his normal cocky self, which was good to see. Riven replied:

> Ta mate. And give my regards to Harve. And I expect an invite to the wedding… INNNIT THO!

And added a random set of emojis because he was in that kind of mood.

Riven made his way to the Outtasight! gallery and to the alley around the back. Here he found a lorry being packed with paintings. The alleyway doors were open, and he walked inside to the under-gallery where he was met by the peculiar scene of a very agitated, screaming Jen and a pleased-looking Dan with a big plaster on his head where Grosvenor had thwacked him.

Riven had checked up on Grosvenor. He had been found wandering and lost a few streets away from the gallery soon after he attacked Dan and was now safe and well and back at his mansion. To Dan's credit, he had decided not to press charges. Riven suspected he had other things on his mind.

Dan stood next to Riven's old friend, Colin Artman, now dressed less formally in jeans and a shirt. Colin's men were also back, busily packing up Dan's paintings that were supposed to form the gallery's next exhibition and taking them out to the truck parked in the alleyway. But it was Jen who drew all the attention.

"How can you!" Jen screamed. "How can you do this!" She stood absolutely still apart from every part of her that shook with rage.

"Calm down, Jen baby," Dan said, seemingly oblivious to her mood. "It's all cool, yeah? Very cool. The coolest."

Jen was aware of Riven's arrival but showed little or no interest in his presence. She was furious and, for such a pencil thin girl, her voice was almost pure broad marker pen. Jen hit Dan with a volley of rather choice and colourful expletives, finishing with, "You're a sell-out Dan! A greedy, self-centred, sell out!"

"Yeah, I am. But I told you, that's part of my art now. A brand-new neo-zeitgeist. I see it, yeah."

"But you're selling your entire collection to Roo Osbourne!"

"Yeah, yeah!" Dan nodded his head in time with his words. "Hundreds of thousands, he's paying. Hundreds of thousands. And with someone like him investing in my work, the Kowalski name is gonna go stratospheric. I mean, it's cool, yeah? Just so cool."

"Are you sure that hit on the head didn't send you crazy? Because what you're doing is insane!" Jen screamed.

"The doc' gave me a clean bill of health. I've got a thick

skull as it happens." He chuckled. "It would be insane to do anything other than sell. You must see that? I can't actually believe it, Jen. And you can be part of my success. For sure."

"No thank you!"

Dan beamed, like he was having an entirely different conversation. "But you wanted us to spend beautiful moments together, remember?"

"Oh, just sod off you pathetic loser!" Jen turned her attention to Colin. "Is Roo Osbourne going to put Dan's collection in storage?"

"My employer is a very intelligent art-buyer and investor," Colin replied tactfully. "And of course, he prefers to protect his investments."

"You see!" Jen screeched, turning back to Dan.

"I understand," Dan said, his vibe seemingly impervious to Jen's anger. "I really do. You're having a bad day. But sometimes you need those bad days, to help you appreciate the good ones, yeah?"

"You think I'm having a bad day? You don't know the half of it!"

Dan shrugged. "You can't afford to limit your joy, Jen. Angry people are never happy people. They're just not. And you don't seem very happy. And you know what they say? …If you lose your temper, you will also lose respect."

Jen let out a frustrated scream, threw up her hands and, angrily pushing past Dan, stormed upstairs.

Dan raised his eyebrows and smirked. "Oh dear. And I tried my best to turn her frown upside down."

Riven wanted to follow Jen, but she was obviously in no mood for more conversation. He decided to let her cool down and to perhaps take her a mug of tea and a conciliatory biscuit.

"That young lady is very passionate about art," Colin said coming over. "And, may I say, she has a fantastic eye."

"Thank you," Dan said, bowing and placing his hands together.

"We're nearly done, just the diptych and a few others," Colin continued.

"Excuse me," said a familiar rough voice, behind them.

Riven turned to see Bill, the rat man, standing next to Joey, his delinquent-looking nephew.

"I'm looking for Monty Fitzhugh or his gallery manager."

"She just went upstairs," Dan said. "She is in quite the mood."

"I did hear shoutin'," Bill said. "I want her permission to take down another wall. You think I should go after her?"

Both Dan and Riven shrugged.

Bill turned to Joey. "You stay here, I'll go and have a chat. An' don't get into any trouble." He went off after Jen.

"I fink I know you," Joey said, going over to Dan. "You're a painter?"

"An artist," Dan replied graciously but with a hint of being slightly miffed.

"I fort so. You were there the day I crashed that tanker into a field." He chuckled at the memory. "I remember you standing there with your mouth hangin' open. You were lucky I didn't crash straight into you. Am I right?"

Dan was suddenly flummoxed and said nothing.

"That was you?" Riven said, also taken aback. "You nearly killed me as well. I wondered what on earth was going on."

"Huh?" Joey said. "I didn't see you. But then again, I ran away from there sharpish."

"You were there as well?" Dan asked, looking Riven up and down as if it was the first time he'd seen him.

"Yeah. I'd been forced to go to a party at one of Landa's overly rich friends," Riven explained. "Her family had a mansion in the deepest countryside. The thing went on into the night. We were on the way back with her and all her drunken friends in some stretch limo when they decided they needed a comfort break and stopped at an all-night garage. I went for a wander, thinking they would be ages, and when I returned, they'd gone off without me. It was a warm summer's evening, so I found a nice place to lie down nearby and went to sleep. Next thing I know, I'm nearly hit by an exploding tanker truck. Shaving foam everywhere. So nothing much out of the norm."

Dan's eyes flicked between Joey and his diptych, and between the stick man and Riven, and drew breath to speak.

"Don't tell me," Riven said cutting him off, "that was quite the coincidence..."

FROM UNKNOWN

WEDNESDAY AFTERNOON, TWO days after the drama at the Outtasight! gallery, and two packages arrived for Jim Riven. He was dressed and ready to receive them. This was the big day, and everything had to go to plan. He'd tried to eliminate chance as much as possible, but there was still a helluva lot of it unaccounted for out there. This made him nervous. Very nervous. What he was doing was so far out of his comfort zone as to be in another zone altogether. One of those difficult zones that no doubt contained such awful terrible things as itchy jumpers, runny noses, and mobile phones that stopped recharging.

At precisely 2pm, there was a knock at his front door. He opened it, relieved to see a well-dressed Jen standing on his doormat, wearing a very smart pair of black boots.

She led with, "What on earth are you doing here?" Adding a heartfelt, "What the absolute f—?"

"And it's nice to see you too, Riven cut, in, smiling. "You got the note about the missing Mondrian, I take it?"

She gave him a sideways look. "How could I ignore it."

"Then come in."

Jen wavered for a few seconds, before angrily walking past him into his recently cleaned and hoovered porchway. He quickly followed her as she stalked down his recently cleaned and hoovered hallway. "This better not be some cheesy chat up attempt," Jen asked rather aggressively, he thought, "because I'm not in the mood for…" her voice dried. Jen's eyes had wandered into Riven's recently cleaned and hoovered living room, and onto the two paintings hung there.

Dan's diptych.

She pushed past him to stare at the two paintings, somewhat clumsily hung, it must be said, but hung all the same. "How on earth?" she ululated, looking at the diptych and back at Riven and repeating the phrase and the move a few more times for good measure.

"Would you like some tea?" Riven asked.

"No, I don't want any tea!"

"That's a real shame as I made a fresh pot in anticipation of your visit. I'm definitely having one, and a biscuit. Let me pour you a mug anyway."

"What are you doing with Dan's… with Roo Osbourne's paintings?"

"There lies a long story." Riven finished pouring tea before adding milk and offering Jen the sugar bowl, which she declined.

"I don't get it. What's going on?"

Riven took a sip of tea. "You read the note, what did it say, exactly?"

Jen took out her phone. "*From Unknown: I know how you can get your hands on the missing Mondrian. Come to this address at 2pm. Dress smartly.*"

"And that brought you here… why?"

"You tell me." She sat down and picked up the tea, cradling the mug in both of her hands and gave Riven the most peculiar stare. "I think I might've misjudged you." Her eyes kept darting to the diptych.

"Yes, I get a lot of that." Riven put a hand into his jean's pocket and pulled out Jen's flash drive."

"You found it?"

"Yes, it's a long story. As was your dissertation…"

Realisation dawned on Jen. "Oh… I see."

"Yes, it made for some interesting reading. Fascinating, to be honest. And brilliant, I would say. Quite, quite brilliant. Now tell me, from the beginning. How did you do it?"

THE THEORY

"**AS YOU HAVE** now guessed, I know Piet Mondrian and his works, his life, everything about him, inside out," Jen began.

"Indeed, you do."

"And I had a theory…"

"Indeed, you did."

Jen gave him a hard stare. "Are you going to let me speak or not?"

"Sorry. Carry on."

"My hypothesis was that during a period at the height of Piet Mondrian's skills, when he famously painted a series of three paintings, known as *3 Compositions with blue red yellow and white*, that he also secretly painted a fourth canvas. A secret Mondrian. Which over time has become known as *The Missing Mondrian*. And that he placed this secret Mondrian behind one of the other three paintings. Not tacked onto the frame, but the same size as the frame with the painting above holding it in place. To achieve this, he used two thinner canvases.

"Why would he do such a thing?" Jen asked knowingly. "The answer is also included in my theory. I believed it was done as a surprise for a married couple—two other artists and close friends of his. I found a draft letter gifting it to them. The translation from the Dutch reads, *For my two inseparable friends, may you be joined together forever.* But for some reason, the painting never got to them." Jen took a deep breath. "The theory of the Missing Mondrian is one of those whimsical art stories that people would love to be true but are seen as pure fantasy. But I believed differently. Especially after I discovered that letter. That letter changed everything. Now, up to very recently, one of those three paintings, one of the *3 Compositions with blue red yellow and white*, was lost.

Riven nodded. "The Mondrian bought by Roo Osbourne, who put it straight into storage."

"Exactly. The other two paintings have been studied and examined hundreds of times and no hidden painting has been found. Which meant that if my theory was correct, the Missing Mondrian must've been hidden behind Roo Osbourne's Mondrian. It had been verified externally but not studied—the provenance was impeccable. And I thought… what if I could get my hands on it? What if I could discover the Missing Mondrian? The idea was a fanciful one, but the thought just wouldn't go away. It grew inside me and began to dominate my life. It was all I could think about. I was working for the Tate Gallery at the time and wanted to get my boss to request the Mondrian for our team to take a look at. But I couldn't give her a compelling reason why. If I'd mentioned my theory, I would've been laughed all the way to the dole queue. The whole thing was driving me mad until… the best friend of Roo Osbourne's daughter bought a London gallery. And before I knew what I was doing, I had resigned my job at the Tate and went to work for Monty Fitzhugh. I had no plan to speak of. No idea what I was doing, but sometimes things just come together, you know?"

"More than you can possibly imagine."

"I was influential from the start. I placed the seeds in first Monty and then Landa Osbourne. How having a masterwork for the gallery opening would be marketing dynamite. But when it came down to it, those two were more interested in trying to impress their friends than getting media interest. In fact, Landa was pretty much against that from the off. The reason, that I know now, is that she'd borrowed the painting from her father without his knowledge. Either way, I couldn't believe my luck.

"When Monty told me the Mondrian was coming to the gallery I could've screamed for joy, but I had no time for a celebration. The painting was to be at the gallery for one night only and I had a lot to do in that one night. You must understand that the art world is a cruel place. If I ever wanted to keep my place in it, I couldn't come up with wild theories without any proof. I needed hands-on time with the painting in question. And if my theory was correct, I needed to separate the canvasses, and to photograph and video everything—a solid timeline of discovery. My plan was to lock myself in with the Mondrian overnight at the gallery after the opening, but Monty got spooked by that money-digger, Harve, and decided to lock the place up himself and take the keys home. A real slap in the face. They didn't trust me."

"But they were right not to trust you?"

"Shut up Riven. You don't know how it felt. All my planning was scuppered. I knew I should've gotten back-up keys, but it happened too fast for that process. I went home Friday night and didn't sleep a wink. Instead, I sat and steamed."

"You may not have had back-up keys, but you certainly had a back-up plan, didn't you?"

Jen nodded. "On Thursday, the day before the opening, Monty had given me the rather menial job of cleaning up that revolver embedded in the under-gallery wall. And after I'd removed the build-up of muck and years of paint, I accidentally activated a fifty-year-old mechanism that revolved the far wall. It screeched like a screaming woman, like thousands of nails being scraped down a blackboard. I almost wet myself. Luckily, I was alone in the gallery at the time, and I was able to keep the discovery secret. I may be an arty type, but my father was an engineer and petrolhead, and he made sure that I knew my way around mechanical devices. The mechanism that revolved the wall was old but serviceable. All it needed was a good greasing. I returned Thursday evening, late at night. I thought I'd brought enough lubrication with me, but needed more, and was forced to use an old can I found in one of the exhibits. It took a few spins, the sound of which I believe finally scared away that tramp living outside, but soon it became almost silent."

"That was quite some discovery."

"It was Outtasight," Jen said with a smile. "The hidden room then became part of my scheme—a place to hide my tools of the trade—and to be a bolt hole should I ever need it. But I was also aware that things might not go to plan, so I painted the inner wall and added the hooks just in case."

"Should your plan fail, or if you needed more time with the painting, you gave yourself the option of revolving the wall to make it look like the Mondrian had been stolen."

"A last resort… or so I thought."

"A last resort you used."

"Yeah, I spent a hard night after the show back at my flat wrestling with what to do. Wondering if I had the guts to do it. Wondering if I'd even get the opportunity."

"But you did. Monty told me you were the first down in the gallery the following morning."

"I had to get to the Mondrian before anyone else and flip the wall. If I didn't, everything was over. After Monty and Harve opened up, I practically ran down the stairs to get to the under-gallery before them."

"You flipped the wall and gave Monty the bad news. That was a ballsy move."

"I thought it would be a hard decision, but in the moment, it was the easiest thing I've ever done. This was my whole life you understand?"

"I do. I read your dissertation. I suppose you had nothing to lose," Riven mused, remembering Dillon's words. "Roo

Osbourne's painting hadn't been stolen—it was just hidden from view."

"Yeah. No theft, no foul. I just needed to get time with it to test my theory."

"And you found that time, didn't you? On Saturday afternoon."

She nodded. "Monty and Harve left, and you wandered off as well. It was easy to create a scene to get rid of Bill and get the gallery to myself for a few hours. Enough time to remove the outer canvas of Roo Osbourne's Mondrian to reveal the Missing Mondrian underneath…" Jen paused, her eyes sparkling as she relived the moment. "Oh my, Riven! It's a superb example of the master at the peak of his powers! You can't imagine my elation. Just me, in that hidden room, dancing around like a loon."

"Then why not go public? It'd be a sensation, wouldn't it? A hidden masterpiece painted by Piet Mondrian. And you found it."

"Yes, that was my plan, but I went a little crazy. Don't you see? I'd found it. The Missing Mondrian. The subject of my dissertation and one of the greatest art finds of the twenty-first century. And it could be all mine without anyone knowing. Mine!" Jen's eyes widened in her face, making her appear manic. "Why give it to Roo Osbourne to hide away forever?" she said angrily. "Keeping it for myself was too much to resist."

"But isn't that a little bit selfish? What about all those other lovers of Mondrian out there?"

Her eyes flicked to Dan's diptych. "Selfish? If anyone is selfish it's Roo Osbourne!"

"But wouldn't you be doing the same as him? Hoarding a Mondrian?"

Jen gave him an exasperated look, before all the anger drained out of her. "Yeah, I suppose you're right. But I'd cherish that painting. I wouldn't hide it away. That's the difference."

"And what about your place in the story of Piet Mondrian?

You're now part of it. An amazing part. You were willing to give all that up?"

"You don't understand. I could own a Mondrian. I could have it with me throughout my life." The manic look returned to her face, although this time it was not as intense. To Riven, it seemed like she was coming down from a drugs' high, where the drug was her own serotonin.

"But I still ensured my place in antiquity," Jen continued. "I documented the whole process. I have copious notes, photographs and videos. Everything to prove its authenticity. And remember proving authenticity was once my job. So I knew what I was doing. One day, when I'm old and dying, then I will tell. I will pass on the Missing Mondrian and my evidence. And I will be tied to Piet Mondrian forever."

"But you don't have the Missing Mondrian, do you?"

Jen nodded, a mixture of anger, sadness and deep resentment crossing her face. "No, I don't." Her eyes narrowed, staring at Riven accusingly. "I'm going to ask you again. Why do you have Dan's diptych on your wall?"

"There is a reason. Not a good one, but a reason all the same. But before we get to that, I need to know one thing. You've told me of your love for Piet Mondrian, and how that love led to a theory, and how that theory led to the discovery of the Missing Mondrian, but what of Roo's Mondrian?"

"What of it?"

"You obviously refixed the original canvas to appear exactly the same as it was before you removed the Missing Mondrian. Same enough to fool Roo Osbourne's art expert. So why didn't you flip the wall and return it?"

"That answer is a simple one."

"It is?"

She nodded. "You."

"Me?"

"Like I told you, hiding Roo Osbourne's Mondrian inside the secret room was a last resort with little chance of success.

I knew that as soon as the art insurance investigators arrived, they would shut down the gallery. We'd all be investigated, and, after that, it might take weeks, months or even years before I could get access to the gallery again… and they might stumble upon the revolving wall, like you did. But the art insurance investigators didn't arrive. You did. *Jim Riven*. A ghost from my past. You were not the rat man, but Landa's investigator. You! I couldn't believe it." She let out a short hysterical laugh. "By choosing you to investigate the disappearance, that idiot daughter of Roo Osbourne gave my improvised plan a new lease of life. Your arrival gave me the time and opportunity I needed to discover the Missing Mondrian. And after that discovery, I thought to myself, why shouldn't I keep the original hidden? I had the Missing Mondrian, and if Roo Osbourne's Mondrian was ever found, I might be a suspect, but they couldn't prove it and they'd be more interested in the artwork's return than prosecution. It was a no-brainer. I'd gone as far as to make it look like it was stolen, so why give it back?"

"And the missing… the new Mondrian? What did you do with it?"

Jen took a gulp from her mug of tea. She was agitated, annoyed, but most of all confused. "I think I may have underestimated you."

"And why do you think that?" Riven replied, also taking a gulp of tea.

"Because you know where I hid it, don't you?"

Riven smiled. "Yes, I do. You used Mondrian's trick of hiding the rectangle of the painting under a canvas of the same size. In fact, hiding it under the larger painting of Dan's *The Stick Man* diptych."

Jen nodded. "The painting bought by Roo Osbourne for over one-hundred thousand pounds that is now hanging inexpertly on your wall."

"And the reason why you've not been able to keep your eyes off it since you sat down, why you were sucking up to that idiot Dan Kowalski when he certainly wasn't your type, and why you went ballistic after you'd found out Dan had sold it to Roo Osbourne. Yes, I can see that you would find its presence here perplexing. Before I explain why and how Dan's diptych is hanging on my wall, I want you to tell me why you hid your Missing Mondrian under his larger canvas."

Jen took a few moments to gather her thoughts. This was a difficult conversation for her. It was also difficult for him. But it had to be done. "I couldn't leave the new Mondrian behind in the hidden room," Jen said. "If it the wall was ever revolved—which indeed it was—it would've been found. I couldn't take it home to be discovered by any art insurance detectives. That would raise too many questions. And of course, I might be spotted leaving with it. I couldn't take that chance either. Instead, I took my cue from Piet Mondrian himself. I hid the painting behind another painting. Dan's diptych had arrived that morning, it was obvious what I needed to do."

"To hide it under the canvas Dan Kowalski was never going to sell."

Jen's face flushed red. "But the sell-out sold it to Roo Osbourne!" She leapt off her chair and yanked the larger painting of Dan's diptych off the wall with a crash, scrabbling at the studs holding the canvas onto the frame."

"I wouldn't do that," Riven said, but Jen wasn't listening.

One side came loose, and Jen yanked it roughly aside, revealing a blank canvas underneath. "Where is it?" she shouted. "What have you done with my Mondrian? What on earth is all this about?"

A loud rap at the door.

"You've not shopped me to the police, have you?"

Riven shook his head. "I think I've done a lot better than that. Take some deep breaths and come with me."

Stephen, Roo's chauffeur waited for them outside. The large Rolls Ghost awkwardly parked in the small access road, looking far too grand for Camden Town. "This way, sir, madam," he said.

"You shopped me to Roo Osbourne, is that what this is about? You took your slice of cash like Dan did and screwed me over?"

Riven shook his head. "I've done nothing of the sort. Roo Osbourne owed me a favour and I used it to get you off. Now get in the roller and let's go and do this thing."

"But where are we going?"

"Just bear with me for the next twenty minutes. It's not far away."

"What isn't?"

"Where we're going."

JENNIFER BOOTSHAMPTON

TWENTY MINUTES LATER, they arrived on Hornsey Road outside the Arsenal Football Stadium amidst the hustle and bustle of outside broadcast vehicles, cables, wires and cameras and a whole host of very excited looking people. Other cars were pulling up dropping off various well-dressed people and there was a buzz outside. Journalists excitedly taking photographs, journalists doing excitable pieces to camera, and journalists interviewing each other with mutual excitement. "The note did say to dress smart," Riven said.

"You're taking me to a football match?"

"Not exactly."

The electric doors of the Rolls opened, and they were met by a stressed looking PA. "You are Jen Bootshampton?" she asked hopefully.

Jen nodded. "Yes, what of it?"

"At last! Come with me."

"Your name is really, Jen Boots?" Riven asked.

"Jennifer Bootshampton, but yes, didn't you know that?"

Riven and Jen followed the PA into the stadium, where they were guided through a series of corridors until they entered the back of a massive media room stuffed to the brim with journalists. At the end of the room, a high stage had been erected, above which was hung Roy Osbourne's Mondrian.

And next to it, covered by a red velvet curtain, was another painting of a slightly smaller size. Underneath stood an empty table with four places and microphones.

"Are you going to tell me what's going on?" Jen asked, suddenly white-faced.

"You're not stupid Jen, I think you know what this is."

"I think I do…"

"Yeah."

"I'm not prepared."

"You've prepared for this your whole life. You'll be fine."

"This way," the PA said, taking Jen to a side door that Riven was not allowed access to. He found a place where he could see the stage and waited. A few moments later, Roo Osbourne emerged from the wings, closely followed by Colin Artman and the presenter Riven recognised as fronting all those late-night arts programs that he never watched, and finally, looking beautiful but terrified, was Jen Bootshampton. They sat down, Roo Osbourne sitting next to a visibly flustered Jen. The room became immediately hushed.

"Ladies and gentlemen, and every gender in between and outside," the presenter said, her voice loud and clear over the public address system. Let me welcome you to, well, to one of the most marvellous events I've ever been a part of. I am privileged to have been asked to present on this historic day."

The hushed audience, if it was possible, became even more hushed.

"Before we reveal what is one of the most astounding artistic discoveries of the twenty-first century, we will have a few words from the experts who are responsible for this discovery. Please welcome, Jennifer Bootshampton, who has previously worked within the renowned Tate Gallery restoration and authentication team, who's incredible theory led to what we be unveiling today, and Colin Artman, Mr Roy Osbourne's personal art expert and curator. Jennifer Bootshampton will be speaking first."

The room applauded and went quiet. Jen sat, stony-faced. "Jennifer Bootshampton," the presenter repeated, beaming at Jen. More applause.

"C'mon Jen!" Riven shouted to a few laughs.

Jen stood, her pencil thin frame shaking. She pushed a strand of pencil-thin hair behind her ear and began to speak in a clear non-pencil thin voice full of passion and commitment. Riven knew what was coming but Jen was magnificent. She spoke for nearly thirty minutes, and everyone was rapt for every single one of them.

After Jen had finished speaking, Colin Artman stood up but did nothing other than to applaud Jen, and the whole room joined in.

Roo Osbourne was next to stand. "My thanks to Jen and Colin. And now, with no further ado," he said in his thick Aussie tones, "it's time for me to reveal to you, the Missing Mondrian!"

He pulled at a ceremonial cord and the new, Missing Mondrian was revealed. It wasn't quite like the others Riven had seen, this one had smaller squares and a tighter trellis. If it wasn't what he expected, it was a different matter for the crowd, who, for a room full of reserved arty types, went batshit bonkers crazy.

THE RING

BILL WARILY ENTERED the hospital ward to find Skanky Mike lying asleep on a single bed in the far corner. He'd had the shock of his life when Sam Smythe had phoned with the information that had brought him here. Her investigations into Skanky Mike had revealed something unexpected. His name wasn't Mike. His name was in fact Wayne. Wayne Robinson.

"So what if his name is Wayne Robinson," Bill had shouted down his phone at Sam Smyth. "What's that to me, luv?"

"Look, I'm doing this as a favour to you okay," Sam had said. "I'm no longer working for the local paper. I've moved on. But the story I was researching was to do with Skanky Mike. I was doing the whole, *let down by family and society* angle. And I'm afraid that my investigations revealed Wayne Robinson, aka Skanky Mike, is your half-brother on your mum's side."

The news had floored Bill. He never knew that he'd had a half-brother. His mother never spoke his name and his father certainly didn't. But Bill realised he did remember him from when he was very small.

"It was your father who was to blame" Sam had explained. "He kicked Wayne out of the house the day he turned sixteen. He didn't want the kid of another man living under his roof. He spent a few months dossing on people's floors before he inevitably ended up on the streets. Ending up outside the Outtasight! gallery. He's your flesh and blood, Bill. Your flesh and blood. But he's in a bad way and being evaluated by mental health."

"And you were goin' to publish that shite?"

"It's my job. And you must admit, one brother abandoned on the streets, the other the owner of the Squeak-End Pest Control franchise, both living within shouting distance in same part of London, was a great story. But you tipped me off about the stolen Mondrian. It was life-changing information, so I thought I'd return the favour."

"Sod off!" Bill had said and offed the phone.

He'd stewed for days, becoming even angrier when he learned the Outtasight! gallery was closed for the foreseeable future and his services were no longer needed. In the end, the guilt of what he'd done to his half-brother—spiking his whisky with LSD seized from his delinquent nephew—had broken him down and he found himself here, at his bedside.

"Who are you?" said a female voice with the hint of a Scottish accent, startling him.

Bill turned to see a grey-haired petite woman sitting on a chair. Her features were pinched and mouse-like. But it was more than just her features that were pinched. He could tell that life had pinched the woman. Injured her. Bill was not normally a compassionate man, and yet he felt sorry for her.

"I'm Bill. Skanky Mike's… I mean, I'm Wayne's brother. It's time his family looked after him."

"Mikey had a brother?"

Bill nodded. "Yeah, but I didn't know about him until a few days ago… And you are?"

"I'm Pauline. I used to live on the streets with Mikey here, back in the day—until I was beaten up and nearly died. I was found close to death on the street."

Bill had heard many sob-stories but something in Pauline's eyes convinced him she was genuine. "I'm sorry to hear that.

But you obviously survived."

She brightened. "It's a long story, but my mum came down to London and picked me up. It was the spur for her to leave that cruel stepfather of mine. And we stayed down south. I'd always wondered what happened to Mikey, to Wayne, ever since. I had no idea he was still living in the same place. Not that I could remember it anyway. That time was a blur. I thought he would've got out and be living his life somewhere like me. But then a reporter got in touch. I heard he in was in the hospital and so I came to give him this."

Pauline held up a skinny hand. Sitting majestically in her palm was the ring that had haunted Bill's life. A beautiful golden feathered serpent inlaid with coloured stones and gems. Even in the gloom of Mikey's room, it sparkled with a life all its own.

"Mikey stole it and gave it to me as a present," Pauline said. "I've always had a love/hate relationship with it. The ring was the reason why I was beaten up. Someone tried to steal it off me. But you know what, if that hadn't happened, I'd still be living on the streets with Mikey, and God knows what would've become of me and my mum. The ring reminds me every day of the bad place I was in at that time of my life, and how I nearly lost that life. But also that without it, I would never have been rescued. I have children of my own now. And I owe them all to Mikey and this ring." She wiped away a tear. "I'm sorry. It's just been a very emotional time coming back here and seeing Mikey like he is now. Maybe the ring will bring him luck as well. Despite everything, I've had a good life." She offered the ring to Bill.

"I know that ring," Bill whispered, his hands remaining at his sides.

"You do?"

"It was a long time ago now, but I was blamed for it goin' missing. And all this time I thought it was the rats." He turned his attention back to his half-brother. "And you're tellin' me it was this thieving little bleeder who ruined my life?" He found a chair and sat down heavily, searching inside of himself for the ever-present anger that had shaped his existence for over twenty-five years, but found it was no longer there. He sighed and, as the breath left him, so did all those years of guilt and pent-up frustration.

"Are you angry with Mikey?" Pauline asked. "I haven't ruined his chances of a better life, have I?" She was genuinely distraught.

Bill shook his head. "You know what? If he hadn't stolen your ring, then who knows what would've happened to me. This ring is the reason why I've made sumfin of my life. I'm the first person in my family to own their own house. And I own two. I'm a bleedin' success story although I never truly felt that until now. I was luckier than I realised." He smiled. "You keep the ring. I'll look after my brother, although I doubt it will be easy. But we'll work through it."

"Are you sure?"

"As sure as I have been about anythin' for years. I owe it to Wayne."

"It's good that he's back with his family again."

"Do you know how much your ring is worth?"

Pauline shook her head.

Bill told her and she nearly fell off her chair. "It's a representation of a feathered Mayan god in serpent form, and very desirable to collectors in South America and others from around the world. Sell it," Bill said. "Use the money for your family and I'll take care of Wayne. And keep in touch. If he gets better, we'll come and see you."

"You're going to take him home?" Pauline said, staring at her ring as if it was for the first time and slipping it back into her pocket.

"Eventually. My guess is that he has a long way to go before then. But I'm going to be here for him. It's the least I can do."

THE LADIES LOO

RIVEN HUNG AROUND for the next few hours desperately trying to get a word with Jen, but she had become quite the media darling. The whole thing was rather tiring, but he couldn't go without talking to her. There was something important he needed to ask.

A tap on his shoulder and he turned to face Roo Osbourne. "I don't know how you've done it," he said, "but I only owe you another bloody favour."

"You do?"

"It's a media coup out there! I'm world news and in a good way. For the first ever time ever! So, I'm in a good mood. This is your chance. What can I do for you Mr Riven? The world is your lobster."

"That's easy," Riven replied. "Stop being such an absolute douche-bag. You're a billionaire, why not try and make people's lives happier, instead of screwing the little guy for a percentage?"

Roo laughed out loud. "You never fail to impress. You ever thought of becoming a politician?"

"Have you?"

"Strewth no! In the meantime I think we'll say that me not ripping your life apart for talking to me like that is your favour done and dusted, yeah?"

Riven shrugged. "Just try and stop being a douche-bag, is

all I'm asking."

"Get lost!"

A long time later, Riven was awoken from where he'd been snoozing at the back of the room by a hoarse-sounding, red-faced Jennifer Bootshampton. She dragged him off into the ladies' loo and into a cubicle. Even in the toilets, people were calling her name and asking her questions about the Mondrian. Riven had had enough Mondrian to last him a lifetime.

"I'm not really one-hundred percent happy being in here," he said. "In the ladies' toilets. And should it really smell this bad?"

"I wanted to say thank you," Jen replied. "What you did. It's the most amazing gift. But I don't get it." She lowered her voice to a whisper. "Why do that whole thing with Dan Kowalski's diptych. Why have it re-canvassed and hung on your wall? What was all that about?"

"That was Roo Osbourne," Riven whispered in explanation. "The deal I made with him. He wanted you to *feel the pinch*, is how he put it. Wanted you to suffer a little bit for what you did. Messing with his Mondrian."

"What an S.O.B."

"I'm not disagreeing. But it was lovely to finally have you under my roof. I wanted to tell you what was happening, but Roo insisted that you had to get here under your own steam so to speak. But don't worry, I wasn't letting you go anywhere. And anyway, I have something important to ask you."

"Okay," she said, her eyes still sparkling from recent events. "Fire away!"

"Yeah, well, I was wondering if you fancied popping out for a curry. I know its ten years late, but I was thinking that—"

"What?" Jen said. "You did all of this, just so you could get a date with me?"

Riven nodded. "Was that wrong?"

"Oh Riven you idiot, there's no chance of that happening now. Don't you see? You've started a non-stop Mondrian rollercoaster. A roller-coaster I'm not going to be able to get off for years. My time just won't be my own. I've been talking to Colin. On the back of the Missing Mondrian reveal, we're off on a world tour, feting the new painting and also exhibiting all those other paintings Roo keeps in storage. It's gonna be non-stop. What were you thinking?"

"A nice jalfrezi, a glass of Shiraz and maybe a traditional snog on my sofa."

"Sounds delightful."

A rapping on the door. The PA again. "Are you in there, Miss Bootshampton? You're needed."

Jen kissed Riven on the cheek and smiled. "You could come with me? It'll be quite the ride."

Riven grimaced. "I'm afraid my sofa is the limit of my ambitions. That world is not a good fit for me. My life is just too complicated, but I really wish I could."

Another knock on the cubicle door. "The car is leaving, Miss Bootshampton. We need you to come now."

Jen smiled apologetically, opened the cubicle door, and left.

Riven sat back on the loo and sighed. "Bugger!"

Everyone followed Jen out of the toilets, and he was left alone with just his thoughts and the rather nasty smell. "Well that was a spectacular success/awful fail," he said to himself just as his phone vibrated. It was Dillon.

Where are you, mate?

The Arsenal Football Stadium in the Ladies toilets

Yeah?

Yeah

You up for a few beers?

Very much indeed, yeah!

Where?

The usual

See you there in an hour?

Yeah

Yeah.

EPILOGUE

INSELBERGS

"**THIS IS IT!**" Dan Kowalski said, repositioning his easel and canvas, whilst performing a little dance, adding "C'mon!" and an awkward fist pump for good measure. His eyes drank in the majestic vista like a thirsty man stuck out on a hot day in the middle the Navajo Nation's Monument Valley Park on the border between Arizona and Utah—which is exactly where he was. The sun was unremittingly hot, but he had chosen this time of day on purpose. The magnificent colours of the extended desert graced with towering sandstone bluffs, known geologically as *inselbergs*, stretched away from him to a horizon dominated by an intense bluer-than-blue sky. There were no clouds at this time of the day, nimbussy or otherwise. Dan loved the name, inselberg. A German word for the isolated, startling, stacks of intrusive, harder-eroding metamorphic rock that dominated the otherwise empty sandstone plains, like islands rising from a sea made from a shimmering heat haze. These buttes of rock were surrounded by miles of flat-topped steep escarpments, other pinnacles, shrubs, trees, and windblown desert sand. The landscape was overwhelming, stark, rough and dangerous, but also spellbindingly beautiful.

Dan smiled. He needed to be right here. It was a scene he'd been searching for ever since he started what he liked to call his *American Odyssey*—driving across the USA from New York to

California in a suped-up VW camper van.

Dan had spent a difficult few months after the sale of his diptych and the rest of his collection to Roo Osbourne. Sure, he'd made a lot of money, and there had been plenty of impressionable young ladies to keep him company—if anything, he'd grown tired of their attentions. It was almost as if they were more interested in his success than they were with him. And somewhere between all the exhibitions, installations and constant sex, Dan had lost his mojo. He wasn't sure when it had happened, although he suspected it had something to do with that Jim Riven character, and the astounding discovery of the Missing Mondrian by the now world-famous Jennifer Bootshampton. Somehow, everything had paled. The world, like his successful and renowned paintings, lacked colour. And yet, now, here in front of this magnificent vista, Dan felt inspired to use his colour palette for the first time in over a year. He stood back, took a long swig from his water bottle, stroked at his now naked chin—the beard had gone a while ago as had his long hair—and smiled. "You've got this, Dan! It's in the bag!"

Dan worked feverishly, his brush revelling in oranges, yellows, browns and blues. Shapes emerged and disappeared as if by magic, his hand darting up and down, and left and right, dabbing at his canvas like, well, like someone who finally knew what they were doing. He stopped to assess the work. There could be no doubt about it, his use of colour and the way he handled the light had been inspired. Even the painting gods had sat up to take a closer look. It was on the way to becoming a masterpiece, but something was missing. He'd fallen out with his stick man motif on this trip. To be honest, Dan had come to see it as a somewhat glib addition, and yet the canvas required something to bring it together, a place for the eye to be drawn to before it discovered the rest of the painting. He found a tube of black paint, and his brush once again dabbed at his canvas, adding that final, masterly touch, still including the stick man, but this time it was distorted by the shimmer of the heat haze. His motif was unmistakable, but instead of being juxtaposed to the landscape it was a part of it.

It was easily the best thing Dan had ever painted. The strange thing was that since he'd found the success he'd so desired, his previous uber-confidence had deserted him. In its place was something akin to humility. The previous Dan could never have painted something like this. Not even close. "You've grown, Dan," he said to himself. A quote by Bertrand Russell flitted into his head, but unlike so many before it, the words spoke to him. *The whole problem with the world is that fools and fanatics are always so certain of themselves, but wiser people so full of doubts.* "I think…" Dan began. "I think I may have been a bit of an idiot."

Chuckling, he stood back to admire his work, astounded to see a familiar black shape emerging from the heat haze in exactly the way he'd just painted it. And even in the intense heat of the desert, he shivered. The black shape approached him quickly, resolving into an unassuming figure of a man dressed in black trousers, black tee-shirt and a black jacket. A man he recognised.

"It can't be," Dan whispered. "It just can't."

"Don't ask!" Jim Riven rasped from a dry throat, before snatching at Dan's bottle of water, putting it to his lips and draining it. He handed the bottle back to the still astounded Dan and sighed in relief. "Yeah, it's been another one of those weeks. Can I thumb a lift?"

END

Yes, We Know All *YOUR SECRETS!*

Unfortunately (for you), this book contains various implanted microchips, hidden-cameras, microphones, and other surreptitious surveillance devices that have been monitoring you very closely. Myself and my publishers now know everything about you including your shoe size, your favourite pizza toppings and… all those naughty little secrets you thought you'd been able to keep hidden. Yes, *those* secrets. Secrets that we will reveal to the world unless you leave *The Peculiar Case of the Missing Mondrian* a favourable review. You know the kind of thing we're after—plenty of stars and plenty more platitudes.

But seriously, if enjoyed this novel as much as I did writing it, can I please ask you to leave a review? Just a line or two. If not, you know what we will do… so it's probably better to not take the risk.

Over to you…

And yes, you're still being watched.

KJ

Keep reading for my full list of books and social links.

About *The Peculiar Case of the Missing Mondrian*

I wrote this novel on a rather awful Spanish holiday. Don't get me wrong, Spain and its people are fantastic, it's just that due to unforeseen circumstances, what was meant to be a holiday away with my lovely wife turned into a two-week vacation spent on my own, sitting in a hotel room with fantastic views, with wonderful beaches, and with my battered old laptop. And nothing much else.

When I started *The Peculiar Case of the Missing Mondrian*, I had no idea what Landa was doing around Jim Riven's flat on that fateful morning, not who or what she was, or what she was going to ask Jim Riven to do, never mind anything about missing paintings or deluded artists, but I found out along the way. And as the Spanish weather took a turn for the worse, with rain pounding down on my balcony, with waves pounding onto the nearby beach, I found myself pounding away at my keyboard. Indeed, I found out a helluva lot more about Landa, Jim Riven and everybody else. I hope you liked what I discovered.

All the very best,

KJ

Acknowledgements

Thanks for the red-pen, scribbling and 'telling me off in no uncertain terms' talents of my lovely editor now turned wife, *Suzanne Heritage* (no one can say she wasn't ambitious). I wouldn't be literally lost without her, but pretty close. And my other lovely editor, *Blossom Young*, whose help on all my books has been invaluable.

Also by K.J.Heritage

Paranormal Mystery

The Peculiar Case of the Missing Mondrian
Emily Crookshanks: Murder in Little Pucklewick

Mystery Sci-fi

Shattered Helix *(Vatic #1)*
Shattered Web *(Vatic #2)*
Blue Into The Rip
Quick-Kill & The Galactic Secret Service
The Lady In The Glass - 12 Tales Of Death & Dying

Sci-Fi Compilations

Once Upon A Time In Gravity City
Chronicle Worlds: Legacy Fleet
From The Indie Side

Contemporary mystery

Dying Is Easy

Fantasy

The Scowl
The Iron Savant *(writing as Heritage Adams)*

Non-Fiction

All About Editing: *55 Easy edits to improve your writing skills forever*
All About Character Flaws: *Making your characters miserable & rewarding your readers forever!*
3000 Writing & Plot Prompts A-C: *Supercharge Your Creativity & Improve Your Writing Forever!*

Online stores

Find all ebooks, paperbacks, hardbacks & audiobooks by *K.J.Heritage* at the following stores:

Amazon & Audible, Apple, KOBO, Barnes & Noble/Nook, Google, Smashwords & more.

Links - Get to know me!

Linktree

All my latest social links (Threads, Mastodon, Insta, Twitter/X, etc.) and my online store homepages, in one easy place.

http://linktr.ee/kjheritage.com

Join K.J.Heritage's *Newsletter*

Sign up and get a free novel of my short stories: The Lady in the Glass and an inside track on all future releases, access to early reading copies (ARCs), sneak previews, and more.

http://kjheritage.com/join

K.J.Heritage Facebook Group: ***Mostly Readers***

Fun chat and posts about reading… mostly (well not at all to be honest. Just mostly a lot of daft stuff). Request to join and myself or a moderator will approve you.
https://www.facebook.com/groups/mostlyreaders

Website

http://kjheritage.co.uk/

Email:

Want to get in touch? Well here's your chance
contact@kjheritage.com.com

DYING IS EASY

Can we ever know the ones we love? A comic seeks the truth behind his girlfriend's disappearance.

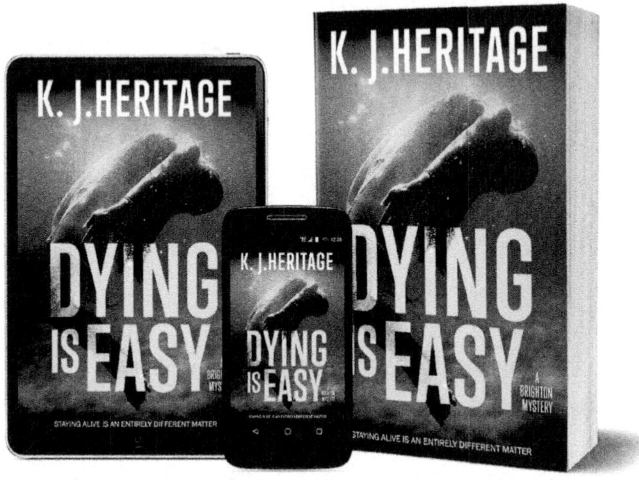

Up and coming comedy talent, Jozee Jackson's life seems almost perfect, until she disappears after a silly drunken argument with devoted boyfriend and new comedian, Adam Hanson. Adam is convinced she's been kidnapped. But by who? And why? Despite all his friends in the local stand-up scene believing Jozee had left him to pursue a new life, Adam suspects foul play and becomes determined to find his missing girlfriend.

After a series of shocking discoveries that shed a new and disturbing light on Jozee's private life, Adam begins to wonder if he knows his Jozee at all. Why are men from seedy hook-up websites visiting their flat when he's supposed to be at work? Who is behind the torrent of vile text messages and emails sent to Adam's phone? And what is the dark secret of Jozee's dead ex-boyfriend?

Adam won't give up looking until he finds answers to these questions - *no matter what the consequences.*

Reviews

"This is a truly unputdownable thriller."

"A wicked thriller with a sense of humour!"

"If you like your crime fiction gritty and uncompromising, then you'll like this one."

"The best time I've had sat on the train with a kindle."

"You'll never watch a stand-up performance again without wondering what nasty secrets lie beneath".

"An absolute gem and enjoyed it from start to finish"

"A surprise ending, but a satisfying one.

"A gripping mystery which gives an insight into the murky world of open mic stand-up comedy."

"The author clearly knows Brighton and stand up comedy well and draws up on both milieus with wit and authenticity"

"This book was perfect. And with all the twists and turns throughout, I just didn't want to be put it down."

"A compelling read you're bound to enjoy. Download it now!"

"An excellent depiction of the open mike comedy circuit in Brighton as well as in London."

"I highly recommend this book, but keep your woobie close by, you're gonna need it!"

Shattered Helix (Vatic Book 1)

The Amazon #1 Bestseller

A war-damaged empath with only six hours to live is forced to solve a series of complex and challenging murders.

A distinguished Company scientist has been murdered.

Vatic, an on-the-run half-alive empath with no memory of who or what he is, will die in six-hours if he can't find out why—or so the Company tells him—an 'added incentive to get the job done'.

Our hero soon discovers he is one of the *Skilled*, a genetically enhanced human—revered and despised in equal measure—a bloodhound with a terrifying past who'll stop at nothing in his pursuit of truth.

And 'the Skilled always get their guy'… *don't they?*

Read what other bestselling authors are saying about *Shattered Helix*

"Gritty, intense, and compelling, Vatic is something you don't run into often enough in Sci-Fi--a cerebral thrill ride you don't want to end." - **Michael Bunker, US TODAY Bestselling author of Pennsylvania**

"Prepare to lose sleep reading Vatic! Delicious Sci-Fiction!" - **Kate Danley, US TODAY bestseling Author.**

"K.J.Heritage's uncanny sense of pacing and story puts him at the forefront of today's speculative fiction writers."
- Samuel Peralta, Amazon bestselling author and creator of The Future Chronicles

"Gritty, detailed and unrelenting. Vatic will take you on a wild ride." - **Peter Cawdron, International Bestselling author of Science Fiction**

About *K.J.Heritage*

"K.J.Heritage's uncanny sense of pacing and story puts him at the forefront of today's speculative fiction writers."
Samuel Peralta, Amazon bestselling author and creator of The Future Chronicles

When K.J.Heritage isn't penning third-person descriptions about himself, he's an international bestselling author writing the books he likes to read. From military/action science fiction and adventure to contemporary mysteries, crime thrillers, comedy, and paranormal fantasy. He should really stick to one genre, but he's not that kind of writer... or reader.

His first short story, *Escaping the Cradle* was runner-up in the 2005 Clarke-Bradbury International Science Fiction Competition. His other short stories have appeared in several anthologies with such self-publishing sci-fi luminaries as Hugh Howey and Samuel Peralta.

K.J.Heritage's short story, *Churchill's Rock*, part of the Chronicle Worlds: Legacy Fleet anthology, will be aboard the Astrobotic's Peregrine Lunar Lander set for launch on the United Launch Alliance's Vulcan Centaur rocket platform bound for the moon in May 2023.

K.J.Heritage has worked all the requisite 'writer jobs' such as driver's mate, factory gateman, barman, labourer, telesales operative, sales assistant, warehouseman, IT contractor, Student Union President, university IT helpdesk guy, British Rail signal software designer, Premiership football website designer, gigging musician, company director, graphic designer, stand-up comedian, sound engineer, improv artist, magazine editor and web journo... Although he doesn't like to talk about it. *Mostly... Maybe a little bit.*

He was born in the UK in one of the more interesting previous centuries. Originally from Derbyshire, he now lives in the seaside town of Brighton. He is a tea drinker, avid Twitterer, and neurodiverse (ASD) human being.

All the very best,

K.J.Heritage